# Lust

## GARNET CHRISTIE

**Cover Design: Cat Imb - TRC Designs**
**Formatting:  Cat Imb - TRC Designs**
**Photographer: Michelle Lancaster**
**Model: Morgan Waterhouse**
**Editing: Salt and Sage Editing**

ISBN Print 978-0-578-89158-3
Kindle ASIN  B08X36HHRT

# Last

GARNET CHRISTIE

# From the Author

**LAST is a full-length, interconnected stand alone that features strong, frequent language, mature scenarios, graphic sexual scenes, and mentions of abuse, alcoholism, and suicide. Reader Discretion is advised, and this book is intended for readers 18+**

I had the idea for Last in mid 2020, and honestly I didn't think much of it at the time. I'd written a few books already, and when the idea for the first chapter popped into my head, I thought it would be a fun "next project" to pass the deary year.  Little did I know that this would be my debut novel, and that Brett and Bianca would take me places I never thought I would go. I've truly enjoyed writing them. I've laughed, I've cried, I've been frustrated, but I wouldn't change one step of this journey. My hope is that each and every one of you enjoy them as much as I have. Side note, Bianca will frustrate you and get on your nerves. If you want to slap her, that's a good thing. She's meant to teach us—to show us how deeply the poisoned words of others can plant into our hearts, and of how we can get in the way of our own happiness. She's also meant to show us that there's a way you can break free and put the past behind you. I hope you feel that when you read this

# Dedication

To the crushed and broken who think their wings have turned to ash—
you will rise again, and you *will* soar.

# Chapter 1

The moment I close the door behind me, dread shoots down my limbs. I already want to leave.

It's a packed house tonight, and I think the whole town is crammed inside this quaint cottage-style home. I duck through the crowd, smiling at the faces familiar to me on this Friday night. I'm at the precipice of the kitchen when I hear a familiar voice.

"Bianca, hi. You're here." My friend Lizzie greets me over the crowd. She raises to her toes and waves from the kitchen island. "Could you please go down to the basement and grab some Cabernet? This one's about gone."

"Sure thing." I wave back, ignoring the fact I haven't been here for ten minutes and she's already begging for help. *Poor thing.*

But I still love her, even if she does end up saying yes to too many folks because she can't turn them away. Saying no is hard for her.

Looking toward the basement door, I sigh. It's inconveniently located at the back of the kitchen. It's a smallish area where throngs of folks are gathered.

I make the swim and say a few "pardon me's" while passing through, loathing the way my head pounds at my temples. Tonight's pain could be from the noise or it could be my ongoing headaches. They've been the norm. At the moment, I can't tell which is the cause of this one—all I know is that it's especially strong.

My eyes bounce around the room with its glaring fluorescent lights and I draw my conclusion. *Yeah. It's the crowd.* And for an understandable reason.

Lizzie's gatherings are chaotic. There's always too many bodies per sane capita in her house. A wince pinches my face tight when a shrill cackle hits the air. I walk faster.

Now I'll do anything to reach that door. Even mash on a few toes if that's the toll. Thankfully, it doesn't come to that and I reach my destination after a few more "excuse me's."

I push out a sigh of relief when the door to the basement latches shut. The lively crowd from behind dwindles out, and the damp, cool atmosphere hugs me. It's inviting after getting slapped in the face from the warmth I felt when walking in. The entire house is hot, heated by the excessive amount of bodies present.

I'd like to stay in here forever, but I can't. If I'm gone too long, Lizzie will notice. A rule she has while hosting is to never run out of drinks.

"Right." My shoulders hunker down with a hard exhale. I almost forgot why I was here. "The wine."

*"Get them happy enough on wine and they won't notice the food ran out."*

That's Lizzie's philosophy. Not that she ever runs out of food though. She's a personal chef, and always prepares a smorgasbord capable of sustaining a small country.

I take my sweet time going down the steps. Her lavish finished basement is what I could call a writer's wet dream.

It's quiet, contained, and the couch alone is spacious enough where I could write for hours in endless positions.

I frown. *Not that anyone wants my books.* None of my romance novels have made a dent in the market for some time now and the fact my agent still believes in me makes me question her grip on reality. By all accounts, I'm a "has been."

A sliver of hurt pokes at my heart. Admitting I've been a failure for the past several years isn't fun. *Dad always told me I wouldn't last.* He was right. I'm simply glad he didn't live long enough to see it. He would have laughed in my face, all while slurring over his words.

*Yeah, thank God he's not around to see me now.*

While that thought needles away, I round the corner and go into an enclosed room.

Judging by the venting on one side of the concrete wall, I think this was a laundry room or was supposed to be. Lizzie's turned it into an impromptu wine cellar.

Bending down, I look at the racks, asking why she sent a non-drinker like me to fetch a bottle. In my mind, it's like sending a monk to Vegas. I have no clue what to do here. My ears perk when I hear a noise. It sounds like the door, but I'm not certain. Most things are muffled in this tucked away area. Tilting my head back, I use my voice. "Hello?"

Nothing.

One more time. "Hello?"

Dead silence.

I shrug and return to the selection in front of me. When I find a Cabernet, I slide it out, cradling it. I'm moving to the door when I stop.

Another noise rings out and I realize it wasn't my imagination.

A shuffle, a moan, and hushed voices. The first one, manly and gruff. *Aching* is a word I use in my books, and I always roll my eyes when typing it. *Effective, but stupid.* However, when I hear *his* voice, I do ache.

"On your knees. Back to the wall."

It's dark and commanding, sweeter than sin, and more beckoning than the idea of going to heaven.

Breath holds in my lungs and my ear strains to hear more.

"Whatever you say."

This voice is soft, flowery, and even familiar, but I can't place my finger on it.

The chime of a belt buckle and the drag of a zipper echo through the cavernous basement. Then a smack. Not like a spanking sound of skin to skin, but of wetness. My eyes widen. A moan from the sin man comes next and when he talks, my knees sway.

"Fuck, yeah. Now, look at me."

I close my eyes and shake my head, trying to force away the intoxicating effects of such a voice. I need to get out of here.

My lips pinch together while I scan my surroundings. I have no idea where they are, but if I don't leave, Lizzie *will* come down here. I'm sure they don't want that. I try to peer around the door, and there's nothing.

Chances are, this couple is further away, and their voices are echoing. The stairs to the kitchen are pretty much a straight shot after taking a hard left. I decide to test my luck and go for it, even though my pulse resounds in my ears. I float on my toes and hunch my shoulders, staying in the shadows if I can.

Several steps in I think so far, so good. There's nothing popping up in my field of vision. Only the sounds of a very obvious blow job breaks the silence. Each second the moans grow in heat, and that makes me want to leave quicker. I'm no prude, but sex sounds are awkward when you're not a participant.

I'm almost to the steps when I stop.

The couple... well, one half is in view. The man. He's standing close, facing the edge of a wall. I've never seen him before. And holy shit. If he's not hotter than melted steel then I don't know what he is.

The red and black flannel button-up, the rolled sleeves showing off corded forearms and swirling tats, the combed back dark hair and smattering of jaw stubble—his look is a sexual hazard... and he's getting a blow job. His pants are pulled down, hugging and straining around his thick thighs. He's also thrusting—causing the woman's head to thud against the wall.

He hasn't spotted me because his eyes are closed. My pulse takes flight when he hisses. It's so indecent to watch, but I can't stop. The sight of his pleasure—his head tossed back while deep moans echo in the air—is my pleasure. My core throbs and my fingers are snaking down toward the button of my jeans. *Shit.* I realize what I'm doing and stop myself.

Unwelcomed jealousy stings my sternum because like writing, I'm not that lucky in love, or lust. Maybe being green with envy that I'm not on my knees sucking him off makes me dirty, but I really don't care.

I venture just beyond the steps to see who the lucky lady is.

My hand covers my mouth and I softly gasp when seeing her.

It's an acquaintance, Monica. Married with three kids. Attractive. A vision really. I'm not bad looking, but I've always been envious of the long midnight hair that vines down her back. A total contrast to my golden locks.

I hug the bottle tight into my chest and scowl. *Why not me?* I'm sure Monica's husband keeps her happy. At least that's what she's told me. I'm also positive my need for action is higher than hers.

Rolling my eyes, I shake my head. Then I look up and blood stops in my veins.

He's staring, right at me. Two black orbs flood with what looks like a combination of lust and anger. His dark groomed brows come together, and he holds my gaze, all while thrusting and pumping in Monica's mouth—his hand on the crown of her head, forcing himself deeper. She struggles not to gag.

My heart batters my ribcage and I skitter backward, careful not to make a sound on the concrete floor.

Then, he scowls. It's dark—fearsome—and there's maliciousness pulling on his mouth. It takes over his face as he licks his lips and moans, all while staying fixated on me, sex and hatred swirling in his eyes.

I gulp and my knees weaken. *He's a devil.* And he knows he's bad—so bad, I'm sure he keeps a pair of horns in his closet for special occasions.

*That's my cue.* With blood ringing in my ears, I back up and leave.

Carefully, I go up the steps, confused, as need pulsates between my thighs. It's mixing in and battling against the anger settling in my gut. Anger stemming from the fact that the douche had the balls to stare at me.

I shake my head on the way up. After I make it upstairs, I go to the main kitchen counter, straight to Lizzie.

"Here." The glass bottle thunks down on the granite. My hold around it is weak. I swallow, hearing his moan in my ears as I try to act normal. "Hopefully I picked out a good one."

"Ha." She smiles wide, her bleached teeth gleaming. "All I buy are *good* ones." Her long lashes cast two shadows over her thin face. "Thanks, Bianca."

"Sure thing." I'm watching her undo the cork, debating if I should say anything about the sight downstairs.

When I think of Monica and how she's betraying her husband, I want to say something...but when I envision her kids, the words tangle up in my throat.

*Those poor babies.*

My big mouth could ruin their whole lives. Every time I see them at the store or church, they look happy—like really happy. Bright giggles are abundant, and toothy smiles are always latched onto their faces, and they hug to Monica's side at all times.

I frown. *I had none of that.* Not even the smiles. For that reason, I'm leaving this alone. I'll hate myself forever if those kids lose everything because of me.

I drop all my thoughts, observing the way Lizzie decants the wine. Part of me gets lost in the process.

"Hey." Lizzie's voice commands my focus. My eyes lift and her brows are sewn together. "You look pale. Are you getting another headache?"

"Eh." I hug my arms around my middle. "I've had one for a while."

Deep blue eyes widen and she sets down the bottle. "Oh, sweetie, I'm so sorry." Coming around the counter, she rubs my arm. "Why didn't you say something? I wouldn't have asked you to come."

My stomach flips at the sympathy. This is exactly why I stopped mentioning my headaches to begin with. I hate it when people make a fuss. My shoulders lift then flop back down. "It's not a big deal—"

"No, don't say that." She frowns. "It's a huge deal. I know how awful they can be for you." Propping her elbows on the counter, she looks deep into my eyes. "Have you made that appointment yet?"

"No. No, I haven't, Lizzie."

She sighs. I can barely hear it over the crowd, but it's there. "Bianca. Really. I don't want to push, but this is serious. You need to find out what's happening."

"I know what's happening." My voice and gut bristle with irritation. "I can't sell anything and I'm stressed. Once I stop being a failure and make sales again, I'll be fine."

"Whatever you say." I see the disappointment brewing in her tight gaze. "But if these headaches don't leave after your next book is a smash hit, I'm taking you to a specialist myself."

"Fair enough." *Not really.* However, arguing with my friend during her party isn't what I came for. I can refuse her help later. In private.

"Go home." Her words are soft. "You look exhausted. I'll feel better if you go home and rest."

I shake my head, my spine stiffening in defiance. "I'm fine. I—"

Out of nowhere, I catch the basement door opening. *Crap.* My heart trombones to my throat when Sin walks out.

I must have been too disoriented to notice before, but he's tall—a good head or two above the crowd, doing anything except blending in. His eyes narrow, and dart around. They land on me and he pushes through the crowd, looking at me like he's plotting my death.

*Crap. No.* Talking to him right now would be too much, too soon, and he doesn't seem pleased with me. I turn my back toward him and quickly slink past Lizzie. "I think you're right. Good night." I try to smile. "Thanks for having me."

"Anytime. Feel better."

Departing the opposite way he's walking, I don't respond. Thank goodness this is an open kitchen with multiple routes. It's my saving grace tonight.

I leave, dodging what I feel is a bombshell of disaster.

When I get home, bed is my destination.

But I don't sleep.

Alone, and bothered with the need for sex roiling in my blood, I slip my hand under the waistband of my silk night shorts and pleasure myself.

I pleasure myself to *him*. To Sin.

The night is spent fantasizing about two dark eyes and the melody of a gruff voice. When I release, I'm frightened by the danger I saw in him, but also yearning to experience it for myself.

I'd never admit it to anyone, but for once, I'd like a bad boy to own me. I just don't want him to keep me.

# Chapter 2

"Eh, I don't know." Retrieving my mug, I recline into my chair at Tanka's Tea and Coffee.

My friends, Lizzie and Cora, are here too, per usual. I love them both. They couldn't look any different from each other. Lizzie dons the soft look of an angel, everything about her light and refined. It contrasts with Cora's dark goth look. Black clothing from head to toe with a short bob sporting an undercut. Outward differences aside, these girls are my tribe and together they form a special type of super glue. It bonds the cracks in my soul. I'd be nothing without them. We've been meeting up every Saturday morning for tea and coffee for as long as I can remember.

"Don't shut out the idea, Bianca." Lizzie circles one of her long nails across the table top. "I think it will be good for you. You deserve a break."

I look at Lizzie and can't help but smile. She's always thinking of me. All those posts about women helping women, adjusting their crooked crowns without telling the world? That's Eliza Morgan.

We met at the grocery store when I came to Copperslane, Washington ten years ago.

Copperslane is the biggest small town I've ever graced. It sprawls itself large, but you'd never know this is a decent sized town thanks to the serious side of cozy it dishes up. I visited because of its picture book aesthetics, I stayed because of people like Lizzie.

In the grocery store, I had an accident thanks to Aunt Flo. That bitch obnoxiously leaked through my blue shorts.

It was Lizzie—a total stranger at the time—who gave me a gigantic hug from behind, acting like she was my best friend. She whispered in my ear about my problem, dragged me off to the bathroom, and gifted me her hoodie. We've been friends ever since.

"Yeah," Cora pipes up, derailing my recall. "Get out of that house. Seriously, the sun misses you."

*Then there's Cora.* She's my kick in the pants.

I met the sassy graphic designer at one of Lizzie's parties. Cora and Lizzie have been friends since middle school, and she and I hit it off on night one. They adopted me into their circle. Cora and I are yin and yang. She may not always agree with me, but she never puts me down or silences my negativity, and she knows how to make me laugh.

But her enthusiasm is a misfire today. I groan and frown. "Did you wait to tell me about this idea until you two were together?" They know the idea they've presented isn't my thing, but refusing them both is a hard thing to do.

"Possibly." Cora's sly voice implies a yes, as do her bright purple contacts.

I shake my head.

This week they've brought some news that doesn't have me leaping out of my seat.

A trip proposal—with tons of people, at some kind of posh log cabin in northern Washington. Everyone is splitting the bill.

Cora's gaze slides over to Lizzie's. "How are you getting out of here again? What about your aunt?"

We don't speak about Lizzie's aunt often, but we do understand that the lady is almost disabled. Lizzie is the only family left to help her and she bears it all like a saint.

Lizzie smiles. "My friend Jake said he'd check in on her."

"Jake." Cora rolls her eyes.

"He'd still go out with you, if you're interested." Lizzie waggles her brows. "He asks about you all the time."

"Shut it." Cora lifts her hand. "Talk about this trip and not that pipsqueak."

After a giggle, Lizzie scoops back some hair off her shoulders and changes the subject. "A getaway of the stars." There's a sound of wonderment in her voice. "Chris Evans rented the cabin we're staying in a while back."

"More like a getaway for the commoners," I mumble out, avoiding eye contact. After taking a sip of Earl Gray, I arch my brow. "I highly doubt Chris Evans split the bill with fifteen people."

"Wrong. Fourteen," Cora corrects. "They'll be fourteen if you come."

My face deadpans. "Oh, that sounds so much better."

Cora snorts and a wry smile cracks across her face. "I knew you'd agree."

My shoulders shake with a laugh as I tilt my head back. Cora always knows how to lighten my mood.

"Laughing is always a good sign with you," Lizzie says. "I think that means you should come."

"No, no." Raising my hand, I wave it in the air. "I didn't say that—"

"No, you didn't," Cora cuts in. "But you do need to come." She rakes her long fingers through the top of her hair. "When was the last time you got away and stopped worrying about things you can't control?"

"I—" I pause, thinking hard. There's nothing. I can't conjure up an instance, so I remain silent. Cora's not lying. It's been a long time.

"Yeah, Bee." Cora rests her elbows on the table and leans forward. "I know what that look is about. You need to break away. Forget about writing. Forget about everything."

I chew on my lip. It sounds tempting and horrible all at the same time. Cora and Lizzie both know I need time to get away. I'm a hardcore introvert and being around people all the time is draining.

Bouncing my gaze between them, my brows pinch together. "It's for five days?"

When they nod, my heart sinks.

Fourteen people and five days. That means loudness, forced dinners with a blob of people, and even late nights where I'll be talking when I'd rather be in bed. And from what they've told me, there are two people in a room, and while I love Cora and Lizzie, I don't share rooms.

I grimace, my stomach tumbling. That all sounds like agony. "Yeah, I don't think—"

"I made sure you'll get your own room." Lizzie drops the comment like it's nothing, but it's more like a mic drop to my soul. She knows that.

"What?" My jaw falls open. "How?"

One side of her mouth flips up. "There's a twin bed on the very top floor." She taps a delicate finger against her neck. "Granted you'll be sleeping with the faces of Elsa and Olaf everywhere, but you'll have your own space. You can go up whenever you like." Her dark blue eyes twinkle. "Plus, there's an amazing view with a pitched cathedral window."

*Glorious.* Just glorious. Lizzie's telling me everything I need to hear. *And the view?* It's like Bianca crack that will hopefully provide inspiration for writing. All my refusals begin to dissolve. "Uhh." My shoulders fall into the seat back. "I hate you both."

"Ha." Cora tips her head back. "You love us and that means you're coming."

"Yes." I sigh. "Damn." A grin creeps across my face, and my fingers are already tingling to type. "You two really know how to seduce me."

"Hell to the yes!" Cora pumps her fist in the air, then turns to Lizzie for a high five. Lizzie swings and misses, which makes us all giggle.

"Gosh, Liz," Cora winces. "We didn't grow up with brothers, and it shows. Anyway," She faces me again. "You're right. We know exactly how to lure our sweet little recluse out of hiding." She winks. "We leave Thursday around noon. We'll pick you up. There's no way we're taking your jalopy."

I ignore the diss to my car and nod. "Sounds good."

"With that settled..." Cora lifts her coffee cup and holds it in one hand. Her tongue pokes out to the side and she waggles her brows. "Has anyone heard about or met the new hot guy that moved into town?"

"Someone moved here?" My eyes widen while I take a sip of tea. Our town isn't that big, but I'm still not as in tune as Cora and Lizzie.

"That's correct," Lizzie says. "He was at my party last night."

*Crap.* A mouthful of warm tea snags in my throat, and my heart pounds in my ears. Not wanting to spew my drink everywhere, I force a swallow and then cough.

Both girls look at me with surprised glances.

"Sorry. Wrong tube." I say it sounding like an old hag about to croak.

Lizzie has to be referring to the guy I saw in the basement, and that makes my cheeks burn for multiple reasons. Not only from what I saw but also because I got off to him again this morning. That's pathetic if you ask me. A rush of heated shame travels down to my toes. *I really need to get laid.* My dry spell has been long-going this time and it's taking a toll.

Completely unaware of what's assaulting my brain, Lizzie continues to talk. "His name is Brett Walker and he came last night because someone invited him. He didn't stay too long, seems quiet. However,"—she drags her tongue over her lower lip while nodding— "he is handsome. Possibly the most handsome man in this town."

"Well screw my luck." Cora drums her knuckles on the table and pouts. "I got caught up doing a project last night for a client. Toby messed up my computer and deleted everything. I had to start over."

Lizzie ducks her head and giggles. "You missed out on the talk of the town because of your cat?"

"Yeah, yeah." Cora flips her wrist. "Don't start. Me and Toby aren't on speaking terms right now. Don't make me feel guilty."

Lizzie busts out laughing, but for some reason, I can't.

*Brett.*

That name is much like the man—an erotic threat. My stomach bubbles with anxiety. A normal woman would be desperate to see him again, but after our meeting, I'm anything but. Placing my teacup on its saucer, my lips pull down. "Why did he move here anyway?" Hopefully, his presence in my social circle will be low to nil.

Cora shrugs. "I heard he buys rich commercial spots and sells them to the highest bidder when a big name wants the deed."

My brow arches. "Sounds lucrative."

"Sounds smart," Lizzie counters. "I wonder what property he's viewing here. I'll ask him next time I see him."

*If she only knew he gets blow jobs in random people's basements.*
*Her* basement to be exact. I doubt she'd be talking to him more then.
But then again, maybe she would. Recalling his voice makes my body
tingle, and I caught him in the very act. *Still.* I hope to never see him
again, and the thought of even locking eyes with him in a crowded room
has embarrassment shooting through my veins, especially after I ran out
on him. I'm a hundred percent certain he wanted to talk to me.

"That's a funny look, Bee." Cora tilts her head. "Whatcha thinking
about?"

I whip out a fib that's resting on the top of my head. Brett Walker's
name will not pass my lips. "My next book idea."

"Oh. Nice." The lie works. She moves to the next topic. "Let's make
sure we all mark down something we want to do on our trip. Sometime
during our stay, the three of us can break off and do something fun.
There are a lot of couples going, we won't want to be stuck with them
the whole time." Her nose scrunches up. "Blech."

Lizzie whips out her cell phone. "I'll start looking right now. Let's
make sure we indulge in some specialty foods. I've been dieting for a
month."

"Good idea," Cora says, pulling her chair closer to Lizzie.

*That does sound like fun.* Sunlight breaks through the Washington
cloud cover and shines down on me. Taking another sip of tea, I smile.
It has to be a good omen. This trip will be perfect for me, especially if
Brett Walker just moved here. The distance will be good.

Copperslane is so tiny, I know I'm bound to run into him again
soon. This trip will give me the time to mentally prepare for him the
next time we cross paths. *Yeah. This trip will be perfect.*

"Wow." My suitcase topples over with a thud while I look around the cabin room days later. I'm the worst packer ever and regardless of the luggage I pick, it always caves to the uneven way I shove things inside.

I have to laugh when I realize Lizzie wasn't kidding about the *Frozen* theme in this room. Elsa's face is covering the entire bedspread, the pillow is Olaf—even the walls are ice blue...but the view? Strolling over to the window, I smile. "Killer."

Powdered sugar-dusted treetops—they span for miles and I feel like a queen residing in a snow globe. I get to see all the wonder of this kingdom from above. Taking in the postcard sight, I rest my fingers on the ledge. My shoulders loosen, my breathing slows. If you can't relax to this view, then you're dead inside.

Sadly, I can't enjoy the sight for long. We arrived at the cabin a few moments ago, and the firstcomers agreed to make dinner. We're doing tacos since that brings joy to everyone...I think. I'm on tomato-slicing duty.

After grabbing a cozy sweater out of my suitcase to combat the nip residing in the air, I saunter for the stairs. I'm ducking past the atrium ceiling and exiting the narrow entry when the voices from downstairs catch my ear.

It already sounds like more people have arrived. Excitement rolls down my spine and finds its way to my fingertips. I wiggle them in happy anticipation. I don't have a headache today and I'm oddly energized and actually looking forward to being with other people.

I haven't been out much since my boyfriend, Lance, broke up with me three months ago. Thanks to him, I've become more reclusive since we fell apart. Getting your heart stomped on after you cared about someone isn't pleasant. This will be a nice change up.

Since all the couples I know are super nice and not over the top, I'm looking forward to seeing them as I round the corner of the main living room. *This is going to be great.* For the first time in forever, my hopes are soaring high, and I have no clue why. All I know is that I like it. I love the optimism.

All those merry feelings erupt into flames when I enter the living room and take note of the figure by the front door.

*Fuck my life.*

I freeze on the spot, my heart pulsing so hard I feel it in my damn feet.

Brett Walker is here, black suitcase wheeling beside him. No doubt about it, he's a guest, and of course, he looks hotter than the devil. His tall and wide frame spans the space he stands on. He's not wearing a jacket and that makes him look like a badass, because all that's covering his torso is a black button-up dress shirt. The fabric strains to accommodate the expansion that occurs with his breath—he's rock solid. I'm sure he could send a marble slab home in tears.

I grow hot under my sweater while drinking him in. Mortification vines around my chest, but at the same time my core weighs heavy with need—the sight of such a man reminds me I haven't had anyone in a long time, and I need that.

On the same token however...

*Why the hell is he here?* Why? He's new, how has he worked himself in with so many people this fast?

I gulp. *So much for preparing myself.* My gaze drops to the wood floor. *I don't want him to see me.* I make a nervous shuffle on my tiptoes. I'm really not ready for this, so I'll deflect to the kitchen. Maybe I can gather myself just enough while I cut up tomatoes.

My feet are sidestepping as I weave through the small gathering. There are people here I know, but I'll say my hello's later. I'm near the opening of the kitchen when my shoes weld themselves to the floor.

Brett's black eyes take note of me and he stares. He's not even blinking. Maybe not even breathing.

*Shit.* I can't hear the room around me—all that exists is a dull echoing in my eardrums. Swallowing around the lump in my throat, I force a sheepish smile.

A huge mistake.

*I want to die.*

All he does is glare, and the repulsion that resides in it makes my limbs go weak from sickness.

It's official. From the look I'm getting, I think Brett Walker hates my guts, and I'm stuck here with him. The. Whole. Damn. Trip.

# Chapter 3

I t's been one night since we arrived at the cabin. Last night's taco night was pretty uneventful—at least for me. After cutting up tomatoes, I hid in my room. My false claim was that I'd had a long week, but in reality I was desperate to get away from the dark eyes of Brett Walker. We crossed paths a few times before I vanished. It seemed like he wanted to say something, but each time, someone was close by and each time, my core bristled with fear and hunger.

It's here now as I catch him emerging from the hallway, a neat whiskey cradled in his hand. The air around him cracks with a quiet authority and the hoopla of our crowd subdues when he enters.

The living room is his. He commands it as he swaggers across the room, It doesn't matter that all he's wearing is a white T-shirt and dark wash jeans. Brett Walker makes this cabin and the rest of us look like his bitches.

My throat goes arid staring at his back. Muscular shoulders blades and lats challenge the fabric of the shirt, and that's hot...but what's even hotter is how that snugness tapers off at the waist. At the torso, the fabric drapes with looseness, and damn. It's just too perfect.

The longer I observe, the more I want to drink him in.

Then he turns around.

From across the room I catch the frost in his black gaze. I *see* his darkness and question if I'm crazy for wanting him. When he looks up and finds me, a shiver trails down my spine. *Yeah, I'm insane.*

There's no softness when we lock eyes. On the contrary, whenever his attention diverts to me, his sharp jawline grits and his perfect eyebrows frame the disgust that swirls in his gaze. What makes it worse is the way he focuses on me. When we're in the same room, I can't shake him.

Which is exactly what I'm trying to do tonight—make him look at something other than me. I can't say it's been working. It's like his eyes are a compass and I'm true north. His gaze is just there. My heart stammers at the attention, but it's also starting to grate on my nerves. I'm not an attention seeker. Never have been, and I'm well past the anxiety that first wove through my stomach. Now I just want him to look somewhere else.

I sigh while skirting around the house, sticking to the wall. *If he has something to say, I wish he'd just say it.* I'm sure it will be about the blow job, but that conversation can't be any more awkward than his searing attention. His stares have been constant, and I'm surprised no one's noticed.

"Texas Hold'Em, anyone?" The boisterous voice of Dan Lowery gets our attention. The stocky man is camping out in the middle of the living room, waving two packs of cards. He tried to get us to bite last night, but nobody did. He's trying even harder tonight. His wide mouth dangles open as he turns in a circle, making his pitch.

"I'll play." Brett's husky voice breaks the silence. He strides over to the coffee table, takes a swig of golden liquid and lowers his frame to the floor.

A domino effect ensues. Everyone abandons what they were doing, opting to meander over to the coffee table. Everyone but me.

"Bianca." Cora pokes her head around to study me. "Are you playing?"

Clutching my Kindle to my chest, I shake my head. "I don't know how."

My spine stiffens when Brett scoffs. Glancing over, I see his lips tweaked up. I see it even though a glass rim parts his mouth while he takes another sip. Unease zaps at my chest when he places the tumbler down and slides his gaze over to mine.

The scowl I've become used to is absent, but there's an overcrowd of intensity in the way he looks at me. It's calm but heated—passionate yet dead—knowing but distant. I'm not sure what he's seeing.

Incompetence for not being able to play? Judgment for not at least sitting with everyone? I have no idea, but I do know I want to shrink away from this look. The angry stares wore me thin. This one has my heart recoiling into my ribcage, and me shrinking away into a seat.

I opt for a cozy armchair in the corner of the room. It's perfect in placement. The way it hooks around the fireplace obstructs my full view of Brett. Happy I'll get a reprieve, I open my Kindle and try to dive into a romance book that I've wanted to read for a while.

Reading as a writer has changed everything for me. I don't merely take in passages, I observe. The usage of verbs, the flow of sentences, the show of emotions, the way this writer brings tension into her scenes. Even her over-usage of the word *surrender*. I take note, highlighting a few passages that really make me swoon.

My focus shatters when the card players erupt over a crazy hand someone played. I look up and spot Lizzie thumping her hand on the table in laughter. I ignore Brett this time, despite my eyes begging me to look at him.

I promptly refocus on my book. I get lost for a while, but another outburst happens. My attention breaks...then it happens again. And again. Each time, I've refused to look up. I want to drown everything... well, Brett, out.

*I won't let him see me looking.* After the last weird pass, I'm done giving my attention to anything he's involved in, so my head stays down even though I'm dying to know what's going on.

That's the game I'm playing tonight—a big fat challenge of don't look.

I'm winning, until one of the ladies lets out a loud shrill. My shoulders lurch, and I plug an ear. *Damn.* She could break glass. My face screws into a wince, then I notice Brett is gone. Nowhere to be seen. The space, *his* space, reverberates with emptiness.

My shoulders deflate with ease, but I grow annoyed at the way my stomach drops at his absence. With my eyes lingering on his open spot, I frown. *I shouldn't want him to be here.* I shouldn't care, but I do, so I'm fixing the situation. I'll make it to where I *can't* look at him.

Closing my Kindle, I weigh my options. There are the stairs which lead to my room. Thinking of Olaf, I shake my head. I'm not ready to snuggle with him just yet. A smile tugs up my lips when thinking of the lower floor. There's a pool table, fully stocked bar, a few couches, and a TV. The best part is no one is congregated there tonight, so it will be quiet.

I slide off the chair, Kindle in hand, and gently depart for the kitchen. Everyone's absorbed in the game, Lizzie and Cora included, so slipping out is easy.

My hands smooth over the paneled wall as I saunter down the steps.

The quiet in here already has my heartbeat slowing down and I love it. Placing my reader on the pool table, I decide to go for a drink...of water.

Thanks to Dad, I never touch alcohol. His bitter words killed my mom. The endless Jack he consumed twisted him into a monster—one that left me only too happy to toss away his expectations of me becoming a lawyer.

To this day, my favorite memory is the one where I told him that I'd switched all my law classes to English lit, writing, and communications. *"Consider it a tribute to Mom."* I said it standing on my tiptoes, sneering in his face. *"You never allowed her to do anything she loved, and it killed her. You won't get to do that with me."*

*"It won't last. Stupid bitch."* I remember how those words sliced down to the quick of my soul. I further recall how I didn't let that show. Even more, I remember the hollowness in his ghost blue eyes, and the way his clothes reeked of piss and drink.

*"She didn't make it because she was dumb. You're the same. Enjoy being a failure because you walked out on the one thing you were good at. Writing won't last. You won't last."*

He was right, of course. My last three books have proven his words. Admitting that hurts like a son of a bitch, but still I smile. I force it to counterbalance the ache in my chest. *He'll never know.*

I'll always have the satisfaction of pursuing something different than what he wanted for me and sticking it to him. As it is, my royalties are enough so I can live comfortably for a while. In a way, I'm not a total failure. I simply didn't last, just like he said.

Running my fingers over the railing of a bar stool, I round the corner. I'm at the edge of the bar counter, about to go behind to fetch water from the fridge.

That's when Brett pops to a stand.

"Shit!" I jump. His eyes go wide, mine go wider, and my nerves take flight, rocketing from the bottom of my stomach. With my fingers biting into the ledge of the counter, my body stiffens.

His black eyes narrow and he sets down a half-full decanter of whiskey. "You." His one word growls out.

It's a one-shot kill to my heart. Hearing all the sex buried deep within it and having it aimed at me sends my pulse rattling against my neck. My knees squeeze together. I end up shuffling backward, right against the paneled wall.

His wide chest lifts with a breath, then he takes four very decided steps and encloses around me. All my hormones go askew just having him near and I'm granted a much-wanted close-up. His eyes aren't black, just an unusually dark brown that lets little light in or out. It makes him even hotter.

I inhale and there's an ungodly calling of soap and earth, and my mind breaks down at the smell. It's clean and unclean, all jumbled into one. When he props his hand on the wall, caging in one side of my head, a fire erupts in my belly. I gulp, wilting under the heat he stirs in me.

But the flames snuff out when he speaks.

"You better keep your damn mouth shut. If you tell anyone what you saw the other night, I'll drag your reputation all over town." He grits his teeth while spewing out his threats, and I finally see him for what he is.

Brett Walker is a bully.

I squint, irritation catching in my blood. "How? You don't even know me."

"Oh, don't I?" His voice darkens, making mine grow stronger.

"You don't. All you've done is stare at me since you got here. What the hell do you know about me?"

My fists tighten when he lowers his tall frame. It brings us closer together, and right now I can't determine if I like that or not.

"Plenty, *romance writer.*" His final two words slice. Hard.

"Romance—" My mouth falls open as I'm blindsided with a verbal two-by-four. "How did you—"

"Think I didn't check up on you?" His gaze hardens and there's steel in it. That cold look lands on my mouth and stays there. "I make it a habit to find out about people who watch me while I get head."

"Mmm." I force a deadened look, even though every inch of me flutters with a nervous yet turned on sickness. "Have that happen often, do you?"

He smirks. It's just as dangerous as I remember. "No," he whispers. "I simply remember the desperate looking ones. Think I don't know you? Your friend Eliza was obliging after you left her party the other night. And from what I heard, you, my dear, are. Desperate."

When his eyes focus on mine, a shiver rips down my spine. *Not* one of pleasure this time, and it renders my limbs tight.

"What's the matter, book writer?" His voice drips with cruel sarcasm. "Your sex scenes not doing it for you anymore?" A harsh chuckle leaves him. "You're so hard up you have to watch the real deal, is that it?"

*Bastard.* My heart quickens its tempo, but I ignore that. Opting to narrow my eyes, I slide away from him, hugging tight to the wall. "You don't know anything about me, and if I do tell Monica's husband about you—"

"Then I'll tell everyone about *you.* That our little single and lonely sex author can't control her imagination. That she creates bullshit lies because I wouldn't talk to her."

The insult makes my jaw clench and my blood bubble with anger. "There's no problem with my imagination."

"I didn't say that, *blondie.*" He says it after taking in my hair. Mirroring my movements, he's stalking me down the wall, ensuring I never achieve the distance I seek. "What I said was that your dreary life lacks excitement. That's why you create stories. Monica Morrison?" His voice spikes with falseness. "Never heard of her. I just moved here."

*Jerk.* But I can't think of anything to say, all that happens is a stilling of my movement. I stop walking, he stops with me, and I look up.

Something foreign seizes his expression. He lets out a long exhale and his hand, resting on the wall near my head, balls up. My gaze flicks over and I watch the black ink of his tats ripple. From a distance, I thought they were swirls. Now I noticed they're huge, ornate cursive letters. One looks like an *A* and it's swooping middle interweaves with a *C*. They wave and conform to the muscle residing in his forearms.

A hard swallow unleashes down my throat. Yes, he's being a total fuckwad, but *God...*

I can't deny that his jaggedness has a way of sucking me in. Poking me in a way that leaves my body thirsty, dying, and desperate to be sliced open. I'm craving to show myself to him. In turn, I want my brokenness to break him open, showing me all the darkness he holds.

For a brief moment, I want that.

Right after I'm done slapping his chiseled face and calling him an asshole.

He leans closer into me, making the wood paneling groan under his weight. My body clenches, even though I hate the reaction—and the idea of Monica being with him leaves a jealous taste in my mouth that I want to erase.

"Hmp." The husk in his voice rushes over me, raising the hair on my skin. "What's the matter? Cat got your tongue, or do you just want me *that* bad?"

It's both. I can't deny that to myself, but to him I deny everything. "I just want to be left alone."

"And I want your secrecy." He grits the words out, but then his vision lowers to my mouth. It stays there. "Give it to me." The way he says it—raspy, dry, and soft. It doesn't seem like he's talking about my silence. It sounds like he's demanding my screams of pleasure. I crumble to it.

Air snags in my lungs and my spine arches off the wood. My breasts brush the front of his marbled frame, and his throat bobs while a moan reverberates from his throat. My mouth dries up and I watch him pant for air.

*I should stop this.* Because this dude has just threatened me and there's nothing hot about that.

However, as much as I want to move, I can't. Just like he commanded the living room, he's forced me to him. I become a slave to the merciless pounding of my heart and his cruel gaze.

The shackles only release when his head lowers, he licks his mouth, and his eyes hood to a near close.

*No way.*

Sure this man is hotter than hell, but he's the biggest tool I've ever met. He won't kiss me—this man will never even graze me with his hand.

I squint. "Touch me and I'll scream." My threat growls out.

He freezes. At first, I think I've wrangled him by the collar—forced this alpha domineering prowler into submission. A feeling of triumph floods through my body.

Until his shoulders shake with a silent chuckle.

Every ounce of that sensation washes away when he lowers his head more, keeping our mouths a few daring inches apart.

"Trust me," he laces his dark utterance with sin—my pulse thrums at the point behind my ears. "I'd have to find you attractive to want to touch you."

The insult kills my heartbeat. I flat line in an instant, then a coldness descends when he rips himself away and leaves the room.

"Damn." I whisper it, slumping into the wall, finally allowing my knees to buckle the way they've wanted to this entire time.

However, while my knees go lax, a sharp twinge sears through me. No matter how much I try to lie to myself and drive his words away, that stung, and it turns out I was correct.

All his hellbent stares are from pure disgust, and I'll need to stay away from him while staying mum about anything that involves Brett Walker. Including acknowledging the way he sets my imagination and body on fire. Yeah. *Especially* that.

# Chapter 4

There's a massive ache wrapping around my head while I share coffee with Lizzie and Cora the next morning. Rubbing at my eye, I sigh and replace my mug on the table.

"Bee, for real, when are you going to get checked out?" Cora picks at her thick leggings and frowns. "I don't think they're getting better."

"I *know* they're not getting better," Lizzie replies. She ignores my scowl and directs her attention to Cora. "But good luck getting through. Little Miss here is digging in her heels."

"Which is ridiculous," Cora says, shifting to better face Lizzie. "I have no idea what's wrong with Bianca, but if I were her, I'd be getting an MRI faster than I could blink."

Lizzie nods. "Or at least getting blood work done. It makes me sad she's so stubborn. We only want it done for her good."

"Bah," Cora waves her hand in the air. "You know she never listens to us."

"Umm..." I hate it when they do this. Talk like I'm not here. It's a running joke between the two of them. They do it to get their points across when they think I'm being stubborn, but it's so annoying. "Excuse me—"

Cora and Lizzie don't make eye contact.

Instead, Cora turns in her seat and faces Lizzie head on, but I know she heard me. A faint smile presses on her thin mouth. "I don't know why I'm still friends with her, 'cause all that girl does is bug the crap out of me."

Lizzie ducks her head and giggles.

I tap my finger on the tabletop, annoyance pricking at my skin. "I don't know why I'm friends with *you*." My eyes narrow. "You know I find this annoying."

I'm granted a sideways glance from Cora. "Precisely why I said you're ridiculous." She readjusts and reaches for her mug. "If it was only me and Lizzie, I would have called you an idiot."

My mouth falls open, more agitation riling in my veins.

"I wouldn't call you an idiot," Lizzie pipes up. She stops the comeback resting on my tongue. "It's foolish not to find out what's going on, but you're not an idiot." Her brows furrow as she pauses and passes that darkened look to Cora, who in return rolls her eyes. "Getting things checked out is scary." Her voice softens. "But delaying will not make things better."

"Exactly." Cora shoves to her feet and snags up her empty mug. "If anything, it will make it worse."

My shoulders slump and temporary defeat slaps me across the cheek. I can't think of a response to deny them. Running my fingers through my hair, a bitter sensation washes over my stomach. *I hate it when they're right.*

Cora's heavy boots break my thoughts when they thud on the wood floor. "I'm gonna pee, then grab a refill." She points to me and Lizzie. "You two need anything?" We both shake our heads, and she strolls away.

"I'll say it one more time, Bianca." Lizzie twirls a strand of hair around her finger. "Go and get checked out. If anything, for me and Cora. We're only pestering you because we care."

A weak smile overtakes my mouth. "I know."

Silence settles and I drain the remainder of my coffee. Recalling Brett's words last night, apprehension pokes at my psyche. He said all his information came from Lizzie. *What did she tell him?* Did she really say I was desperate?

I scratch at the back of my neck, uncertainty rolling through my limbs. Lizzie's always been in my corner, so I doubt she meant to put me down in any way, but still, whatever she told him, Brett is using that.

And my time with Brett this morning wasn't much better than last evening.

He stalked me around the house, giving me pointed looks. I think he's keeping tabs on me to make sure I keep my mouth shut, but I can't be certain of that. Maybe he's just trying to annoy the hell out of me instead, sending out a reminder that I can't have him. I don't know. All I comprehend is how he grinds my nerves into powder. I seriously want to slap him each time we lock eyes.

"What's the matter?" Lizzie's voice rips away my train of thought. "It seems like something is bothering you."

Clearing my throat, I tug at the small pendant resting around my neck. The once pointed edges of the letter *K* are smooth and cool against my fingers. *K*—Mom's initial. Anxiety makes me touch it, the feel of it leaves me calm.

"Bianca," She brushes long hair off her shoulder and leans forward. "That look isn't good. You're upset. Did I do something wrong?"

A soft sigh slips out, and I have to smile. Lizzie is always concerned about others. I decide to not tag her along in suspense and be as upfront as I can about my situation with Brett. "Did you say anything about me to Brett Walker?"

Warm, large blue eyes light up. "Oh, boy. I'll say I did." An indecent yet gentle smirk captures her fine features. Judging from this reaction, I think she has the impression she's done me a favor. "He was asking all kinds of questions about you after you left. What you did and if you were seeing anyone."

A lump forms in my throat, stopping the swallow I'm trying to force. "Wh–what did you say?" My question comes out weaker than intended thanks to my knotted-up gut.

"That you were a writer and single." Her brows waggle. "Very. Very. Single."

The urge to slap my palm against my forehead and groan is strong. Given the weighted way she's saying that, I can see why Brett thinks I'm desperate. I hug myself around my middle. "You didn't happen to tell him in passing that I'm single by choice, did you?"

"It slipped my mind, Bianca." Long black lashes flutter. "When I was looking at him, all I could think about is how you deserve someone that gorgeous."

"Thanks but—"

"Sweetie." Sympathy flashes in her soft gaze. "I know Lance hurt you, but not everyone is going to be like that."

*Lance.* His name is like salt to the soul. He ended up being a dick, sleeping around on me and using me for money. A bitter experience considering he was so sweet for a while. It was after he dumped me I decided I was done with relationships. I swirl my finger on the table, letting those painful words re-loop. *Nothing lasts.* Not even relationships, which is why I refuse to get entangled with anyone these days.

"I doubt Brett is cut from the same cloth as Lance. Brett seems like a strong person. I hope it's not rude to say this, but Lance always reminded me of a weasel."

I stop a snort. She's not wrong. Looking back at it now, there was something shady and not forthcoming about Lance. For the most part, I know what field Brett is coming from.

"It's time you move on from that." Lizzie's voice breaks off my thoughts and her cheeks round with a soft smile. "He seemed super interested in you."

"Yeah..." I wring my hands together, sickness weighing me down in the chair. "I wouldn't call what Brett holds for me 'interest.'"

"Okay. So Brett is obviously not marriage material." Her slim shoulders lift then fall. After looking around, she leans across the table and lowers her voice. "So he wants to bang your brains out? What difference does it make?"

"No—"

"Who wants to fuck whose brains out?" Cora belts out the question and every head in the coffee shop turns as silence hits the air.

Lizzie and I both wince.

"God," Lizzie grits her teeth and tugs at Cora's shirt, yanking her down into the chair. "This is why I can't take you anywhere. You're so embarrassing."

"What?" Cora shrugs. "What did I do?"

"Don't look now," I say. "But everyone is watching." Unlike my friends, I have a head-on view, and I'm praying for the floor to suck me up as I shoot a strained smile to our onlookers.

Lizzie glances over her shoulder and turns ten shades of crimson. "Oh, holy..." She snatches up her purse and bounds to her feet. "We're leaving."

"Good idea." I'm already standing.

"No, we're not." Cora points to her house coffee, fresh and steaming. "I have—"

"Ruined everything." Lizzie latches onto her arm and pulls.

When Cora refuses, I grab her other arm and yank her to her feet.

We're shuffling out of the coffee shop, fast as our feet can keep up. The whole time I'm partially keeping my head down, partially granting everyone awkward grins.

A whoosh of needed cold air encompasses me after we step outside. Even that isn't enough. I undo my jacket as we stride along, Lizzie and I trying to keep up with Cora's longer legs.

"Golly, dum-dum." Lizzie hip bumps Cora.

"Ouch!" Cora leans closer to me and rubs her hip. "All I said—"

"Dropping F-bombs like that is never cool, Cora." Lizzie's breath trails in the air as she sighs. "Seriously, what happened to your filter."

"Bee broke it." Cora jerks her thumb towards me.

A laugh busts out my lungs, echoing in the air. She always knows how to make me laugh. Catching my breath, I shake my head. "You're so full of bullcrap."

"I agree." Lizzie is anything but giggles as she squints. Bundling her coat around her, she wiggles her finger in the air. "When we go to dinner tonight, try to not say outlandish things like that so loud."

"I'll try." Cora's brow lifts. "No guarantees."

I smile. *Dinner.* It's only brunch, but a puddle of drool is already living in my mouth. There's a divine Italian place we're hitting up tonight, and Italian food is something I'd die for. It's my favorite. Peeking around Cora, I address Lizzie. "What time are we going and who's coming?"

"Seven." Lizzie's mouth lifts. "And last time I heard everyone is coming."

My mouth falls open. "Everyone? Like 'everyone' in our cabin everyone?"

Cora snorts. "Is there another kind of *everyone?*"

And just like that, my happy hopes die. That means Brett will be there, which no doubt means more staring. My eyes glaze over as I flick my vision to the sidewalk. "Great." If I sound flat, I don't care. "Can't wait."

"Hey, don't sound so put out." Cora's arm rubs against mine. "Our hottie Brett Walker will be there."

I gulp, dread winding around my core. *That's what I'm afraid of.*

Cora makes a throaty *mmm* and laughs. "Dinner and a show, am I right?"

"Yeah." My laugh sounds weak, but probably only to me. "I guess you're right."

*A show.* More like a circus. And now I can honestly say I'm not looking forward to tonight. Brett Walker is turning out to be my final lemon in life. His ugly stares are souring everything about my getaway weekend, and I don't know how to make lemonade out of this situation. To be frank, I don't know how to make lemonade at all, and I've been out of sugar for years. At the moment, I'm pretty sure life is decidedly against me.

I take a deep breath, for once trying to stay positive. *Two more nights.* Two more nights and I can escape back home and not have to worry about ways to avoid Brett. Two more damn nights.

*I can do it.* I hope.

# Chapter 5

**M**y stomach growls, the need for pasta is heavy, and Lizzie and Cora are waiting in the car for me. Rounding the darkened corner of the hallway, I'm ready for dinner. I've dressed in my favorite sheer cream blouse and snug jeans. The blouse was Mom's. I always wear it for special occasions.

After many years, I still get compliments on this thing, proving it's a classic, like a little black dress only better. The oversized floppy bow at the collar is my favorite detail.

I'm looking down, retucking the blouse into the waistband of my jeans, when I have a crash landing—one that's hard enough to make me bounce back a step.

"*Umph.*" Immediately, I know the maker of that gruff voice.

*Brett.* My knees sway at the sound, but a mixture of annoyance and disdain swirls through my core.

This is the first time I've seen him since this morning—mainly because I've been hiding out in my room like a grounded teenager. I tried to outline a few things for a new book idea, but I didn't get far. All my plots were dead ends. I spent most of my time getting ready so I'd feel pretty tonight...which thank goodness for that.

I need this confidence to not faint under his suffocating intimidation. It reeks from the man, residing in his spread-out stance. In the partial darkness, I see the workings of a heated glare while he peers at me past the end of his nose. I waste no time sending the look back.

Pocketing his hands, thumbs out, he encloses my space by moving forward. I don't know why, but it's a total turn on. Lust bolts from my clenched thighs to the floor, making my toes curl along the way. *Crap.* I despise how helpless I am to control my reactions, which only happens when we're together.

When he swallows me in his shadows, he flips the switch on an emotional dryer. Everything in me ends up jumbled and full of static.

Sexual static in this case. The fact he's narrowing his eyes doesn't change what he charges in me. Same goes for when he finally addresses me. "What did you and your girls talk about today?"

He's not being nice, but the man still has my stomach exploding with butterflies. *I'm deranged.* That's the only answer to my bizarre hot and cold energy.

He lowers his head and a spearmint scent lightly floats across my skin. "I asked you a question. What did you say?"

*I bet he tastes good.* But I don't want to find out.

"Blondie?"

I like how it sounds when he says it. It leaves me thirsty, drying all the saliva in my throat. After managing a dry swallow, I steady my voice. "Not about Moni—"

"Don't." His voice snaps like hard leather. "Don't even say that name."

"Why?" I shuffle toward him, cinching my arms across my chest. Our body heat collides and I hear the pace of his breath quicken. "Last time I checked, she isn't Voldemort. Death Eaters aren't going to descend if we say her name."

His brows furrow, and the floor creaks while he shifts his weight to the opposite foot. "I haven't a single fucking clue as to what you're talking about."

My mouth dangles open. "Seriously? Don't you read or watch movies?"

"Don't have a need for movies. Reading? Paperwork? Things that make me money? Yes." An evil smile passes across his mouth, and I can sense the jab that's about to occur before he spits it out. "Fiction? Made up shit that brings no purpose to the world? No."

"Mmm." My head bobs as I refuse to feel the lashing of his words. "That explains it."

His nostrils flare, and that satisfaction of watching him get trapped in his own game sends me flying higher than a ball sailing out of the park in a home run. However, some of the victory deflates when he shuffles closer. Our shoe tips rub against one another, and again, he smells amazing. I'm praying he can't hear how hard my heart knocks at my sternum, because I feel it's waves in my heels.

He threads a large hand through his gelled back hair. His black, medium-length hair kisses the nape of his neck and there's a wispiness to it. A slight crunch occurs when he flexes his fingers. A few springs come undone as he frowns. "To answer your question, I don't need any slip-ups from you. If people suspect anything happened, all my plans are trash."

"Plans?" My ears pique with interest. "What plans?"

"Ha." His laugh is dark, but a lightness takes over his eyes. He almost looks amused. "Why should I tell you anything?"

"Humor me." I cock my head to the side and bite my lower lip, rolling it through my teeth. "Perhaps a better understanding will encourage my silence." I lower my pitch at the end to sound ultra calm and enticing, but all I feel is hot blood sludging through my veins and my knees weakening.

All thanks to the way he stares at me.

His jaw clenches, and there's a flicker occurring in his eyes while they fixate on my mouth. I bring a hand to my throat when he takes a breath so deep the buttons strain across his chest. There is no exhale.

It renders my limbs useless and my core heavy. *Shit.* Heat creeps upward towards my cheeks, and I don't want that. I don't *want* to respond to him.

The wood floor groans as I step back, retreating into the darkness. "You know what..." The words want to knot up in my throat. "Just forget it." I take a side step, preparing to dart around him.

"Her husband owns land." He sounds normal while addressing me, and whatever that was a second ago has passed. No space is given while he passes into the dark, joining me in it. "Land that I need. *Really* need."

I watch his wide silhouette move as he rubs at the nape of his neck. He's a specimen of power, and I'm grateful he can't see how rounded my eyes are, or how bright my cheeks flare. The dark we're sharing tells me lies, making me feel intimate with him, and even though we're anything but, he has me captive. My vision traces the outline of his shadowed thighs. They're perfectly widened against his narrowed waist, playing in harmony to the span of his chest. He creates a beautiful $X$ shape. One of muscle—of pleasure.

*Sadly, not my pleasure.* I'll never experience any of it. I make a note to write about this body instead. My shoulders tighten when Brett's voice rumbles in the dark, reminding me we're talking about Monica.

"If her husband finds out what happened, he won't sell me the property, and that's a problem. I need your silence."

His words slap the heated desire I've been feeling for him right out of me. Bile hits the back of my throat and disgust twists in my stomach. "That's it?" My voice goes hard and flat. "That's your reason?"

*Please tell me he isn't this selfish. Please tell me I didn't just meet the biggest dick-bag on the planet.*

"Yeah."

I refuse to believe it. Brett must care about jeopardizing Monica's family—he must. Even if it's only a little. My nose screws up. "You mean that? That's your *only* reason? Not because you feel bad for using her or possibly getting their marriage in trouble?"

"No...I mea—"

*Scratch that.* Turns out he *is* the biggest dick-bag on the planet.

"That's pathetic." Aversion carries my legs as I skirt past him. I'm running a little late and upon hearing this, I'm so done giving him my attention.

"Excuse me?" What sounds like shock laces in his deep voice.

"You heard me." I spin on my heel after coming into the light. "Thinking only of yourself and not caring one iota for possibly troubling their marriage is pathetic."

He doesn't move, but there is a hard scoff. "I didn't ask for your opinion. I'm telling you to keep your mouth shut."

"You don't get to tell me what—"

"Mouth. Shut." He whispers it, but damn, it's harsh...but still not harsh enough.

Bitterness coils around my tongue. It stands equally next to the anger shooting through my raw nerves. My eyes narrow. "Fuck your plans. They suck."

I swear he gasps. "Bianca..." That *is* shock I'm hearing. His voice is easily an octave higher.

The utterance of my real name makes me pause, forcing my attention. Not in a good way. My fingers dig into the frame of the large wooden arch before the last flight of stairs. "If I have to tell someone, I will." There's no warmth in my voice for him. Brett has killed that tonight.

"You wouldn't dare. You're not serious." When he finally comes out of the shadows, his mouth is wide open.

I take it as a good sign and nod. "I am. Your plan sucks, you're a douche, and I'm not guaranteeing you anything." My teeth grind together. "Now leave me alone."

"Bianca."

Tearing myself away, I scurry down the staircase, not looking back, not acknowledging him as he says my name once more.

I'm halfway down when I hear his low laugh, and I do mean low. It's continuous, dark, maybe even a little unhinged.

A chill brushes up my body, and I rub my arms. I have no idea what that reaction means, but I have a pretty good inclination I'm going to find out, and I don't think I'm going to like it.

# Chapter 6

"That blouse always looks so nice on you." Lizzie's finger trails down the sleeve as we wait to be seated. "It was your mom's, wasn't it?"

A smile perks up my mouth while I stroke over some of the fabric. "It was."

"I'm sure she'd love to know how much you cherish it." Her voice is hushed in our gathered crowd. Anytime she refers to my mom, she does this. I think it's her gentle way of connecting. Both of her parents are gone, and while we rarely talk about the loss, I sometimes wonder if she hopes talking about our moms will make it less painful someday. That will never be the case. At least not for me.

I don't talk of Mom much, of her struggles and tragic end, but Lizzie knows how close I keep her to my heart. Kathryn Stanley has been a driving force in my life, even writing is a memory to her. I did it because she never got to do the things she loved. All Dad did was squash her interests and control her. And Mom? Well, she was tender. Never using a harsh word, or loud voice. She wasn't born to be a fighter, and so she died.

Because of Dad.

He drained all the color from her, leaving her to believe her world was pale and bleak. In reality, the only thing dreary was my dad. Dad didn't suck all the vibrancy from me. Thankfully, there's enough fire in me that I still fight. Mom's ending will not be mine. If anything, I fight harder because of her.

*But I still miss her.*

That thought is hammering in my skull, pulling my heart down when the restaurant doors open.

Brett steps in, and our crowd sounds happy to see him with their bright hello's. The only thing I can conjure for him is a scowl.

*Inconsiderate prick.* He's the douche we've been waiting on since they won't seat an incomplete party. Everyone has been here for a while. Except him. *Not that he cares.* He's proven he doesn't think about anyone except himself, which is something I should have seen from the start. Ogling him this entire time has been foolish on my part, but I won't do it anymore.

Contempt is easier than breathing now. Observing him from across the room, my mouth snarls up when taking in his bare forearms. Once again, the sleeves to his button-down dress shirt are rolled up and there's no coat in sight.

"Doesn't he own a damn jacket?" It's freezing balls cold outside.

Cora is the only one who hears me above the commotion. Ducking for my ear, she snickers. "Do men that hot need one?"

"Last I checked he's human." My voice has a hard edge that I can't hide. "Yes, he needs a jacket."

Cora's thin brows quirk together. "Someone's in a bad mood." Her lips purse out. "You haven't eaten much today. Let's get that hanger out of you, huh?"

"I'm not hangry. I'm—"

"We're being seated," one person from our group calls out, and my words die.

A shuffle occurs as all fifteen of us reposition. Some people meander over to form groups of who they want to sit with. Then we start a line. Either way, we'll be seated between three tables. I'll of course be with Lizzie and Cora. Besides them, I'm good with just about anyone else—except Brett. I know he won't sit by me. Not after the words we exchanged.

I'm relieved, really. Our distance will mean dinner will be better than I expected. *Maybe our fight was a good thing.* I'm claiming that while draping my coat over the seat-back. I'm at the end. Cora will be at the head since she's a weirdo who needs her space. Lizzie will sit next to me.

"Mind if I sit in between you two beautiful ladies?"

I'm pulling my seat out when my spine stiffens. *Brett.* Holy shit, it's Brett, and his voice oozes like dark corn syrup. When I glance over my shoulder, he's addressing Lizzie. She's all giggles with a high flush in her cheeks.

"Oh, of course," Lizzie says, sliding down to the next seat, sweeping hair behind her ear.

There isn't room for me to object—that makes my stomach plummet. This is most likely blooming from the laugh I heard earlier. Whatever idea Brett concocted after our discussion, I'm sure it's rooted in this.

*Damn it. Damn it.* More reason to stay in my room after tonight. My decision concretes itself as he sits next to me and then has the nerve to prop his hand on the back of my chair. What's also not helping is how he's angled, facing me. His muscular leg encroaches on my square of land. I snatch up my menu, working hard to shut him out.

"What do you like to eat?" Brett's voice is the dictionary's description of considerate, and I know he's addressing me, but I act like I don't hear him. "You strike me as a pasta girl. Maybe lasagna?"

My lips press together in a firm line.

"Bee?" Cora's not going to let me ignore him.

Resting the menu down, I shoot him a stilted smile. "I hate lasagna, and hopefully I order something you find revolting."

He actually laughs. It sounds real, not like the dark one from earlier. His shoulders shake with the husky sound, and if I wasn't pissed, I'd swoon over it. Lighter tones of brown spark in his gaze as leans toward me. "I'm sure you have great taste. I'll order whatever you're having." He smiles so amiably it could melt the panties off a blind grandma.

I tap one finger on the tabletop, agitation bundling in my nerves. "Please don't."

"Bianca." Lizzie locks eyes with me past Brett and frowns. The rebuke in her voice is soft, but you can't mistake it for anything else.

Brett shrugs and briefly gives his attention to my friend. "Is she always this sassy?"

"Gosh no." Lizzie's reply is weak and her shoulders curl inward.

"That's a shame," Brett says. "Because it's cute. Don't scold her." He brings his head closer to hers. "I like it."

*Dear Lord.* The tone of his voice...if this is how he charms his victims, it's a total slam dunk. If he hadn't poked so many holes in my perception of him, I'd be scolding me too.

Lizzie doesn't utter another word. There's a tremor in her hand and crimson in her ears. If there was a wine glass present, she'd be clutching for it. She always crumbles with strong male attention.

Brett redirects his focus on me. "I'm a veal man myself."

"Calf murderer." I mutter it, snatching up my menu, refusing to spare him a glance. Annoyance threads through my chest when he chuckles, forcing my body to stiffen.

"Hey," Cora pipes up. "I like veal too, so cast some stones this way."

"Awesome." Brett's voice is so fake and happy it turns my stomach sour. "Looks like I'm in great company."

My heart sinks to my toes when Cora responds by laughing. *Great. Just great.* In less than five minutes, he's hooked my friends in his snare. Debating openly won't work and will make me look bad. I'll need to talk to both of them in private since I'm sure that whatever I do at this table, Brett will flip it on its head.

*Looks like my night is going to blow after all.* My shoulders fold into themselves, making my frame smaller—it's a stupid, futile gesture, but physically retreating makes me feel a bit safer from the deceit Brett spreads out.

Some unease flits away when silence overtakes us. Brett's presence is throwing any conversation we would naturally have off kilter. The off timed throat clearing and sighs of Brett, Cora, and Lizzie catch my ears. I never look or make a sound, opting to keep my face in the menu. I'm sad knowing the waiter will take it away soon. It's a great shield—the perfect Brett deflector.

"So," Cora knocks her knuckles on the table, shattering our quiet. "What are the plans for tomorrow?"

"Bianca wants to go check out that Apple Cottage store," Lizzie says, which puts unwanted focus on me.

"That sounds interesting." When Brett says it, my nails bite into the menu. "I heard about that place and wanted to check it out. You're going tomorrow?"

My mouth opens to object.

"Sure are." Cora cuts me off. "We're leaving at ten, just so you know."

*No. Shit. No.* I clamp down on my tongue. Anxiety swirls inside. The Apple Cottage is a store off the beaten path with a certain amount of kitsch. I found it online and they sell slices of homemade apple pie and cobbler. You can eat and shop. I've been pumped about going here, and I'll be damned if he ruins it—which he's going to do.

"What kind of vehicle did you ladies come in?" His shoe brushes my leg as he props an ankle on top of his knee. I feel like it's on purpose. Since I won't give him my attention, he's doing everything he can to remind me he's still here. "If there's room, we could all go together."

The menu fumbles in my hands, and the words have my stomach in my throat.

"Oh." Cora's voice slides up to a higher tone. She seems pleased. "That sounds great."

Looking at her, my eyes are wide. I shake my head.

She doesn't pay me any mind. "We're in my Crossover. There's lots of—"

*Damn.* "Actually." The menu falls from my hands, floating down to my plate. Screw Brett. I'd rather miss out on the trip than be miserable with him. "I'm not going."

"What?" Lizzie and Cora say it in unison.

"But you've been so excited about this." A strand of Lizzie's hair dangles on the table when she bends over, staring at me with an open mouth. "What changed?"

My gaze flicks to Brett. *Bastard.* The smug smile tweaking up his lips sends a pulse down my fist. *God, I'd love to punch him.* He knows exactly what he's doing. An old adage plays in my mind. *Keep your friends close and your enemies closer.* And right now, if I'm reading this right, he's opted to keep me close. Very close.

Folding my arms across my chest, I lean back in my seat. "My agent wants to talk to me about some book ideas I have."

"Really?" Cora tilts her head, and through the haze of those purple contacts, I watch her try to dissect me. She probably knows I'm lying. "What book idea is this?"

"Mmm. This one's really interesting." Fatigued at the way Brett encroaches on my space, I cross my leg at the knees making sure my shin rubs against his foot. My pulse stutters when he clears his throat and shifts.

At least I have some effect on him, and that's the best feeling I've had all year.

Tilting my head back, I keep my vision locked on Cora. "It's about this douche, who's nothing but a piece of crap and only thinks about himself. I haven't worked out all the details yet, but his ending is going to be sad and lonely, where everyone despises him." I shrug. "I might even kill him off in the final chapter."

Brett coughs and pats his chest. Cora's brows squish together.

"That sounds awful." Lizzie's soft voice sounds flabbergasted.

"Yeah," Cora winces. "Even I have to agree with that. I'm not sure I'd read it."

"Well, I would." I tug at my ear and fake my best doe eyes, gazing up to Brett. "Would you read something like that?" I fake a sugary voice.

"Uhh," The ire in his eyes fades and a warmness creeps in. He darts his vision away from me, scratching at his nape. Even under the dim lights, I notice a slight pink shading his tan complexion.

It's my first time witnessing this alphahole falter. I have to say it's a beautiful sight. One that sends satisfaction humming through my limbs. After a second longer, one side of his mouth raises. It strips away the natural brood, and for a flash, I see a softness that wasn't there before—it forces me to wonder how deep it goes.

*How deep is his well?* Is he all dried up, comprising of deadness and cruelty? I'm not sure, all I can hope is that he's not like this with everyone and that I'm merely seeing the worst version of him.

"I...uhhh." He chuckles softly. "I don't actua—"

"Are we ready to order?" The server appears out of thin air, killing our discussion.

We order, and sure enough, Brett copies my choice of chicken marsala. And maybe I'm being petty, but knowing he's experiencing what I am spoils my dish. Especially as our night drags on.

Anytime Cora and Lizzie try to start up a conversation with me, he interrupts. It doesn't matter what we're talking about. Makeup, music, movies, getting our nails done...he has some kind of input that always ends up cutting off my answers—but he does it so obligingly that my friends can't see it for how it's intended. The only signals I get are the occasional cocky smirks he sends my way. Each one strips my composure that much more.

*He's trying to control me.* That thought circulates through my brain an hour and a half later. I have to think that Brett is so hellbent on getting me to keep my mouth shut that he doesn't want me to talk at all.

I frown. *Dick-bag is ruining everything.* Light glints off my silver fork as I swirl it through my pasta with zero gusto. Our meal is winding down. I've hardly eaten, thanks to his innumerable interruptions and my jumbled nerves. It gets worse. My shoulders tighten at the tone of his voice.

"Bianca, you've hardly touched your food." I smell peppermint and red wine embanking me on the right. Glancing over, Brett's infringing on my space yet again, fake concern playing in his eyes. "Is there something wrong with it? We've been here a while, but I could send it back."

Aggravation grinds me raw, to my marrow. Brittle composure

snaps inside me like a dead stick. I squint, unable to live under the thick cloud of lies he's trying to sell. "Don't." The word growls out.

"Don't?" He cocks his head. "Don't send it back? But if you're not happy with it—"

Cora and Lizzie are both absorbed in their phones. We're undetected. "Stop."

"Stop?" He uses a confused voice, and God, it's infuriating, igniting hot blood in my veins. "Stop what? I don't understand."

*That's it.* I'm so done it's not even funny. I sneer and look away. Pushing hair off my shoulders, I sit higher in my seat and force a louder voice. "Has anyone heard from Monica?"

Brett goes rigid beside me. He stiffens more when Cora places her phone down.

"Ha. No." Cora rests her elbows on the table. "I haven't seen her for a while."

"I have." I feel Brett's eyes digging into my back, but I don't care. This is what he gets for threatening and harassing me—a huge warning shot. I'm not ready to out him yet, but I will if I have to. Hopefully me mentioning her scares the shit out of him. "I saw her the other night at... AH!"

Liquid hits my blouse. There's a shatter of glass while something collides on the floor, but it drowns out in the distance.

*No.* Looking down, my heart shreds in two. There's a red splotch on Mom's blouse. Wine. Red alcohol bleeds through the sheerness of my top, marring it for life.

Hot tears streak my vision. My hands shake. I can't breathe. "Oh..." The singular sound wrangles out of me. The longer I stare, the more my stomach knots into sickness.

"Damn, Bianca." I hear Brett's voice. It pulls me back to the land of the living. My blurry gaze locks on the two cold, distant eyes of Brett as he lightly dabs at my shirt with a napkin. "Me and my big arms. I shouldn't have put my glass there."

The false apology swirls painfully in my ears, growing when a mocking smile passes over his mouth. Anyone else would miss it, but he lets me see it long enough to get the point across.

I hunch over, clutching at my chest. "You—you—you..." Finishing my words isn't possible. Not when my heart just shriveled up and died. A sob breaks free.

"Bianca?" Brett's voice deepens, and his large hand cups my shoulder. Trembling, I look up and notice his disdain falling away. What looks like genuine concern brings his brows together, and a paleness splashes across his features. "Bianca?" My name comes out breathless and his thumb grazes across my shoulder.

His touch and voice are revolting. "Don't." I jerk away and stand— my skin crawling at the sensation of him. Jerking to my feet, my chair topples over.

He's towering over me before I can comprehend him rising from his chair. "Bianca?" When he holds his hand out, I back up.

My feet tangle around the legs of my fallen seat. I wobble but catch myself, aware of only one thing—the hole in my chest. A massive, burnt, bleeding, aching hole that Brett's placed there. My blouse is ruined. Mom's last article of existence is ruined because of this monster.

Tears slide down my cheeks. Then I notice the deafness swirling in the air. Everyone is watching, not moving or breathing. Cora and Lizzie are on either side of me, and I'm only now noticing them.

We've created a ruckus, and I'm the focus when I'd rather be under a rock. Glancing up at Brett once more, I can't stop the trembling of my lip, and the workings of a wail climb up my throat—so I leave.

Scooping up my purse and jacket, I dart away from the scene.

"Bianca, wait!"

I ignore the sound of Brett's voice and run out the restaurant, its walls smearing around me, while I gasp for air.

Brett's destroyed my most loved possession on earth. I hate him for it. I thought this man was a thorn in my side, but now I know him as someone who further breaks the jagged pieces of my heart, and I can't forgive him for that. I just can't.

# Chapter 7

**M**aybe it's ridiculous to be in emotional shambles over a ruined blouse, but that's what's happening. Tears trickle over the bridge of my nose and slide down my cheeks before seeping into the pillow beneath me. Clutching the shirt against me, I sob once more, unable to breathe through my nose. I still can't believe it happened, and while it shouldn't seem like a big deal, it is.

A frown captures my mouth while thinking of Mom. Envisioning her causes my fingers to dig into the article of clothing, almost like she's still here and I'm clinging to her. But she's not here, and she left far too soon.

Accepting that all over again sends a fresh burn through my sternum.

I was a junior in high school when it happened. Mom and Dad argued while I was staying over at a friend's house. Hearing that Mom fought with Dad that evening always struck me as odd. It wasn't something she'd ever done—but neighbors told me Mom could be heard that night, screaming at my dad to stop hitting her.

By the time police arrived, Mom was already gone, checking into a hotel, and Dad wasn't arrested because what occurred was 'just a little tiff' according to him.

*Some tiff.*

A hotel worker found Mom in the bathtub the next morning. Two slices to the wrist. That's the end she chose for herself. She only picked it because of *him*. Whatever Dad said to her that night, it killed her.

Waking up to a phone call the next morning and receiving that news was like having your heart ripped out while beating and then watching it get smashed. What followed was worse. I went home the next day to find Mom's belongings destroyed.

Every picture of hers? Burnt. Jewelry? Sold to a pawnshop. All her clothes? Cut into squares with a pair of scissors. I lost every piece of her. Except for the blouse. It was in my closet because I had worn it for school pictures earlier that week. I snagged it because I loved it and thought it was the most gorgeous thing I'd ever seen. Mom had been pestering me to give it back. Thank God I didn't.

When I confronted Dad about what he did, he claimed it was because he couldn't deal with the grief. Looking back, I think he was pissed because he couldn't control her anymore.

The blouse became my world for the first few years. When the pain of her absence became too much, I'd take it to bed with me and cry. Tonight, I've come full circle. Years later, my head is buried in a stranger's pillow to muffle my cries, the shirt nuzzled into my neck.

I'll never be able to wear this and be connected to her again. That's Brett's doing.

He's sullied my last piece of her. It's like I'm losing her all over again, and loss aches heavy in my chest. Like before, it's going to take a while to seal. All I can do right now is let out the grief.

A few hours later, my tears dissipate, and I roll to my other side, determined to sleep, hoping tomorrow will be better somehow.

That's a struggle. Dad's voice disrupts my attempts as his drink ridden tone loops viciously in my head. A haunting shiver races up my spine.

*"Nothing lasts. You won't last. Your mom didn't last. Nothing lasts."*

He's proving himself right. More so in death. Nothing is lasting for me. Not even the memories of Mom.

*Mom.*

I grip the shirt tighter, then exhaustion wins the fight against my eyes and sleep takes over. Sadly, I slumber to Dad's words, and maybe I'm beaten down right now, but for the first time I feel myself agreeing to what he spoke over me.

Nothing lasts. In the end, everything good slips away. Even those we love. *Especially* those we love.

# Chapter 8

"Oh la-la," Cora's voice rings out over the gathered crowd at the lounge as I enter. "Look at what the cat dragged in."

We have two nights left of our 'vacation' and a few of us have decided to hit up a posh lounge and upper-class rec bar in town. I almost didn't come, but after a lot of thought, I knew it would be best. People will know I'm still alive. And while I'm not over the idea of Mom's blouse being ruined, I'll survive.

Arriving this late, I'm pretty sure I'm the last one here. It was by choice. I enjoy slipping into places undetected—the dim blue lights melding around the walls thus chilling out the entrance seems like the perfect opportunity for a sneak in.

However, Cora has ruined that. Several heads turned when I stepped in.

"Thanks." I grit my teeth. "Pretty sure everyone heard you."

"Good." She props the sole of her chunky boot on the wall behind her, clear drink in hand. Most likely vodka. That's her go-to. "You look hot."

A giggle slips out. Running my hands down my torso, one of my shoulders pulls up. "Not too bad, huh?" I roll my bottom lip through my teeth and give her a wry smile. It grows when she gives me a once over and nods.

I've picked a silver mesh bodysuit, black wash jeans and nude heels. The top shines metallic under the rotating lights above, and it's so form fitting I'm wearing a corset underneath. I've also gone heavy on the cat eye and smokey shadow, playing up my blue eyes. *Yeah, not bad at all.*

"Wanna drink, babe?" A silvery voice catches my ear. Looking over my left shoulder, I make eye contact with a guy who stands just a few inches taller. Not bad looking, but not my type. Too preppy for my taste with his sweater, collared shirt, and oxford shoes. The glasses on his thin face aren't helping, and to be frank, I'm surprised a squeaky-clean looking guy like him says the word 'babe.'

I shake my head, tucking a tendril behind my ear. "No thank you, I don't drink."

His altar boy expression disintegrates, and a cruelness twists up his features. "Sure you don't. That's why you're here." One of his shoes drags on the floor with a step he takes—it looks too heavy for his medium build, and the way his balance teeters tells me he's drunk. Usually I can see it in the eyes right away, but his glasses concealed it from me. "Come on, sweetheart."

"Hey, Yale." Cora attaches herself to my side, cutting this douche off. "You heard her, she doesn't drink. Now go away."

"Excuse me?" Our prep boy furrows his brow, giving Cora a confused look. "Who are you?" He looks at her clothes and wrinkles his nose. "Did you miss the rock show?"

"No." Her purple gaze goes hard. "But you're gonna be missing your teeth if you don't get the hell away."

He puts two hands up. "Fine." Hanging his head, he saunters away. "Enjoy being average."

I snort. Now that's the type of insult I expect from a guy like that.

Cora releases a low scoff. "Enjoy looking like Harvard barfed on you."

Only I hear it, but it has a laugh busting out of my chest.

"Seriously," Cora says through a chuckle. "What is it with you and jerks? You haven't even been here five minutes."

My shoulders fall with a shrug. "I don't know." I push some of my weight against hers. "Thanks for having my back."

"Anytime." She takes a sip. "You feeling better from the other night? I've never seen you so upset."

I push out a deflated sigh. "I think so." I feel the lines appearing between my brows as I scowl when recalling a certain someone. "Stupid Brett."

"Oh, Bee, you know that was an accident." Her voice is gentle yet correcting.

"No way. He—"

"We gave him an earful for what happened."

"What?" A sickness grabs hold of my stomach, dragging it down to my toes. I swear to God they better not have told him it belonged to my mom, because if there's one person who shouldn't know anything about me, it's Brett Walker. A weak swallow washes down my throat. "You didn't tell him—"

"That the blouse was your mom's? You can bet your ass I did. So did Lizzie."

*Great.* If I haven't been brought down low enough already, now he's privy to knowing my mom died.

*Check.* One forever single, failing author, with a dead mother and a ruined blouse...it sounds like a lonely hearts advertisement or the start to the worst novel ever. Nothing about my life speaks of empowerment. No wonder he looks down at me, past the end of his nose.

I wrap my arms around my middle and frown.

"Geez, don't look so beaten down. Trust me, we got the point across for you." One of her brows wrinkles. "He felt terrible about what happened."

"Yeah." The reply is weak. "I'm sure he did." *Of course he didn't.* Whatever they saw spins from the lies and fake persona Brett displayed that night. Hearing Cora's story, it sounds like he continued to sell the show, even after I left.

Since that's the case, I'm deciding to not push this issue right now. Calling Brett an asshole after I'm the one that had a public meltdown is not the tactic of champions. All I'll sound like right now is defensive and bitter. I'll save this war for another day, when I'm calm and have Cora and Lizzie all to myself.

Thinking of Lizzie makes me realize I haven't seen her walking around, but I know she came with Cora. "Where's Lizzie?"

Her lips flip up. "Talking to a hot guy." She flicks a long finger to the opposite corner of the room. "See?"

Ducking my head, I peer past the gathered bodies and through the blue lights. There's an area filled with black sofas. Sure enough, Lizzie giggles it up, looking mega hot in a red bodycon dress that shows off more leg than what she's usually brave enough to wear. The dude? Totally her type. Lean, tall, and tawny with a built-in surfer look. She's probably in heaven.

Like we're reading each other's minds, Cora and I bump arms at the same time and glance at one another.

"What d'ya say?" Cora rakes through the top of her hair. "Think we should let them be?"

I slowly nod. "Absolutely."

That's what we do. Cora and I hang around each other, just mingling with the crowd in the front part of the lounge. We enjoy the drum of music, harmony of lights, and the natural excitement in the air. Most of our company is people from our cabin—the nice ones. Brett is nowhere and thank goodness for that.

After an hour, I'm certain my bladder is about to pop. "Where are the bathrooms?"

"Mmm." Cora finishes her third and final drink for the night. She never has over three. "Past the bar, into the second room. Walk straight, then a sharp left before the pool tables."

"Thanks." I slide past and make my merry way.

The second room spans out like a football field, one littered with recreational fun. More dim ambient lighting acts like a haze. It's hard to see every detail, but there's a lot more people in here. Most are just talking, holding pool cues in hand if they're standing by the billiards area, or a drink if occupying the sleek bar to my left.

The bar is the area I'm skirting past when a familiar voice catches my ear.

"Sugar?"

Smacking face first into a concrete wall couldn't stop my momentum more. I'm actually wondering if my feet are tacked to the carpet as I look over my shoulder. My heart bottoms out, not stopping its fall until it hits the floor. It's Lance.

My ex.

This dude is the reason I've decided to stay single for life. *Talk about good things not lasting.* Somehow he bundled me so tight in his deceit that I couldn't see him for what he was. A cheater who was using my cash to spoil other girls and then spending the weekends professing his love to me.

A large scar of pain lays across the span of my heart, all because of this snake—one who, even now, has me wondering why I wasn't enough. I'll never admit it, but having him near and knowing we're forever apart makes my soul reverberate with an emptiness and the bitter reminder that relationships end in heartbreak.

My nails bite into my palm, but my voice is weak. "Lance."

"Thought that was you." He climbs out of his stool, staggering to one side with a step. He's gained more weight since he broke up with me, but he still looks comfortable. Normal. Easy going. His relaxed blonde hair and penetrating hazel eyes always had a way of unlocking me and my tongue.

*But I can't trust him.* He may look the same, but I've tasted him for what he really is. *I'll never open up to him again.* Not even as he stops in front of me and gives me a glimmering once over. It's familiar since I always witnessed it right before he'd drag me off to bed.

Tonight, I'm retracting from it by taking a shuffle back.

"You look amazing." His voice flows like honey, but I know it's a web of entanglement. After he broke up with me, he went all over town claiming I'd come running back to him if he made an offer. I think I'm experiencing that talk right now.

Rolling my shoulders back, ice coats my heart. "Good night, Lance." I manage one step when his hand latches around my wrist.

"Don't be like that." An attempt to back away fails. He tugs me toward him and he's always been deceptively strong. I stumble forward. "All my friends are here. I want to show them the hottie I used to dick down."

"You're drunk." The stench of alcohol swirls up my nostrils with each word he utters.

"Drunk on you." His hand grips around my waist, pressing into the fabric of my shirt, clenching deep in my corset. I feel his heated hand through it all. A slither coils down my spine at how his touch hasn't changed.

My heart teeters on a dangerous edge, wanting to fall and experience Lance again, but Dad's words mingle in, breaking up the strange craving racing through my skin. *Nothing lasts.* This might mark the first time I re-loop the saying in a positive way—because I'm no fool. If I go crawling back to Lance, he'll be sleeping with someone else the next day.

After taking a deep breath, I attempt to free my hands. He washes away my desires for him when his grip tightens so hard his fingers crunch against my bones. A fire erupts at the base of my stomach. "Let go." The heated anger tingling through me fuels my voice and my glare.

Too bad it explodes right in my face.

"Don't be like that, Bianca." There's no time to think. His free hand threads through my hair at the base of my skull, and his lips collide on top of mine.

I squirm against him, striking at his chest in futile attempts to break free. He's rougher than I remember, and I despise it. Plus, the taste of the Jack he's been hitting reminds me of Dad's tainted breath. I want to cry as nausea roils in my stomach while I hear his friends hoot and holler. I raise a foot off the ground, preparing to kick his shin.

Turns out I don't have to.

A hard thunk vibrates in the air. Lance's hold vanishes. I spring, sky high.

A large hand connects with his chest, shoving him away. His eyes widen. He stumbles over his Timberlands, unable to catch himself. Sailing back, there's a thud as he lands flat on his ass, wincing with the connection of the floor.

"WHAT the fuck are you doing? Who the fuck are you?" The question is a pissed off growl...but I can still identify it.

*No way.* It wouldn't be him. It couldn't be. But when I crane my head back, my mouth dries up.

Brett Walker is standing beside me, looming over my ex, jaw and fists clenched, eyes black as night. He looks angry enough to commit murder, and when he speaks again, his tone has my heart binding in my throat.

"I'm not going to ask again, fucker." He points a finger toward Lance. "Who the fuck are you and why are you kissing my girlfriend?"

# Chapter 9

"G irl—girlfriend?" Lance's voice squeaks, and his eyes grow wider.

"That's what I said." Brett settles beside me. "You stupid, ugly, *and* deaf?" If my world wasn't rocking already, he goes further, blowing up my universe when he gathers me in his left arm.

The frame I drooled over a few days ago is nestling up to mine. Our hips and thighs collide and rub in all the ways they shouldn't, yet I shift against him once more, enjoying how he melds to me. More than that, how he sends my pulse rattling down my throat.

Lance climbs to his feet and scowls. "I've never seen you before."

"That's not what I asked, fuckface." Brett repositions his hold, hooking his thumb on the waistband of my jeans. His large fingers grip into my thigh, and he vacuums us together. "I asked why you were kissing my girlfriend."

My pulse sings at the connection and the words. *This isn't right.* I should hate it, loathe it—instead I curl into Brett, claiming his natural heat as my own. When the fragrance of fresh soap descends, a shiver travels downward and lands in my center. Disliking him isn't possible. At least not right now.

My eyes shutter closed for a brief moment. He feels...perfect, and nothing about his touch is light. It's weighted, like he could pin me down with one hand and master me in whatever way he pleases. *Holy crap.* My skin heats at the thought.

I know there's lust swirling in my vision when I clash eyes with Lance. I also discern Lance sees it and understands he's not the cause of it. One of my brows arches. "What's the matter, Lance? Didn't think I could do better than you?"

He opts for an open-mouth stare.

Cocking my head to the side, I smile. "People upgrade, you know."

Brett's body quakes with a deep, smooth laugh, and it's the most sin-filled thing I've heard yet.

The sound has me grinding the side of my tit into his ripped torso. A spontaneous gesture that's definitely rooted in lust, and he responds in kind. A dark moan rumbles out. It's hardly audible, but I feel the workings it makes in his chest all the way to my damn core. He shifts, forcing the connection again, and my frame arches into him. When we both smile, I know we're in trouble.

*Shit.* I'm liking this far too much. Liking *him* in a way that's unhealthy.

Thankfully, Lance breaks up our charade with his whine-filled voice. "You'll never get over me." Spite cracks in his harsh stare. "Nobody knows you like I do. Nobody."

"Yeah." Brett's doubt-filled voice beats any reply I can form. "Sorry." He *tsks* his tongue. "But I can guarantee she's not thinking about you at night. Not from the way she says my name."

My cheeks flare with heat, but there's no time for me to respond.

"Fuck you—" Fire erupts in Lance's eyes and red hues splotch across his face. Clenching his fist, he hurls it back and unloads.

*SMACK*

Brett stops the punch, midair, with his palm.

He does it without moving an inch. He does it, keeping his thumb hooked in my jeans and not flinching. It's the most badass thing I've seen.

Lance gasps, then winces.

It happens when Brett closes his hand, locking Lance's fist inside. His knuckles whiten and a crunch crackles in the air.

My blood stops when a few of Lance's friend's clamor to their feet. I can't swallow while picturing the fight that's probably about to break out.

Brett's hand finally falls off me as he shoves against Lance.

Once again, my ex tumbles head over boots, unable to control his landing. This time he groans. I'm sure his tailbone is going to feel the aftereffects tomorrow.

Brett faces the group of friends. His figure dominates the room as he plants his feet on the ground in a wide stance and places his hands around his hips. He stares each man in the eye, going down the line, his gaze pure black. "Anyone else want a taste, and in which order? One at a time, or all at once?"

The friends must sense the danger in him, just like I did. Do. They shake their heads in what looks like forced disinterest and mutter "no." It doesn't take them long to retreat to their seats and pick up their drinks.

Brett looks at me. His hand extends and my pulse springs alive as he drapes his arm around me.

Sparing one more look to Lance, he points his finger downward. "Touch her again and I'll snap you like a fucking twig." The growl and threat sounds real.

I notice the hard swallow Lance takes, and then we're leaving.

Brett pushes us through the crowd, his hand at the small of my back. We exit the pool hall area. When we cross into the main room, we don't stop. Brett moves in front of me and his hand grabs around my wrist. Thanks to how tightly he's wound me up, I'm anticipating the hottest exchange of my life.

He tugs me behind him. My shorter legs struggle to keep up with his longer strides and by the time we reach the front entrance and step outside, I'm a little winded, the cold stinging my lungs while I muffle my gasps for oxygen.

Frosty air encapsulates me as I'm twirled around. After catching my bearings, I discover I've been spun so my back is against the brick building and Brett is in front of me.

The burning attachment that linked us in the lounge dies to ash as he frees me from his grip and scowls. The hardness returns all too fast. "Consider that an apology." His dark voice threads with a frigid chill, and he looks pissed.

"Apology?" My head tilts. "For what?"

"For the shirt." He smacks his hands on his thighs and grunts. "Fuck. How was I supposed to know you were sentimental and wore your dead mother's stuff?"

Irritation flares up in my veins. Man, he knows how to ruin a moment. I cinch my arms across my chest and give him a deadened stare. "Wow." My tone matches my face. "How touching. I just adore the heartwarming way you said that."

He rakes his hand through the sides of his hair and laughs. "I don't warm hearts. I was made for fucking over people who stand in my way." After the laugh dies, his top lip pulls up. "What you did was make me feel bad, and I fucking hate it when people do that."

"Oh, boy." My vision goes skyward. "Having a conscience is a terrible thing, isn't it?"

"God…" He breaks away, paces in front of me, and scrubs over his face. "Would you please get out of my head?"

"*Your* head?" My face wrinkles in disgust, and I kick myself for loving the way I felt in his arms. *Why did I enjoy him?* There's nothing *to* enjoy. He's harsh, crass, and rude. "I'm just a desperate writer, remember? So please, tell me how I'm in your head."

Coming to a stop, he pockets his hands and huffs through his nose. "You." He gives me a side eye glance. A ghost of a smile presses up his mouth, but it battles against the frustration I see snapping in his gaze.

He takes a deep breath, then pushes it out. "You know, Mom used to read romance books. Dad always said they were garbage and probably written by lonely, abandoned women." His eyes rake over me in a slow fashion, starting at my feet. When he reaches my gaze, he scoffs. "I'd say the stereotype is right."

I should walk away, but it's too easy. Cruel words don't cut me—they fuel me. I learned that about me with my dad. I'd rather dish back what he's serving and be granted more frustration. With anger bristling up and down my spine, I stand up straighter, pulling myself as high as possible. "Then I bet your stereotype fits the mold, too. It's pretty common, you know. *My* kind writes about it all the time."

"Really? And what stereotype is that?"

"Hmm." I take him in, ignoring how my head is starting to hurt. There's a tender spot forming behind my left eye, but I shove it aside and focus on the vexation in front of me. The bare arms, the medium length wispy hair, the tattoos and natural scowl. Drawing conclusions of him isn't hard.

"You're a bad boy. So let me guess and say that you probably have some sad, shit story."

His chest expands, but he doesn't make a sound.

"I bet that either your parents died or your dad was a jerk."

His jaw flexes and his eyes grow wide, but he still doesn't say anything.

Drawing my vision away from his angled jawline, I focus on his two voided eyes. "You've had a hard life, and whatever happened killed your faith in humanity, but not before it rotted out your soul, because all you are is black, and you have one of the darkest auras I've seen."

He stops breathing, and what looks like horror and shock floods his gaze.

Puckering my mouth out to the side, I buckle a knee, still battling to shut out the ever-growing pain in my head. "What? Too close for you?"

The horror and shock ebbs away, and I see a calmness. "Close?" His voice is so dark it makes my legs clench together. He gives me another once over. This one's different from earlier...it's fever...it's fire. It slowly incinerates my skin as his eyes comb me, following the patterns of my curves. "I'll show you close."

I blink, and he's there. Right in front of me, two powerful arms caging my body on either side. My pulse slams against every part of me, the back of my knees included. He lowers his head, bringing his mouth inches from mine. My stomach flips.

"Damn." He huffs out the word, and it spears into my core. "You cut deep when you want, kitten. Be careful with those claws, you might hurt someone someday." I try to look away, but he hooks his finger under my chin, forcing our gazes to meet. "Thankfully, I like a little bit of pain, but not everyone is twisted like me."

I've never been more aware of how loud my swallows are or how hot my nape grows, but I don't acknowledge them. Instead, I force my eyes to narrow and create an edge in my voice. "Maybe I like hurting you."

"Don't." The command is gruff—sounding like something he'd use in the bedroom. His hot breath washes over my cheeks with an exhale, and I get lost to the scent of whiskey and mint. "You'll make yourself unforgettable, and you don't want that."

He's right, I don't want that. I know I don't, but I can't convince my heart of that while it jackhammers away at my stomach. Right now, loud thuds tell me it *wants* him to remember me, regardless of if it's good or bad.

"Now." He takes a long inhale, one that has him looking like he's grasping for control. "I'm sorry about your mom's sweater."

"Blouse."

His jaw clenches. "Whatever. Now leave me the fuck alone."

I shake my head, aggravation licking at my composure. "Last time I checked, I didn't ask for your attention. You're the one bothering me."

"No." His teeth grind. "You're the bother. In my damn head when you shouldn't be." The lids of his eyes hood over. "Go away."

"You first." I raise up to the tips of my toes. "I was here before you."

"Shit." The words are grunts, and he claps one hand to the brick wall. "Stop it. Stop being difficult." He groans, and if I didn't think my heart could thud any harder, I was wrong.

*Shit.* I muffle a whimper when he wraps one hand around my waist and tugs at the fabric of my shirt. I'm keeping myself from grinding against him as his minty breath trails into my mouth. That's how close we are.

A growl leaves his throat. He tugs harder at my top. "I don't have time for you."

My pulse booms like a cannon, and I'm certain he hears it. Somehow, I keep my hands at my side and stand against him, half hot, half cold.

I hate him and despise his actions and brutish words. Yet, he does the unthinkable to me—dragging my imaginations and desires through the mud, making them dirty and unsavory. I want to be bad. I want to be wild, but only for him, and only when he's near. Whatever disdain I plant inside of me for Brett shrivels when we're together.

I can't help but think he feels it too. He concretes the notion when his throat bobs and he sucks in air through his gritted teeth. His fingers bite into my waist that much more, and his gaze sinks to my mouth. "Fuck, Bianca. Just..."

I can't hate it. Anticipation and lust mix together, pooling in between my legs. My eyes begin to shut as his head comes closer to mine, our lips promising to meet. We jump when the lounge door flies open and three giddy girls exit the building. Their loud shrills cut through the sky, demolishing our intense focus on each other.

"Shit." Brett hisses the word out. He rips himself from the wall, from me, and strolls away without a look back. Like I mean nothing. And to him, I probably don't.

Without him in front of me, the nip in the air works itself under my mesh. It makes me shudder and I hug myself, desperate to feel the heat of another person. His. But it doesn't last long.

A sharp twang cracks through my head. "Ah." I cover my eyes with my hand, and my face screws up. I gasp, losing my breath when white lightning shoots through my skull. My knees almost buckle. *If I can just make it inside.*

But I can't. One step and I collapse. A bundle of pain wraps itself around me and I can't shake it. I sit on my ass, tugging my knees to my chest. *It will pass.* It's just stress. Brett's shown me that tonight because he stresses me out.

"Bianca?" My head lifts at the sound of Cora's voice. Focusing is hard since she's doubled, but I know it's her. I can also hear her concern. "What's wrong?" She falls to her hands and knees. "Bianca?"

I open my mouth to speak. *Shit.* There is no complete sentence. Pain strips me of words. "Cabin." That's all I can say and it slurs.

"Shit, no." She's grabbing my arm, propping me up. "The hospital."

I shake my head, regretting it as more pain collects. "Cabin. Sleep." All I need is sleep. I know it.

She huffs hard through her nose. "If I take you back to the cabin, you have to promise me to go to the hospital after we get back home, okay?"

I nod, and Cora takes me to her car. I can't sit in the front, sitting up is a bitch.

Instead, I collapse in the back seat and lay on my side. I'm thankful for the dark and close my eyes. *Stress.* I repeat it. This pain will be gone in the morning and then I can go on and get back to what I was doing.

Trying to write and being mediocre at life. But most importantly, disliking Brett Walker. Screw his apologies. I hate him, and after the way he left me tonight—cold with a splitting headache—I'm going to ensure each of our run-ins is unpleasant and leaves him wincing. It's the least I can do. After all the douchery he's subjected me to, he deserves it.

I'm going to make him regret walking away from me. I'm going to make him regret it for life.

# Chapter 10

The metal spiral bindings of my notebook indent and press into my chest while I walk into Giuseppe's. It's a popular Italian restaurant here in Copperslane. Rustic red brick and a bright green canopy give this building a Disney look, making you think it was constructed in another world—same goes for the inside with its low lighting and checkered tablecloths.

Its location is perfect too.

The restaurant is in Historic Downtown. A picturesque area with cobbled stone streets, storefronts out of a magazine, and restaurants galore. Simply put, if you want to have a quaint time and forget your life sucks, come to the fantasy land of Downtown and grab some food, either at a posh place, or from one of the multiple food stands in the square.

I'm here for my usual Friday night bite. Any weekend, you can catch me at this place with my notebook, trying to scrounge up ideas for writing.

Plotting and brainstorming for anything new is still a bitch, but I'll be damned if I'm just going to give up. Or perhaps it's the food I'm not willing to part ways with and I'm eating under the guise of writing. I'm not sure.

What *I am* aware of is how happy I am to be here, especially while strolling up to the entrance. The owner, Mr. Giuseppe, is present tonight and the smile on the stocky, round man leaves his cheeks plump and high.

"*Signora* Stanley." He claps his hands together, taking a large stride toward me. "You came."

"Of course." I squat, lowering down to his level to receive and exchange a kiss on both cheeks. "You didn't think I'd miss my weekly session, did you?"

"No, no." He laughs, belly bouncing, hand waving in the air. "I know you wouldn't let that happen." Resting his hands on his rotund stomach, he winks. "Your table is already prepared. Water and your menu are both waiting for you."

Damn, that's good to hear. It's people like this man that make life sweeter. A giggle slips out. "At this rate, you'll be serving the food before I get here."

"We could, if you wanted." He gives me a wide grin. "Chicken marsala, correct?"

"Always." Patting him on the shoulder, I slide past.

"You want a host to take you in?"

"I think I know my way around by now." We exchange one more smile and I cross the entrance.

Closing my eyes, I moan. It's the same comforting scent that weakens my knees each time—warm bread and fresh pasta. My shoulders already lose their natural tense state at the soft music playing over the speakers. It's serenity to the soul. Honestly, it's nice to be home. That cabin trip was for the birds.

It's been a week since that talk with Brett. I also haven't had a headache since. The last one knocked me on my butt, forcing me to stay in bed for the rest of the trip. But maybe that was a good thing. I haven't seen or heard of anything concerning Brett since all that mess went down.

I'd like to keep it that way.

*Fat chance of that happening.* I feel that's what life says to me upon reaching the main area of the restaurant.

He's here, sitting at a table, an untouched plate of food in front of him. Across is a thin chick with dark blonde locks and a tight, blood-red dress.

My feet anchor themselves to the floor and I stare far too long, not sure if I'm repulsed at the enticing way he smiles at her, or if I want it for myself. The only reaction I identify is my heart, which taps harder at my throat.

I'm chewing the inside of my cheek, trying to sort out what I'm feeling, when he laughs. The noise is dark and sultry, and a pang of envy needles through my core. I clench my fist. *Why can't he be nice to me?* He seems decent to everyone else. Seems. From our talks, I know he doesn't think much about others, but shit...at least he manages to smile and laugh with them.

A filter of green overtakes my vision when he reaches across the table and pats her hand. He keeps it there, then drags his thumb across her skin. My teeth grit. I know what that touch feels like, and remembering it has me recalling the promise I made after he walked away. *Make him regret it, right?* I set my plan into motion and bee-line for his table.

Contempt carries my legs, making them move faster than normal. *Make him regret it.* The statement loops like a broken record.

Make him regret leaving me with a splitting headache.

Make him regret the pathetic way he makes me feel, *and* for the low dig at my mom's blouse. *Fuck him.* That piece of clothing meant everything to me, and he's talking about it like it was nothing.

Like a port in a storm, I spot the water glass near his hand. I want to pick it up and splash the contents of it on his face—but that will be obvious, and paint me as a crazy-looking bish. My plan will have to be much more subtle. Instead of loud and messy, I opt for a backlash that's quiet and controlled.

Finishing my traverse across the room, I rest my hand on the checkered tabletop, nonchalantly sliding my hand forward in a smooth motion.

Brett's head is just beginning its swivel in my direction when my wrist knocks his tall glass.

It topples.

Water rushes, ice clatters, and it finds him—dumping happily onto his lap. My only regret is that it's not wine.

"Shit!" He pushes his seat backward and his date gasps. A redness flares in his face and his voice is gruff while looking up. "You stupid id—" His gaze goes wide. "Bianca." He sounds winded and I don't know why.

Biting down on my lip, I serve up the nastiest stare of my life. "That's for abandoning me outside and not following through with your stupid kiss."

"Kiss?" The blonde's question screeches, but Brett doesn't look in her direction.

Neither do I.

We're the only two in this area as we command each other's attention, yet his stoic face isn't something I'm able to decipher. "Is that what you thought I was going to do?" There's a graveling edge in his voice tonight and I hate how sexually charged he always sounds.

"Wasn't it?"

His arms fold across the span of his chest and he nods to a nearby space. "Why don't you go stand against that wall over there and find out?"

"You would like that since that's where you always put me." I scoff, clutching at my necklace, the edges cutting into my palms. My mouth twists up the longer I stare at him, forcing my words to prod deeper. "Is that the only position you have, or are there others?"

His teeth grind, causing a vein in his neck to form. "I have *a lot* of others, Bianca." His voice is low, flowing with an edge of danger. "Would you like me to show you?"

*Shit.* What on Earth did I just unleash? I'd love to backtrack, but doing that seems like a total cop-out. Instead, I hide my suddenly shallow breaths and purse my lips out in an attempt to look bored. "Sorry, but I know whose mouth has been on you and I think leftovers are disgusting. Besides." I arch my brow, ignoring the loud rush of blood in my ears. "I doubt you have any position up your sleeve that could surprise me."

"Excuse me?" Brett's date speaks again. "I think that's enough."

We still don't look at her.

Instead, the air changes, and I watch him shift under the dim lighting. He inhabits the other persona I know him as.

Sin.

It oozes off him, residing heavy in his dark eyes which dip and then pull across my breasts. He groans, his tongue pokes out, and air slowly rags from his lungs. "Trust me, little one."

*Damn.* My eyes squeeze themselves shut—my stomach matching the action at the guttural usage of his ending words. Maybe I shouldn't have come to his table.

"I have more positions than you can dream of. I have..." His voice falls off.

Opening my eyes, I'm flooded with the vision of his gaze dancing along the swells of my hips.

"Fuck." He whispers it, rakes through the sides of his hair, and pulls to his feet.

A gulp lodges in my throat—my eyes gluing themselves to the worst area possible. His cock.

An outline of it displays through his wet pants. The shape is wide and solid. Upright, rigid. *Perfect.* Its *T*-shape pushes against the fabric, leaving zero room to the imagination of what he's been blessed with. I wonder how Monica handled it all and I end up biting down on my lower lip so hard a copper taste hits my tongue.

"Look up here, kitten." Brett's raspy voice forces my attention away from his obvious erection. "Like what you see, Bianca?"

Our eyes clash. My core tightens, and I think I'm overheating. It suddenly feels sweltering in here. I keep my breathing in check. When I speak, it's hardly above a whisper. "No. I—"

"Okay." The blonde speaks once more. "This is ridiculous and disgusting. If you—"

"Leave." Brett never looks at her, only angles his head a little to make it clear he's addressing her. "This doesn't involve you." One of his brows arches. "Sorry for a shitty date."

Her loud sigh hits the air. "Exactly why I drive myself." She collects her things, mumbling cuss words about men under her breath, and then she's gone.

With the two of us alone, he cocks his head. "Happy? Now you have me all to yourself."

Shock palpitates my heart when I realize what's happened. Brett's just dismissed his date and told her to go home...all because of me. I'm not sure if I love it or hate it. I came over here to be a pain in his side.

All he's doing is turning on wild emotions and giving me all his focus.

It's annoying as hell.

My eyes narrow. "If you think I like your attention, you're dead wrong."

"That's too bad, because the attention is your fault." He flicks his eyes up and down my neck. "I told you not to make yourself memorable. Blame yourself."

My teeth grind against each other, hot annoyance prickling at my skin and steaming up my face till I think makeup is about to smear. "Fuck you."

"I wish you would, just once so I could get you out of my system."

The anger peaks, flaring up my body, forcing me to want distance. I stumble backward and bury my nails in my palms. "I'm sorry I came to this table." Everything's backfired but hindsight is twenty-twenty. I should have just strolled on by and eaten my meal in peace.

At least I can still do the latter. Twisting on my heel, I resecure my notebook under my arm and try to head to my usual table.

"Don't leave, Bianca."

My body obeys the request to an extent. I don't turn around, but my head strains over my shoulder to look at him. "Don't tell me what to do. I'm sick of it."

A hard huff hits the air. "Then don't come over here, ruin my date, and expect to get away with it. Sit with me."

Looking at his pants, a smirk captures my face. "Don't you need to go home and change? I'm sure sitting in wet pants isn't fun."

"It isn't." He shrugs. "But I'll live. Trust me, I've had worse things dumped on me. Now sit."

"No." My foot steps out.

"Yes." He catches my arm in his hand.

"Brett—" Tugging away is pointless. He's much stronger, easily directing me back to the chair that was his. He applies pressure to my shoulders, plopping my ass down in the hardwood. Water soaks through my jeans. I squirm at the cold contact. "It's wet."

"Perfect. Now you're as uncomfortable as me. Also, damn. You're so fucking difficult," he grunts. "Frustrating too." The chair next to me creaks as he settles his weight into it. "Anybody ever tell you that before?"

"Several times." From Dad. After I dropped out of law school, he was quick to remind me that I was a source of major pain in his ass.

A weird ache of remembrance whips across my chest, and I rub at my sternum. Somewhere deep down, I think I always hoped Dad would come to accept the choice I'd made for myself—maybe even like it. Support it. Support me. That never happened. He made certain to prove that point. His will reading was the final blow to any hope I tried to hang on to. He cut me off from his estate and gave everything to my estranged cousin.

His last words to me being:

*And to my daughter, Bianca, I bequeath the lasting gift of wishful failure. May your writing career and your hopes die, just like your mother.*

I take a deep breath, letting his hate fuel me for a second. All it does is make me want to write harder and actually succeed this time. But I don't want to focus on it. Instead, I force all attention on the current annoyance. Brett. If Dad soured life, then this man is souring my dinner. "Why do you want to talk to me all of a sudden?"

"Sudden?" His brow raises. He almost looks annoyed. "If you knew me, you'd know this isn't sudden."

Knowing him sounds like the worst idea in the world. I pass over the subject and look at him past my shoulder, furrowing my brows. "You do realize that I came here to enjoy myself? You're ruining it."

"Me? Ha." His shoulders raise with the fake laugh. "Let's talk about what you did. You've screwed over a date I've been trying to land since I got here, dumped ice water on my dick, and given me a public erection at a family restaurant." He rolls his eyes. "You've botched my whole night."

"Good." The pleased word purrs out.

"Good?" A darkness flashes across his gaze and his jaw clenches. "I have half a mind to shove you to the nearest wall and finish that kiss you bitched about, making it last long enough to where you're begging for more."

A cold thrill rushes down my limbs. I grab at my necklace, clutching so hard it hurts my palm. "You wouldn't." For some reason I can see him doing that, and I bet he's skilled enough to make that threat come true.

He squints and I'm leaning back, desperate for space as he closes our gap. "No. Instead..." His chest lifts then deflates. "I'm going to try to talk to you."

I frown. "Why?"

"Because communication is what separates us from the animals, and I need that reminder right now." A shiver runs up my spine when his eyes go pure black, burning out all the brown. "I didn't want to make time for you, but I might as well if you're endlessly going to be bugging the shit out of me."

I'm turning my head away faster than I can blink, afraid the fire I see in him will singe me, leaving me desperate to be totally consumed.

He doesn't say anything for a moment, and the silence is kind of nice.

Resting my elbow on the table, I prop my chin on my palm. An odd tug makes my heart beat out of control when I noticed he's ordered chicken marsala—my usual. I adjust my gaze to the ground, not wanting to see that. My fingertip taps on the table in a nervous rhythm when he finally speaks.

"How's the head? You've been to a doctor yet?"

"Ugh." This time I tap my finger in frustration and jerk my line of sight to him. "Wow, great. Do Lizzie and Cora just blabber everything about my life to you?"

He scowls. "Jesus, Bianca. Everyone at the cabin was talking about it. I mean, shit, you were alone in your room for two days." He raises his arms, shrugs, then allows his hands to plop against his legs with a drop. "Excuse me for having ears and being worried about you."

"Oh. Nice." A hot seethe unleashes down my body. "Real good communication, Brett. Your gentleness is really going to encourage me to open up."

"God." He rakes through the sides of his hair, even in the dark I spot a crimson tint flooding the shells of his ears "Why are you like this?"

"Like what?" I push his plate away from me, becoming irritated by it.

"Just, just..." A large hand scrubs over his face. "Shit. You really are the most...the most..."

"Say it. You think I'm annoying as hell, right?" Sitting high in the seat, I brush my leg against his, loathing the tingle it sends through my jeans.

His hands drop. "I wasn't go—"

"Because that's how I feel about you." I bite the inside of my cheek, grinding away at the tender area, hoping to work away some of my frustration. "You're so fucking annoying that half the time I want to slap you, and the other half of the time I want to kill you. There." *I said it.* I finally worded most of my frustration.

A short burst of gratification works down to my toes. But it withers faster than it appeared.

It happens as a frown casts over his carved features. When he breaks our gazes by jerking his head off to the side, it's more like a flinch. "I wasn't going to say that." He sounds...disappointed?

Hurt?

I'm unable to place my finger on it, but something's there, and it's sending my heart into a free fall plummet.

*Shit.* I despise this feeling. The tops of my shoulders knot up and I try to form a sentence. "Wha-what were you going to say?" My voice is weak, almost getting lost in the low music.

His vision flicks to mine. "Seeing how you just spilled your feelings..." His wide chest expands. "Maybe you don't want to know." His response is softer than mine, and that softness creeps up into his expression.

"You're right." I hug my arms around me, walling myself off from him. "I don't want to know."

He sighs. Something about it works down to my soul, and each muscle in me tenses. I attempt to suck in a breath, but there's nothing. My chest is too tight, too full, vicing around my lungs as he reaches his hand out and wraps his finger around the top spoke of my chair.

He squeezes so hard his knuckles whiten and his shoulders tremble. A pit shreds my stomach when he swivels around, facing me head on. "Bianca." My name drips off his tongue and like slow-flowing honey, his eyes dip to my mouth.

*Holy shit.* I want to run away and hide in a corner. Instead, my ass seems to glue itself to the seat. "What?" I manage the response, but it sounds dry.

"The real reason why I asked to talk to you is because I'm tired of this." He keeps his eyes locked on my mouth. "Let's call a truce. I want to start over."

"After everything you did?" One side of my nose curls up. "Why would I be interested?"

"I don't know." If he's trying to take a deep inhale, it fails. It looks shallow and strained. "All I know is that I'm sick of fighting with you. Let's be fri—"

"Friends?" I jerk away, like I'm electrocuted by the word. "Fat chance in hell. Not after you ruined Mom's blouse and threatened me."

"Fuck." He lightly knocks his hand on the tabletop and shakes his head. "Will you please stop making me feel bad about the damn blouse? It was an accident."

"You seriously expect me to believe that was an accident?"

"Do you really think I would have purposely ruined something that meant that much to you?"

My eyes narrow. "I think you're perfectly capable of that."

"Then you don't know me very well."

"Don't want to." I shimmy my shoulders away, wanting distance.

"Well, even if you don't, I'd like some peace, and I regret fucking up your mom's blouse. *Now.*" He takes a long inhale and pauses for a beat. "Tell me what I need to do so we can avoid frustrating each other in the future."

The answer is simple, winding up and out of my mouth before I can even think about stopping it. "You can leave."

His frame turns rigid and a hard gulp toys with his Adam's apple. "Leave?" He sounds unsure. "As in leave this town? You mean there's nothing I can do to try and fix things?"

"Yep to the first one, nope to the second." Crossing my legs at the knees, I recline. "We're never going to get along, Brett. Not after the way things started. This town is too small to keep our paths separate, so we're always going to continue running into each other, and we're always going to be like this. I think the sooner you finish your business here and go back to wherever you came from, the better."

Wide shoulders deflate like a popped balloon. "You don't mean that." He whips his gaze to mine, but it's not fiery. It's rounded and I hate the guilt it stirs up at the bottom of my stomach.

I curl my shoulders inward, trying to freeze out the unwanted feeling. "I do mean it." My heart flutters in my neck as he leans in close. Close enough to make me aware that there's the scent of leather cologne mingling with the usual fragrance of soap.

"Prove it." His eyes wash over my face, scanning every inch of it, testing my resolve. "I see something different every time I look at you."

"Then you're delusional." I peel my shoulder blades off the seat back and jut my chin out. "Whatever you think you're seeing doesn't exist."

At last, I think I've gotten through. He hangs his head and sighs. "I think the mistake here is me. Go to your table. I shouldn't have asked you to sit with me."

Blood stops in my veins at the defeated way it sounds, and my heart sinks to the floor. Maybe I was too harsh. I shake my head, trying to soften my approach. "No, I didn't—"

"Go." His head snaps up, and he scowls, dark red eating up his natural tan complexion. "Get to your table. Fuck trying to talk things out."

"Brett..."

He cuts me off by grabbing ahold of my arm and forcing me out of the seat. "You're right. We'll never get along, and I'm sorry I thought we could. Goodbye, Bianca."

Regret pins me to the ground for far too long, and I stand there, ignoring the chill from the air-conditioned surroundings which nips at my damp ass through my jeans. My mouth hinges open to speak, some sort of apology resting on the tip of my tongue.

"Save whatever it is, Bianca." He shoves to his feet, muttering what sounds like 'fuck,' then he leaves, maneuvering around me quicker and vanishing faster than any reply I can conjure.

*Damn.* I stare blankly at his empty seat. Somehow he's taken the life with him, unleashing a deadness in the atmosphere—one that has me hugging around my middle for warmth and comfort while a giant hole gnashes away at my stomach.

Safe to say nothing went as planned just now, but nothing ever does with him. I cock my head, trying to understand the conundrum of conflict coursing through my limbs.

He's gone, and while he probably won't leave this town, at least he's out of my hair for now.

So why don't I feel better?

Why is remorse yanking at my chest so hard it has my frame slouching? And worse, why do I feel like I made a mistake by chasing him away?

# Chapter 11

"Gone?" The teacup shakes in my hand. I decide to place it down before I drop it. "What do you mean Brett's gone?"

"Pretty sure gone means gone." Cora keeps her head down while answering. She's too absorbed in adding more sugar to her coffee. "He left a few days ago."

My mouth drops open as the room swims around me for a beat. "But, I mean, he's coming back, right?"

Lizzie finishes her sip, shaking her head. "I don't think so. He told a few folks yesterday that he came to snag some property. I guess he got it, so now he's gone."

The explanation sounds logical, but being privy to certain details makes the situation coat over like the biggest lie of the century.

Today is Sunday—we passed words on Friday. He's gone.

*Coward.* I shove away the guilt lying in the corner of my brain when I think of one of the last things I said to him.

*"You can leave."*

It appears that's what he's done, and screw him for listening. My stomach sours on top of it all when I think of him accomplishing all his plans. After using Monica and keeping it from her husband, he got his land and left. *Disgusting.*

"What's that grumpy look about?" Cora's voice breaks through the contempt swirling in my head, and I realize it must be written all over my face.

A coyness plays across her aquiline features. "You look pretty upset. Miss him?"

"What?" My head jerks back. "Eww. No way."

*Of course I don't miss him.*

"Not even a little?" Lizzie's brows hit her hairline.

"No." Swiping up my drink, I take in my friends widened stares. "Are you guys sad he's gone?" When they don't say anything, my shoulders deflate. Their silence makes them look so guilty—like they are disappointed but don't want to voice it. *Great.* My eyes roll. "Please tell me I'm not the only one who didn't like him?"

Lizzie averts her eyes after taking an awkward-looking gulp. "I didn't *dislike* him. I mean, sure he was kind of standoffish—"

"And intimidating," Cora says.

"Agreed," Lizzie says. "But we all thought he was cool. Kind of like he was too good to be with us, so were all in awe of him."

*I wasn't.* I bite the words back, afraid a can of worms will burst open if I say them.

"He did have that way about him." Cora crosses her legs at the knee and rests into the seat back. A shiver trails down my spine when she looks at me and waggles her brows. "He took a special interest in you. Everyone saw that."

*Special interest.* I go queasy. That's one way to put it. I put up my palm, dismissing the remark. "Trust me, he wasn't interested in me. *"*

"That so?" Cora rolls her brown to-go cup between her palms. "Then he must not have told you about how concerned he was with your headache episode."

"My headache?" A crease forms between my brows. "He mentioned something, but I doubt he—"

"Told you." Lizzie throws Cora a sideways glance. "I told you he wouldn't mention it. Guys like Brett don't talk about things like that."

Curiosity is so strong it has me leaning halfway across the table. "Like what? What didn't anyone tell me?" Frustration batters my nerves. Once again, I feel like I'm the last person finding out about my own life.

Lizzie rests a finger to her chin, tapping it lightly. "When your headache hit, he was always the first person to ask how you were doing after Cora and I checked on you. Always."

My mouth drops open.

"Yeah." Cora folds her arms across her slim chest. "And I found him pacing outside your room on one occasion too. He even stopped me at the grocery store after we got back just to ask about you."

My throat dries up. "He did that?" Cora nods, and I sense every ounce of blood drain from my face. "No." I set my cup down, almost too hard as irritation and horror ripples in my stomach. "He didn't do that. I don't believe it."

"Then don't." Cora's voice is flat. "It doesn't change what he did. He may have seemed a bit of an intimidating bad boy to us, but with you, he was all hung up."

"And you guys didn't think to tell me?"

Lizzie ducks her head, her voice going timid. "He practically begged us not too. I would have felt bad if I went back on my word while he was in town."

"Same here," Cora chimes in.

I scowl. Cora and Lizzie wouldn't lie, but it's too bad they can't see Brett's motives for what they were. *He didn't care.* He only acted that way to see what I told them.

*That's all it was.*

And if I am wrong for some reason, then screw him and his concern. I don't need it. *It can all go to hell.* But I won't tell them that. Using silence as my weapon, I give them a stiff smile, pick up my cup, and take the longest sip of my life.

"Anyway," Cora slides her attention from me, giving it to Lizzie. I can't help but think she knows I'm deflecting the topic of Brett. "How are things with Kace?"

A high flush hits Lizzie's thin face, but it looks weak compared to the smile on her mouth. Turns out the guy at the lounge is working his way into her heart pretty fast. "He's super sweet. I really like him."

"Oh, we can tell." Cora smirks. "We haven't seen you since we got back. You're either working or with him."

Lizzie trails a long finger down her neck, tilting her head. "I won't apologize for that."

"Real talk then." Cora nestles deeper into her seat. "What's he like in bed? Does he fuck hard?"

"Cora!" Lizzie smacks her friend on the arm.

I almost spew out my tea.

"What?" Cora's eyes widen. "I'm just asking. Besides, we're all adults." Rubbing at her arm, one side of her lip puckers out. "Plus, I want to make sure you're happy. He looks really skinny. Can he work you good enough?"

"He has some muscle."

"Some?" Cora snorts.

I bite back my laugh, not wanting to knock Lizzie's choice in men.

She's always hanging around blond-headed, slim-chested guys. Totally not my thing, but hey, to each their own.

"Yes." Lizzie's brows fall, darkening the color of her deep blue eyes. "I shouldn't even be entertaining this, but he can get around just fine."

"Well, you look happy," I say, picking up my cup. Poor Lizzie's endured enough for one morning. "I'm glad it's working out so far."

"Me too." There's a brightness in Lizzie's gaze, and she's sitting ten times higher than normal. This girl is the happiest I've seen in a long time. She's always trying to act like she enjoys the single life, but I know she despises it. If anyone deserves their HEA—writer's talk for happily ever after—it's Eliza Morgan.

I'm savoring my spot of tea when Lizzie sends me a pointed look that causes my spine to stiffen. Breath stalls in my chest when her eyes narrow. "What?" I pull my head back. "I don't think I like that look."

"Neither do I." Cora's sitting straighter than me.

"Sorry." Lizzie muffles a giggle and ducks her head. "I wasn't trying to be weird. It's just that..." Her words die, and she wraps a long strand of hair around her finger.

"Oh God." Cora chuckles. "Just spit it out, Liz."

"He has a brother, and he's single." Lizzie rushes the words out and then grins at me. "I told him—"

"Lizzie, no." The thought of sitting at a restaurant, waddling through the unsettling small talk and the whole "what do you do" thing, has dread circulating in my limbs.

"Bianca, please." She bats her eyes. "His name is Cliff. I met him last week, and he's *so* nice."

I groan, slumping in my chair. "It will be awkward."

"It won't be." She raises her hands and waves them back and forth. "I can be with you, and it doesn't have to be a date."

"Sheesh." Cora frowns. "Am I dead or something? What about my dude?"

"Hush." Lizzie pats Cora's knee. "If you're not getting set up it's because you're so darn picky." She narrows her eyes. "No muscles, remember?"

"Blech." Cora's face scrunches up. Resting her elbows on the table, she bobs her head. "Yeah, never mind. Forget I'm here."

"Thank. You." Lizzie twists her shoulders around, facing me again. "So, what do you say? It doesn't have to be a date."

"What are we going to do then?" My stomach sinks, telling me this is a terrible idea, but damn. Saying no to Lizzie is hard.

"Hmm." Her eyes flick to the ceiling. "Kace and Cliff are both out of town on a construction job. They'll be gone for a month. But..."

"Poker night at Jensen's house?" Cora asks.

Jensen is a local guy who hosts poker nights at his place once a month. It's kind of a staple thing to attend if you're in our circle of friends, even if you don't play the game.

"Now that's a good idea." Lizzie bites down on her lip, a twinkle in her gaze. "Perfect, actually. They'll be getting back in time, and you two can hang out and get to know one another with no pressure."

I cringe. "I mean—"

"Here." Lizzie whips out her phone faster than I can blink. "This is what he looks like."

My shoulders shake with a laugh. "Damn, you're selling hard." Stretching my neck across the table, I squint. *Not bad.* A little too thin, of course, but he's not ugly. Wavy blond hair. Stormy blue eyes, dark lashes. Yeah. Not bad at all. And while I'm not looking for a relationship, I sure am tired of staring at my computer and then going to bed with it. A smile creeps over my mouth. "Eh, okay."

"Really?" Lizzie bounces in her chair. When I nod, she springs more. "Yes! Yes. I'll tell him about poker night and to bring Cliff."

I nod, but a tightness creeps into my throat. *Crap. Why did I say yes?* But now I don't feel like I can retract that. Finishing my tea, I try to focus on how happy Lizzie is and use that to find some sort of silver lining.

Lizzie is sweet, so she'd never set me up with a jerk.

*It will be fine.* I take a deep breath and repeat it. All I have to do is get past the hard part. Finding something to talk about and not being totally awkward. Thank God I have a month. *It will be fine.*

# Chapter 12

"So you don't play poker?" Cliff asks, extending his hand to help me out of the car.

Climbing out, I shake my head and promptly drop his hand. "I never learned." My steps slow and we dance around each other while coming up the sidewalk.

A month has come and gone since Brett first left, and it's been paradise. Not having to avoid gatherings to dodge his blistering stares. No worries he'll cage me against a wall and make my hormones go batshit crazy with attraction and anger. Zero occurrence of him sidling up to my friends under false pretenses to keep tabs on me. None of that. I've been able to live in a normal way and do the things I enjoy. It's been amazing.

Tonight, though, is less than stellar. Especially as I teeter on my tiptoes once more to avoid crashing into Cliff. The entrance to Jensen's house is way too narrow for two people. Unless you're Lizzie and Kace.

Those two love birds are snuggled up, arm in arm, a few yards ahead of us, giving sweet giggles to each other. A smile spans over my face as I watch. They seriously seem like a match made in heaven.

Kace's brother on the other hand? It's been awkward as hell. I was right—Lizzie didn't set me up with a jerk, she hooked me up with a bland piece of unbuttered toast. He's dry, boring, and leaves me cringing every time we try to talk. Our whole night has been chock full of awkward shuffles, apologies, strained bouts of silence after we try to start sentences at the same time, and abundant throat clearings. *I should have stayed home.*

"If you can't play, then why do you come?" Cliff's voice derails my thoughts.

Looking up, I see the only pleasant sight of my evening. Dark lashes, gray-blue eyes, and tawny skin. And I have almost a full-on view since Cliff isn't much taller than me. With my heels on, his nose is a shave higher than mine.

Finally I shrug, answering his question. "Sometimes it's nice to get out and spend time with others, even if it's not your thing."

He frowns and shakes his head. "I don't think that at all. Standing around is going to be weird." We reach the door, and he hurries to it, opening it for me.

I let a sigh out. *"Not as weird as you."* The phrase mutters out under my breath.

"I'm sorry, I didn't hear you."

"Uh." A stiff smile hits my lips. "I said I could use a beer or two."

He frowns again. "I don't drink."

*Of course not.* So far we haven't lined up on anything we've discussed. I don't drink either, but retracting that statement will make me look stupid and add to our strained time.

Opening the door wider, he gestures for me to go in. "Kace does, but I'm always telling him to quit. It's bad for the mind." Staunch disappointment laces through his voice. Honestly, even to a non-drinker like me, it's a total buzz kill.

Suppressing a groan of anxiety, I slide past his narrow frame, entering the house.

The noise of the small crowd instantly washes over me, and turning around, I pipe my voice up to make sure Cliff hears me. "That's very, uh…" I struggle to find a word that won't come out like a putdown. "Gallant of you." *Damn it.* That sounds horrible.

The way his face screws up informs me that my attempts have failed hard core. "I'm not gallant. I'm just a man."

Oh, boy. *More like a stick in the mud.* I stop a deadened stare. When my gaze flicks to Lizzie and her guy, I'm feeling less jovial than I was a second ago. *Never again.* This is why I don't even bother with dates. Screw relationships.

I plaster on a fake smile as Lizzie and Kace slide my way.

"Want to grab some food?" Lizzie grabs Kace's arm and sways it back and forth. "Jensen always has bomb finger foods."

All Cliff does is frown. Again. I swear that's all the dude does. This time it looms over us, and I see a rounding in Lizzie's eyes. She's probably worried she said something wrong. I try to break up the doom and gloom feel by injecting enthusiasm into my voice.

"She would know." I bob my head, looking at Cliff. "She is a personal chef."

"So I've heard." Cliff being tortured probably couldn't sound more depressing, and I question if he has a personal vendetta against food or anything fun. But hey, at least he takes the lead and shoves off in that direction. Too bad he kills it with his droopy self along the way. "I guess we'll eat."

Falling behind, I allow my eyes to roll. I've been wanting to do it all night, but I've stifled it till now.

I'm forming the end of our squad when Lizzie stalls so I can catch up. "Has he been like that all night?" There's regret swirling in her gaze, and I don't know what it is but seeing her sad or worried always makes me check myself.

I shake my head, allowing a lie to coat my tongue. "He was nice at dinner." *Nicer.* I think.

Her shoulders loosen in relief and the apples to her cheeks round. "Thank goodness. I was afraid I set you up with a dud."

"No. He's great." The words leave a bitter taste in my mouth, but I'll be damned if I hurt her feelings.

We pass through the kitchen and our heads bound up to the voice of Cora. "Well, look at you, hotties." She ditches her plate and swims through the crowd. An easy thing for her thanks to those long legs.

"Gosh, I'm glad you're here." I bump shoulders with her and flash an honest-to-God smile. She's the best thing I've seen all night. "I didn't think you were going to come."

"Ha. Sorry." Her laugh climbs in volume over all the other voices. "You can't keep me away, and actually, I just got here."

"Us too." Lizzie joins our huddle. "Should we grab a plate and go to the den? Sounds like that's where most of the people are."

"Heck ya." Cora reaches for her loaded dish. "Let's chow and find out who all's crammed in this place."

Lizzie and I rejoin with Kace and Cliff, with Cora tagging behind. After brief introductions, and a dull "how do you do" from my date to Cora, we pile on some snacks.

It doesn't take long for Lizzie and Kace to fall behind. They're flirting heavily by feeding each other and exchanging giggles. We leave them, our trio meandering toward the den, allowing them to catch up.

The bustle climaxes as we near the area. Loud shouts ring off the walls of the very obvious bachelor pad. Professional photographs of various European cars cover so much square footage it could classify for wallpaper. There's no 'woman's touch' in this vicinity, but there's a grunge to the atmosphere. It's the perfect setting for animated poker nights and keeps every gathering buzzing with animation. Tonight is no exception.Heavy chatter can be heard and it's obvious someone is raking in the winnings, has been for a long time. We make our approach to the archway and—

"Shit." My heart and stomach swap places.

"Oh, no way." Cora sounds as shocked as I feel. "What's he doing here?"

"I don't know." I barely hear myself. I double blink, thinking he'll vanish. He doesn't.

Brett sits at the middle of the table, a nice pile of chips at his hand.

I swear he feels me. His head lifts and a carnal vibration zings across the room when he spots me. It grows when he *doesn't* scowl. His eyes peel up my body, making me feel naked in a room full of people—bare even though I'm wearing a bulky, soft sweater and snug camo jeans. When his dark gaze lands on mine, I'm locking my knees for support.

Somehow, through the bustle of the crowd and the haze of my head, I hear Cora's voice from behind. "Who the hell is *that*?"

My gaze slides to the right and damn. My visuals are assaulted.

Sitting next to Brett is a fantasy of a man. Whoever created him decided to curse the rest of us with ugliness. Dark sun-kissed skin, ink-black hair that's combed back and piled high, a wide jaw, chiseled cheeks, and fern-green eyes. He doesn't even look human.

Pretty sure they're together too as this guy leans toward Brett, enclosing on his space to say something to him. By all appearances, it looks like a familiar exchange. Especially as Brett leans toward him.

"Fuck." Cora's loud voice catches in my ears. "Which one do I look at?"

"Good question." I mutter, a little breathless. My vision bounces between both. The longer I stare at the newcomer, the more I like him.

He could be a bad boy, but he's too composed with the way he sits. He fills out the chair like it's a throne, and even though his deep voice is barely loud enough to reach my ears over the crowd, everyone looks at him—waiting patiently while he takes his time playing his hand.

*Not a bad boy. Just sheer authority.*

He's quiet control, our CEO. If Brett makes us his bitches, this man is the one releasing the order to make it happen.

"Shit. Look at his chest." Cora's breath hits my neck. "Hot bod squad much?"

She's right. He's just as ripped as Brett. The workings of pure muscle ripple through his tailored black blazer and white silk dress shirt.

"Make me stop watching, Bee. I think my panties are going to catch on fire."

A laugh nearly slips out, but it's cut off.

"Oh." A sound of dismay hits my ears. It's Lizzie.

She's joined us and in noticing her, my instinct is to put my hand out and smooth it down her shoulder. "Lizzie, what's wrong?"

The natural pink that usually lives in her cheeks isn't there. She's pale, and a tremor radiates through her petite body. Her cornflower blue eyes are wide, wider than I've ever seen, and they glue to our newest arrival.

When I look back to the guy—*Whoa.* Those crystalline greens are pinpointed on Lizzie.

His gaze is not like Brett's—a scorching, hot tidal wave. This one is tender, like his heart melts just by looking at her. Like he's already lost in her without touching her...like he'd guard her with his own life.

It's powerful enough to send my heart drumming in my throat, and it's not even intended for me.

Lizzie must sense it too because she flinches, backing up, crashing into her date. "Come on, Kace, we're leaving. I have a headache all of a sudden." Her voice is tight.

"Lizzie." I grab around her elbow just as she turns around. "Do you know him? What's going on?" We've been friends for ten years. I've never seen this from her before. Panic. It's strange to me.

She gently pulls away, shaking her head. "I'm fine. He doesn't know me." I can see the lie. It's tight in her wild spinning eyes, but I'm not going to push it.

I let her go. "If you need anything, call."

"Thanks." There's a tight nod, and then she's gone, pulling Kace behind her almost faster than he can keep up.

"Oh, great. They ditched us." Cliff of course is less than thrilled, but I can't focus on that. Besides, I don't know what he's bitching about—he's in his own car.

Spinning around to face Cora, my brows furrow.

"What do you think that was about?" Cora's expression matches mine while her line of sight darts to the mystery guy.

"That's why I'm looking at you. You don't know?" When she shakes her head, my mouth drops open. "But you two have been friends since middle school."

"We sure have, but I don't know him, or what that was about." Her eyes narrow. "Something's up though."

"For sure." I chew on my cheek, biting down harder as worry grinds in my gut.

"Don't worry." Cora winks. "We'll get it straight."

My lips set in a grim line and I nod.

"Well, since Kace left, guess I'll deal in." Cliff's voice catches my ear, forcing the situation with Lizzie away. For a moment, I forgot he was here. He breezes past me and snags an open seat at the animated table.

His odd comment and behavior makes a deep line crease on my forehead. "Really?" He won't drink, but he'll play poker. *Weirdo.*

But he really does play. For a long damn time.

Standing behind Cliff, my night with him takes a positive turn. When he plays a good run, he looks back at me and grins wide. After a while, my hand is propped on his shoulder and he's showing me what he's about to play, and I'm sorry I didn't see this side sooner.

Then there's Brett.

It's too bad I'm seeing him at all. *He shouldn't be here.* The last month has been amazing because he *wasn't* here. I fold my arms, allowing disgust to settle in my chest while I observe the game.

The house deals the cards. Brett extends his hand, mutters something to our newcomer, and laughs. The sound is low. I hate it. Then he looks at me. The smile doesn't leave. It stays in place, growing wider—softer.

I scowl, narrowing my eyes and shaking my head.

Deep browns come into play, there's a glow, followed by a gentle crease forming around his eyes. Then he winks.

My stomach flips in distaste. *Gross.* I twist on my heel and walk away. Looks like I'll be sticking around Cora thanks to that.

I find her in the living room and stay there.

Cora and I don't have a further chance to talk about Lizzie. There are too many folks around, so we circle the room together, talking to all the people we know. Time passes. Swallowing, a dryness scratches at my throat—I'm more dehydrated than my neglected house plants. I go to the kitchen to grab a cold bottled water. They're all gone, but I know there's usually some in the fridge in the garage. Those are always free game. I head off in that direction.

The door is latching shut behind me, and the silence is beautiful. No noise or unexpected loud laughs. No—

"Missed me so much you had to come find me?"

*Well, it was for a moment.* Brett somehow magically appears from behind the open fridge door. I should leave, but again, running away is too easy, simple, dull. Ignoring the mixture of strange excitement and irritation swirling in me, I venture further into the garage. "Jensen ran out of water."

"I noticed." A smirk curls up one side of his mouth and his gaze trails up my body till it hits my eyes. He peers inside the fridge, breaking our stare. "Who's the Gumby?"

My head jerks back. "Gumby?"

"Yeah. Your guy? Green shirt, big lips, skinny, gross. He reminds me of Gumby. Who is he?"

"His name is Cliff." I fold my arms across my chest, my body temperature rising with a flash of anger. "And I like him." Tonight, the lie feels good coming off my tongue.

"Do you?" His short question has a way of stabbing at my fib, almost like he's calling bullshit. "So that's your type?" He gazes at me past his shoulder, slyness dancing in his dark expression.

"Yes." I force the answer out, averting my line of sight to the gray floor. Too much of that look and Brett will tear my lie wide open. My throat tightens with the swallow I take. "I like short guys." Damn, it's painful to say that, but I press on. "If they're too tall and strong..."

Words die when Brett's shoes stop in front of me. I've been fighting so hard to block him out that he's closed the fridge and crossed the room without me noticing.

My head cranes back, and the strong scent of zest descends. His nearness bristles me the wrong way, causing me to shimmy away from his closeness.

He cocks his head and grins.

Staying was a mistake. It always is with him. "You know... ? Never mind." Taking one shuffle to the right, I try to move beyond him.

"No." He stops my attempt, moving with me. "I'm dying to find out where that was going. If they're too strong, then what? Then they can't stop a punch from someone like, uh, what was his name?" His vision floats to the ceiling for a moment. "Lance? Wasn't that his name?"

*Jerk.* I scowl.

"Man." His wide shoulders rattle with a chuckle. "Watching bean poles getting pulverized gets you going, is that it?"

"Why are you back?" I can't hide the snark in my voice—don't want to either.

"What?" There's a brightness in his expression. I find it more upsetting than the fearsome stares. "Is there some sort of committee in this town that determines when I can come back?"

I huff through my nose, sinking deeper into growing irritation. "I'm just surprised, that's all. I really don't see what kind of attraction this town holds for you."

"Ha." The outburst rings off the walls, only his gaze is much too soft, and he keeps it that way while his eyelids droop and his voice darkens. "You'd be surprised what I'm attracted to." His growl at the end can't be missed.

"Don't." My nose screws up, and a flush hits my cheeks. "Don't look at me like that."

"Why?" His voice deepens. "Because you like it?"

"No." I stumble back a step. "Because I hate it."

"Your eyes and cheeks say otherwise, little one."

Air involuntarily snags in my chest. I've never heard anything more sexually tangible in my life, and my core has never clenched harder in the process. *Damn it.* My body needs to get in sync with my mind, because he doesn't deserve this reaction from me.

"What's the matter, Bianca?" He utters my name in a way that's only decent for a bedroom.

I skitter away from it, afraid to be sucked up in it. Afraid of liking it.

"Discovering you might like me more than you thought?"

"Hell no." Revulsion ripples across my chest and I cringe. "I don't like men who screw with married women, and I still don't know why you're back. You got your land. Isn't that enough?"

"Oh, I got land all right." He scrapes his palm over the stubble on his jaw. "But not the one I came for."

"Well, if you didn't get it the first time, maybe it's a sign you shouldn't lie to men after messing around with their wives."

His jaw grits, but it lacks its usual cruelty. I want it to be more.

Hating that he's not loathing me like I've grown accustomed to, I narrow my gaze. "I hope your precious land gets swallowed up by a sinkhole."

He snorts. "Do we even have those here?"

"I don't know." Twirling on my heel, I move for the door, deciding to forego water.

"Would it help if I told you I didn't know she was married?"

I want to keep walking, but my feet cement themselves to the floor, and his voice forces me to glance over my shoulder.

"What?" My response is weak, zapped from the shock flooding me.

"I like sex as much as the next guy." He rubs at his nape and shuffles toward me. "But I don't sleep with married women. Frankly, because I don't have to. I met Monica at a bar earlier that night, she told me her husband had just died. Turns out he was only gone for the weekend.

And before I went back upstairs, she told me that if I slipped up and mentioned anything, that she'd call rape and have her husband run me out of town. And what man wants that?"

My jaw dangles open. "You mean—"

"She threatened me."

Doubt forces my head to tilt as I study him. Would Monica really be that spiteful?

"Oh, come on, Bianca. You don't believe me?" He finishes closing the distance between us. "When have I ever bullshitted you?"

*Never.* At least not that I know of, but I won't admit that. Instead, I fake a detached stare. "Then why her? There are lots of girls in this town, so why did you pick her up?"

"She was attractive, so I thought I'd have a bit of fun." His jaw clenches. "Imagine my shock when she got a phone call in the middle of blowing me and then slipped up by saying it was her husband?" Sucking in air through his teeth, his eyes widen a touch. "Then imagine me finding out her husband is the guy who owns the land I need after she's threatened me." A frown paints over his mouth and he jerks his line of sight away. "A huge fucking mess."

Sincerity weaves itself into his voice, and I almost feel bad for him. Almost.

*No.* A flicker of aggravation drowns out that notion while recalling how he treated me. He could have been nicer. He could have been honest, sparing me multiple bouts of anxiety and anger.

I fist the hem of my sweater, confused by his confession, yet mad I had any empathy at all. "Why are you telling me this?"

His shoulders rise, then fall. "I don't know. Maybe because I'm tired of you looking at me like I'm the biggest piece of shit on Earth." Coasting one hand through the top of his hair, he sighs. "I mean, sure, my life isn't going to earn me any gold stars, but I have my limits,

Bianca." He drops his hand. A sprig of hair falls forward, swooping down to rest on his forehead. "You said I used Monica, but actually I'm the one who's been used. You think I don't feel that?"

"I..." A sudden intense thrum occurs behind my eyes. It's strong enough, stripping me of the words I want to say. I squeeze both eyes closed, pushing the pain away. When I reopen them, Brett's frame blurs, but I force myself to speak the first thing that comes to my mind. "Why didn't you tell me this before? You should have said something."

He laughs, but it's cold. "Ha. Excuse me for not spilling my guts to a group of strangers, and for craving some privacy."

"Strangers." The thrum turns to a sharp needling pain. I close my eyes, pinch the bridge of my nose, and groan. "I saw you getting a blow job, I think we automatically skip the stranger stage."

He grunts. "You shouldn't have been down there in the first place." The familiar snap in his voice makes my eyes pop open. When he comes into focus for a moment, his hard-set scowl floods my vision. "You..." He eyes me up and down. "You just shouldn't have—"

"No." A wave of angry heat floods my limbs, and I'm climbing to my tiptoes faster than I can stop it. "This isn't on me. Don't be pissed off at me because you can't keep it in your pants." Hot breath sucks in my lungs with an inhale. "I'm sorry Monica lied to you and did all those things, but you have to blame yourself too. If you weren't getting blowies at random parties—"

Red lights up his face. "God...shitty...fucking..." He grunts and breezes past me. "Why? Why do I even try with you?"

"If this is you trying, then I'd really hate to see you *not* try."

"You're not giving me a chance."

"No." I rub at the tender spot rising up at my forehead. "You just suck at doing anything nice." A sneer forms on my mouth. "Even your apology about Mom's blouse—"

"Shit, Bianca. I said I was sorry. Will you please stop making me feel fucking bad about that?"

"See." Aggravation ruptures through my body. "This is what I'm talking about. You..." A crack splinters down my head. I wince as painful white encircles me, cutting off my words and train of thought. "Ah." Shielding my eyes, I hunch over. "Shit."

"What's the matter?" Brett's large hand encloses around my shoulder. "Another headache?"

"Dammit." The word slurs. "This is your fault. I only get heada—" I can't speak as a sharp twinge makes me gasp.

"What can I do?" Concern weighs down his voice, and he tugs me into his arms. Just like I remember, they're heavy, weighted, commanding.

"Don't." His wide frame engulfs me, as does his scent and warmth. Even through the haze of pain, my pulse accelerates. I try to pull away, knowing distance is the only thing to keep me safe from him.

"Bianca, stop being difficult." He yanks me flush into his chest. His two heavy arms wrap around me, and a hand glides down my back. "Let me help you."

I try to wiggle free. "Don't hold me like that."

"I'll hold you however I want, damn it." His hands drop, strong fingers dig into my hips, and he takes a deep breath.

His chest presses into me, and his marbled frame against mine sends my pulse soaring—each tap shooting down my spine. He smells so damn good, and molds to me like a blanket of comfort. I end up collapsing onto him. Even though I want to reel back and push him away, I can't. I finally accept him—loathing and all.

"That's it." His fingers stroke through my hair, and his deep, gentle voice coaxes me to relax more. "Now, tell me what to do."

"Take me to Cora." My brows screw together in pain, causing me to put additional weight on him. "Don't tell her I have a headache. She'll make me go to the doctor if you do that, and I flat out don't want to go."

"Then what do I tell her?"

His voice is distant, but I still comprehend it. I think hard for a second, battling through the pain. Finally, I land on my best bet. "Tell her I tripped, sprained my ankle."

He swallows hard. "If that's what you want."

"I do."

"Very well." His chest rises with a large breath and then falls. "If we're saying you sprained your ankle, I better carry you."

Panic surges through my limbs and my throat closes. "No, I don't want that. I don't—"

He bends down, and one arm scoops behind my knees. I'm promptly swept off my feet as he secures the other arm around my back. *Shit.* My arms fling around his neck and my nose is nestling in the crook between his head and shoulder before I can even stop it. I use him to block out the glare of lights which only serve to increase my pain.

"Are you sure you don't want me to tell her you have a headache?"

I grab the collar of his shirt, squeezing it tight. "Tell her and I'll chop your balls off."

As he carries me out of the garage, I hear what sounds like a sigh of frustration. "Fuck, you're stubborn."

All I do is close my eyes tighter. I don't say anything and allow him to carry me to Cora. I let him do it while hating him every step of the way.

Somehow, Brett always sees me when I'm weak. And I can't stand that—I can't stand *him.*

# Chapter 13

"**Y**ou're awfully quiet today." Cora picks up her coffee and observes Lizzie's withdrawn frame. "Everything good with you, or are you still keeping mum on a certain subject?"

Lizzie shakes her head. "I didn't sleep well. That's all." Lizzie is a quiet creature by all accounts, but today she sounds weaker than normal—it's been that way ever since she laid eyes on that guy last weekend.

Through the grapevine, I found out his name is Saber DuBois—uber fancy name if you ask me. Some say he lived here years ago. There has to be some connection between him and Lizzie, but she won't say anything.

I've asked about it, Cora's badgered the poor girl about it. Nothing. Lizzie is a vault of secrets concerning him. She clams up and pinches her lips anytime he comes around or is discussed.

"Hmm." Cora arches her brow, rolls her eyes and shakes her head. "You're gonna have to talk sometime, Liz."

Her dark blue eyes glaze over. A chasm couldn't make me feel more divided from her as she glues an indiscernible look onto her heart-shaped face. "I don't know what you're talking about." Her voice is icy while saying it, and coming from her, it's enough to shut Cora up on the subject. Probably because it's such a rare occurrence.

Cora sighs, runs her long fingers through the back of her bob, and slouches down in her seat. "Anyway, speaking about last night—"

"Good morning, ladies."

My fingers grip anxiously around my cup at the sound of Brett's voice, but there's a flood of butterflies pulsing at the base of my stomach as well.

"Brett," Cora's voice rises over Lizzie's to greet him. "Whatcha doing here?"

"Meeting a friend. We got some business to discuss."

Looking over my left shoulder, there he is—all of Brett Walker. Impeccable collared shirt, rolled up sleeves, and roped forearms. *Damn.* I still hate him after that whole incident with my head last week. I think.

"Mind if I join you all till he gets here?"

*Please no.*

"Sure," Cora pipes up. "Have a seat."

*Dang it.* And of course he sits right across from me.

"Hi." He gives me a sly smile.

"Hello," I grumble out the greeting and avert my eyes to the table.

Replays of last week flash across my mind—replays I don't want. The warmth of his hands sliding down my spine, the span of his solid chest pressing into mine, the way he picked me off the floor like I weighed nothing. It was sexy as—*No.* I force all of it away and dare to look him in the eye.

"How's the *ankle*?"

"Better." That's all he's going to get from me.

"Good." The deep coy residing in his tone sends a ripple down my spine.

I can't stand it. Especially when it's backed up by the gentle glow swirling in Brett's gaze. I miss the days he used to scowl.

Turning my face away, I remind myself of the inevitable truth. *His niceness won't last. Nothing lasts.* The thoughts fall away when the table groans from Brett putting more weight on it.

"Bianca—"

"Coffee and a bagel." Thankfully the moment is broken up when the server brings Brett his order. She places it down, bats her eyelashes at him, and darts away. Whatever Brett had planned to say vanishes with the server.

The silence lingers while Brett takes a few sips and bites while looking down at his phone.

"Ugh. There goes Miss Slut."

My head bounces up at the voice of Cora. She's glancing out the portrait windows of the coffee shop.

Lizzie's brows furrow and she knocks her on the elbow. "That's rude, Cora."

"Rude but true," Cora counters.

I strain over my shoulder and tilt my head. "I didn't see anyone."

"That's 'cause you're blind, Bee."

Brett's chuckle rings out. "I didn't see anyone either. I also didn't know this town had sluts."

"Oh." Cora's face screws up. "We do. Well, one anyway."

"What?" My shoulders lift in a confused shrug. Everyone here is amazing. I can't help but poke. "Who on earth are you talking about?"

"Shame on you, Cora." Lizzie sighs, wrapping her hands around her mug. "She's talking about Monica."

My eyes go wide. When I shoot a sideways glance to Brett, his are wider.

Lizzie shifts her line of sight to Cora. "You shouldn't be saying things like that in mixed company." She grants Brett a passing glance.

"Sorry not sorry." Cora slumps hard into her seat back and taps a fingernail on the table. "Usually I can keep my mouth shut when it comes to her, but after last night, I can't."

"Last night?" Brett's voice rises in interest. And it has me leaning across the table top.

"Yep." Cora nods.

"Cora." Lizzie's voice sounds more like a warning shot.

"Then you don't care?" Cora arches her brow. "It was in your basement after all."

"*Mph.*" Brett sputters on his coffee and promptly places down his cup. He masks his shock through a cough. "Sorry. The coffee is hot today."

I sit higher in my chair and flick my eyes over to Brett. He's already staring at me. Both of our gazes are a bit wider than usual, but that's all we're showing. But I don't doubt he's feeling so much more.

"Oh gosh." Lizzie sounds sick. "Do you mean she was with someone else *again*?"

My brows rise high at the last word.

"Who was it this time?" Lizzie rubs a hand over her eyebrow, something she only does when stressed. "I can't tell you how many times I've asked her to stop doing crap like that at my parties."

Cora sighs and shakes her head. "Well, she's still doing it. It was that pot-bellied dude who works at the furniture shop. Are you gonna tell her husband this time?"

Lizzie's shoulders slump. "What's the point? He didn't listen last time when I caught her with his own brother."

I muffle a gasp.

Brett twists in his seat. I swear his face looks green, and while I'm sure we both have things to say, there's no way they'll be aired out here.

"You need to have a talk with her," Cora says, tapping her nail rhythmically on the table.

Averting her large blue eyes, Lizzie pulls her lower lip between her teeth. "I want to, it's just...well, you know. After what she said two years ago..."

A long heavy pause dangles in the air. It scoots me to the end of my chair and I'm gripping the edges till I think a nail is going to break. When it becomes clear they aren't going to go further, I snap. "What did she say?"

Lizzie pulls her mouth inward—she's a tight vault. I won't be getting info from her. Cora on the other hand twists her head, looking around the room, and then leans part of her upper body across the table.

"She said someone took advantage of her last year. Forced her into doing a blowjob or something."

A gulp gets stuck in my throat. When it finally washes down, there's a pool of sour acid in the base of my stomach. I push my drink away, the words spoiling my appetite. And while I feel bad for doubting Monica's credibility, after what Brett told me I'm struggling to accept it at face value.

I dart my eyes to Brett. There's nothing. His head stays down more than normal, but I can't make anything out. I look back to Cora and Lizzie. "Do you guys believe her?"

Cora shrugs, plopping her shoulders back into her seat.

Lizzie's eyes tighten and she brushes back a hair that I can't see. "It's hard to say. The guy she accused gave an account for everything that happened, but he also didn't live here." Her slender hands wrap around the mug. "Monica's husband almost went to jail because he got in a fight with him and forced him to leave town."

*Damn.* I shake my head, and Brett finally meets my gaze. I've never thought his eyes could be so down-turned, and his usually hardened features are twisted and broken looking. A frown tugs down his mouth as Lizzie carries on.

"I guess I can't invite her anymore. Regardless of what happened that summer, it's disgusting she doesn't even care about her family. Same goes for those guys she's with. Shame on all of them." She gives her focus to Brett, and an embarrassed-looking wince pulls at her lips. "I'm sorry you had to hear all of this. It's definitely *not* appropriate for table talk." Her face sours and she directs it to Cora.

All Brett does is dismiss it all by shaking his head—but I see something working in his eyes.

Embarrassment. Betrayal. That's what I sense as he shifts in his chair while rubbing at his nape. He doesn't speak another word until the bell chimes, announcing another guest.

Brett shifts his weight, waves, and pulls to his feet when the person he was waiting on shows. He leaves our table without a glance back or even a goodbye.

Time drags on, but I can't keep my eyes from watching him, and I can't shake his reaction. The longer I think about it all, the more my shoulders deflate. They sink even lower when his words ring in my head.

*Used.*

He said he felt used. Not to mention he was threatened, and if my senses are right, she's done this before.

I can't take pleasure in Brett's circumstances, and now sympathy is beginning a slow brew at the bottom of my stomach. I mean, who knows? Maybe he was really excited when he met Monica and she hurt or disappointed him. Either way, she's blackmailing him, and he's keeping his mouth shut probably praying he can get his business taken care of and then leave. Honestly, that sounds miserable.

*Damn.* I take a sip of tea, not fully listening to Cora and Lizzie's conversation, guilt knotting up my insides.

After a while, I look over and air sucks into my lungs. He's looking straight at me, and something about the sad tightness ripping across his gaze makes me pause. It makes me pause long enough to feel him...to *see* him. To make me realize that he's human too, and human enough to get hurt and feel things. Like everyone—like me.

My eyes snap away, but I can feel his staying on me, and the longer I sense him, the more his gaze scrapes at my preconceived notions of his true motives. When I think of being in his arms, and how he held me in all the right ways, and even lied to Cora for me, I wonder if maybe we've been the victims of a terrible start. Maybe we could start fresh like he suggested at the restaurant. Maybe he's not as bad as I made him out to be. Maybe he's a halfway decent guy, and I kind of like him a little.

Maybe.

# Chapter 14

A shiver is ripping down my body and drenched clothes cling to my skin like a thin blanket that's been dunked in ice water. *Fuck my life.* I'd say the curse out loud, but a chatter steals the words away. Safe to say, tonight hasn't been a highlight for me as I stand out here in the light drizzle.

It's early evening. A damp breeze nips at my skin while it works under my sopped shirt. I'm in a bit of a jam. My old jalopy of a car has decided to die on the 285—a highway lined with an evergreen forest. It exudes postcard vibes on most days. Today, it's a road trap of nightmares. Making the situation all the better is how my driver's side window decided to fail while I was inside during the worst part of the downpour. I can't even be mad about it. Honestly, the situation is my damn fault. Cora always told me this car would die at the most inconvenient time and she was right.

So now I'm standing on the side of the road since it's drier out here and waiting for a ride. I've called Jensen, the guy from poker night, since Cora and Lizzie are both not available.

Cora's at a workshop of some sort. Lizzie? I think she's here in town, but laying low for whatever reason. Either way, I'm at the hands of someone else's mercy and even though it sucks, at least Jensen is nice enough to come help. Although, I did bribe him with a steak dinner.

At last an engine purrs, heading this way. My head bounces up and a sleek black and red sports car drives by. Spoiler alert, this is *not* Jensen.

"*Shit.*" I already know the owner. It's Brett. I've seen his vehicle here and there. It's hard to miss and even harder to forget. *Lovely.*

I fold my arms, hoping he can't see me shivering. *Maybe he's not here for me.* I'm praying that as he rolls past.

However, it's just wishful thinking. There's a screech of tires on asphalt and his vehicle whips around, doubling back, stopping when it's exactly across from me on the opposite side of the road.

"Great." Looks like he'll be seeing me at my worst yet again. It's impossible to be enthusiastic about this knowledge. I slouch against the car, resting my shoulder blades on cold, semi-ruined metal and paint. My pulse staccatos in unsteady beats when Brett climbs out. Of course he looks hot—hot enough to make me forget the chill in the air for a flash.

He's in a light blue denim button-up, ass-hugging black dress slacks, and aviators. It's enough to make me want to drool. When he cinches his thick arms across his bulging chest and smirks, my tongue wants to poke out and wet my mouth.

*Asshole.* Him looking this good is just wrong. I should be fighting the Brett effects harder as he still doesn't deserve my reactions, but for some reason, I'm less prone to fighting them this week. I allow some of the attraction coursing through me to settle in my chest and nod his way, raising my voice so it reaches across the road. "Make service calls, do you?"

"Sometimes."

"I called Jensen." There's a deadness in my voice, but it lacks the go-to harshness.

"And he sent me."

I tilt my head. "Did he?"

"Of course. I was standing right next to him when you called." He chuckles and slides off his glasses, hooking the earpiece on his shirt front. "I was going to drive by and splash you, but..." There's more brown swirling in his gaze while he examines me. "You look pretty pathetic."

"Mmm." I feel the displeased lines crease my forehead. He's probably teasing, but it manages to make me feel weak. I hate that and possess zero guilt about letting *that* dislike swirl inside me. "How gallant of you."

"Isn't it though?" He cringes looking at my jalopy. "Not sure I can help that, but undo the hood, book writer. Let's see what we got."

*Book writer.* That's always been used as an insult, but tonight there's no snide attached in the way he says it. An odd wave of satisfaction rolls up my spine, and I hide my face so he can't spot the warmth living in my cheeks.

*Damn it. Get it together.* One week and I've gone from not wanting to look at him, to him being the only sight I want my eyes to drink in. The closer he gets to me, the more frantic my blood pumps, and while I want to feign staring up at the sky, I can't. Like all the times before our battles, he commands me. Swaggering across the road, his movements are liquid meth to my senses. One view and I'm hooked.

Stifling a squirm, I turn around, ducking my frame inside the car to open the hood. I stay there. Conversing with Brett wasn't in my plans tonight, and I have to look like a drowned sewer rat, so I'm going to avoid him.

His dress shoes stroll through the uneven mossy terrain, crunching through a mixture of loose rocks and dirt. I expect to hear a squeak from my hood, but there's nothing...for longer than I expect.

"If you're wanting to get on your knees for something, Bianca, you're in the wrong place. I'm over here."

I grunt. Irritation twists up my nerves, forcing me to stand. "Really? Not funny after the position I caught you in."

"Precisely why I made a joke about it. If we can't laugh about it to each other, then who with?" A wry smile draws up his mouth. "Come join me."

I walk around hugging my arms around my middle and coolly keeping my eyes on the hood, driving away the butterflies lifting off in my stomach.

His large hand feels underneath the lip, then a rusted squeal breaks out as he forces the top upward. Out the side of my vision, I see his eyes widen once he gets a view of the engine.

"Jesus, Bianca. You ever heard of a tune-up?"

I pucker my mouth out and arch a brow. "What's that?"

Large shoulders shake with a silent laugh. It vanishes quickly. "How is this thing still going?" His finger brushes over a collection of black tubes snaking around and under each other. "Even without maintenance..." He motions for me to back up and lets the hood fall. It lands with a resounding slam, and he swivels his frame to face me. "You need a new car."

"No." My heart sinks. "But it's paid off."

"*Pff.* I'd hope so."

*Prick.* I swat at his arm. "How dare you—"

"You *can* take it in, but if someone offers to fix it, I'll strangle them myself because that dick is ripping you off."

I release a sigh and my shoulders deflate. All this is the news I *don't* want to hear. The idea of looking for a new car and picking up an extra payment sounds like a huge inconvenience. "That bad?"

"Hopeless. I'm not even going to try and jump this." His voice is flat while he unpockets his phone. "I'll call you a tow truck and take you home, so you can cook me that steak dinner."

"What?" My brows snap together, annoyance flaring at the base of my stomach, stemming from his quick assumptions and his lack of courtesy to even ask if he's welcome in my home. "I'm not cooking for you."

"Like hell you're not." He widens his stance by spreading his feet apart and his voice snaps. "I didn't come out here for nothing."

*Presumptuous asshole.* The flare explodes, dousing me in a quick burst of anger. My nails bite into my palms. "I'd rather walk home than cook you steak."

He smirks. "I highly doubt that. But hey..." He backs up a step or two. "I've been wrong before. If I am, then there's the road." Pointing to the yellow dotted line on the black asphalt, he shows me his back and starts his departure. "I'm sure you know the way back. Hopefully, you don't live far because that's the only way you're getting out of making me that dinner."

I scrub over my face. Even with his hot as sin expressions and voice, he still manages to button smash the worst reactions out of me. "*Stupid. Annoying. Idiotic—*"

"Hey, Blondie!" Brett's voice reaches from across the street. "You coming or what?"

Defeat sinks in, smoothing over the aggravated edges of my composure. "Yeah. Yeah." I can't be too upset. He's exasperating, but he's here and he's helping. Kind of. I snatch my purse out the open window of my car and sling it over my shoulder.

The whole time I'm ignoring the voice in the back of my head that dares me to give in and show him a smile and thank him. But I'm not ready for that yet.

Especially when I reach the passenger door of his car. A gulp wedges in my throat when I think of us being together and him being in my home, seeing me where I'm most comfortable. My fingertips graze the handle of the door before I pull them away, almost like I've been shocked.

I'm wondering if the walk home would be the better option when the window smoothly lowers. The black film disappears into the car, allowing me a full view of its impossibly awful, yet sexy, driver.

He peers at me through the opening. "There a problem?"

Rubbing at my arms, wet sleeves stick to my skin, bunching together with my upward stroke. "I'll ruin your seats." I'm still soaked and his car is all pristine leather and fresh smelling carpet. Also, this is probably an excuse to stay away, but I'm good with that.

"Cool." He stares ahead at the road, idling the engine harder. "Don't care. Get in."

I give the handle a slow tug and open the door. Unlike my car, these doors don't shriek.

"I've got the seat heater on for you."

"Thanks." The word sounds strained. No doubt because these are the nicest things we've spoken to each other since we met. With the door shut, I lean into it and away from him.

One inhale tells me I've been tricked. I thought the car had that new car smell.

It doesn't.

There's a strong zest permeating the space. Last time I experienced it this strong, I was being held in his arms and carried. Being this close to it now has the moisture evaporating out my mouth. I take a dry swallow and wonder if he can hear it.

"Okay." He flicks the gear shift down. "Where do you live?"

The question and nonchalant behavior tells me he doesn't know how jumbled my mind is, and thank God for that. I wrap my arms around my soaked middle, still chilled and shivering, and try to smile. "House 28 on South Purdue."

His brows touch his hairline. "Fancy for a single gal. Don't those places have three bedrooms?"

I nod, and my thighs tighten when he chuckles. It's deep and sexy. All the things it shouldn't be.

"All right. Sounds like I made the right call in picking you up then. Let's see this fancy place, huh?"

He peels out and takes me home—my home. With my fuzzy state, I don't know if I like it or not. Since I can't decide, I lean my head back and stare out my window.

We drive to my house in silence, but I know that's not going to last.

# Chapter 15

My heart drums hard at the bottom of my throat as I enter my kitchen. I've dried and changed while Brett "hung out." Me being naked while he was a few steps outside my bedroom door wasn't awkward. No. No. Not at all.

Being out here with him is a different game all together. Brett's strong and authoritative stride follows close behind, and I still can't believe he's here. My awareness of him reaches the top of the pendulum as he passes through the entrance, joining me.

I keep my back to him, not certain of what to say. We've never been "alone" alone and because of that, I've never been more in tune to the vibrations he lets off.

Without looking, I'm sensing every adjustment he makes, hearing all his small inhales, burning underneath my clothes while I feel his eyes linger on me. Goosebumps prick on my skin and the annoyance from him finding me stranded on the road drains away.

"So this is it, huh?" There's an underlying current to his tone, almost like he's impressed.

Butterflies flutter at the deep melody of his voice—ones I attempt to stamp down. Poking at the bag of marinated steaks, I fight the tenseness in my shoulders and ignore how shallow my breaths are. "What were you expecting?"

"I'm not sure. Cats maybe?"

I snort.

"But you have nice taste." He ventures further into the kitchen, coming to the attached dining room. His dark eyes bounce off my deep aqua walls, widening when he spots my high tea station—a grand white cabinet adorned with porcelain tea pots and ornate cups. "Very nice."

"Thank you." The compliment unleashes a warm flush down my body.

He glances past his shoulder to grant me a smile and...

*Damn.* I have to be closer to this man. Every fiber of my body demands it. My legs carry themselves to join him. Having Brett in my house makes me realize how long it's been since I've had a man here—and that maybe I'm a little lonely. I gulp through a dry throat, fighting my hungry instincts. *No.* I won't let my vision rest on the muscle stretching his shirt sleeves. And I certainly won't focus on my curling toes while recalling the weight of his hands. No, I won't focus on any of that.

"What's this?" He sidesteps, observing the long rectangular chalkboard which hangs off the wall.

My stomach sinks, the same way it does each time I look at it. "Nothing." I mutter it, regretting not taking it down last month.

His brows wrinkle together in what looks like confusion. "Obviously it's something." He points to the top. "It says 'storyboard.'"

A bitter laugh rolls out, and I cinch my arms across my chest. "It used to be." He nods, urging me to continue. "I used to write down all my book ideas on there."

"Then why is it blank?"

"Because I can't write." My voice falls flat and I drop my head, staring at the floor. A second later my gut winds into a knot. "At least not anymore." I mumble the last part to myself.

"Yes, you can." His face catches me off guard. Serious lines course his face and a tinge of defensiveness pulls up his vocal cords. He talks like he's had some personal experience with my writing, and that's just strange.

My head jerks back, and my face screws up. "How would you know?"

His eyes widen a millimeter or two, then flick to the ground. "I mean..." He takes a deep breath. "I'm sure you can."

"Thanks." The mini pep talk fails to conjure up any confidence. Shuffling back a step, I shake my head. "But I really can't. At least not anymore."

Abandoning our conversation, I scurry over to the stove, pat the steaks down after removing them from the marinade, and prepare to cook them. I begin with pulling down some oil.

"No butter?"

My heart flutters in my stomach when he comes up from behind. The natural heat from his body wraps around me and I freeze, my fingers clenching around the bottle. "I usually don't use butter." The response is dry, sticking in my throat.

"Then it's not a steak." His thigh brushes against me, indecently, striking up the dirtiest parts of my imagination while he forces me aside. "Let me handle this. Make something else. Where are your pans?"

There's zero room for objections, and frankly, he seems more fit for the job than me. I point to a cabinet near the stove. I'm forced to have confidence in his skills while he fishes out a cast-iron skillet from a cabinet and fires up the stove. There are ready-made sides in my fridge raring to go, so I focus on dessert.

Brownies, to be exact. I'm fishing out flour, cocoa powder, butter, sugar. All the fixings for a proper, chewy brownie. I've just finished stirring a pinch of salt in my chocolate mixture when Brett speaks over the hissing and fizzle of the stove.

"You make them the way Connie made them."

I tilt my head, continuing to mix my batter. "Connie?"

"Yeah." He clicks the tongs in his hand and leans his butt against the lip of my counter. "Saber's mom." His gaze flits away when he says it, a coldness slamming down in his gaze. "One of my guardians."

I can't breathe. *Guardians...*My gut leaps up into my neck. *Did his parents...?* It's like he's thinking my thoughts as he continues.

"You guessed right that night at the lounge." He folds his arms across his chest, his lips pulled into a grim line. "Both of my parents died when I was young."

Guilt ruptures down my spine, flowing into my limbs. I end up clenching the whisk till my knuckles whiten. The words he uttered that night strike like a hammer.

*"You cut deep when you want, kitten."*

More remorse compounds, snuffing out the air in my lungs when I think of the sad look on his face that night. My heart jumps to life when I notice he's looking at me, a strange, half-cocked grin on his face.

"Don't look so horrified, Bianca. It happened when I was young." He turns his attention to the steaks, flipping one on its side, dousing it in butter, pressing it hard to the pan till it browns.

It sounds like Brett doesn't want me to be dramatic about it, and that's what I'll do. Diverting my attention back to the white ceramic bowl, I stir away, trying to keep my voice easy yet serious—because there's no way I'm letting this go. He's just dropped a bombshell of info.

"Do other people here know?"

He scoffs. "Please. Hardly a topic to bring up at casual dinners." Metal tongs scrape against dark iron as he flips the other steak. "I usually don't talk about it."

"Mmm." A weak nod lifts my head and flattery swells inside. There's a notification dinging in my brain—one of me learning that he's telling me something he doesn't share with a lot of people. I scrape down one side of the bowl, still keeping my head down. "So your time with your guardians...was it good?"

"Ha. No." A hard edge slices through his voice.

"*That's* why you don't talk about it." I sense him turn around to face me but I don't look up. "If it was a good experience, you wouldn't mind talking about it."

He grunts, but it's soft and low. "I guess you're right."

The dark brown batter swirls in the bowl, and I pause, staring at the mixture. If it were me, I wouldn't want to eat something that dug up the past. I frown. "If this reminds you of her, should I not make it?"

"Oh, she was fine. An angel, actually." He shuts off the burner, flings open the oven door, and puts the cast-iron skillet inside. After he does that, he snorts, giving me all his attention. "It was *him.*"

"The dad?"

His eyes roll. "He was no dad." The counter is quick, razor sharp, and there are heaps of bitterness mingling in the way it's spoken, hurt too. Loads of it swirls in his blackened gaze. I think he's trying to shut it out, to still be the badass he shows to the world, but here, with us all alone, I see the rawness bundled up inside him. I *feel* it.

The tops of my shoulders tighten and while I want to apologize and tell him I'm sorry that I was right about him having a shitty life, nothing comes out. All I muster is a weak swallow and probably a sad smile.

My knees weaken when he combs me over. It's slow, and the

further he gets up my body, the more he shuffles toward me. When he reaches my eyes, he's standing over me, and I'm not sure he's breathing. I know I'm not.

He diverts his attention to the tattoos on his right arm, coasting over the *A* and *C* initial with his finger. "I got these because of him. They're my parents' initials. Alison and Carson."

I tilt my head, fighting the urge to nestle closer to him, drowning in his heat and smell. Observing the markings, I'm a little lost at his meaning. "Because it helped to remind you what you've been through? Or...?"

"To hide the scars." Peeling back more of his shirt sleeve, he puts his arm closer to my face. "It's hard to see them now since they're so old, but look close." One finger tracks in the middle of the swooping *A*.

At first, there's nothing. Then he flexes his forearm and twists it. I catch a glimmer of old silver and uneven grooves flowing under the ink—and like a veil's been lifted, I follow it up and down his whole arm. There are lots of scars. Lots, tattering his smooth skin until it looks like a roadmap.

My heart falls to the floor. Clenching my fingers into my palm, I notice my teeth are gritted. "What happened?"

"*Field* work." He draws out the first word, hard and angry. Dropping his arm, he sighs and rests his hip against my counter top. "Saber's dad owned some land." He huffs through his nose. "He owned a lot of things, but there was a ranching field in particular that he would graze cattle on at times. It was my tenth birthday, and I'd lived with them for a while at this point." Shifting on his feet, he looks at the floor. "So he drops me off in the middle of a field I'd never seen, out in the middle of nowhere and said there was some fencing work being done. He gave me half a canteen of water and half a sandwich. He said the guys were working on the south side and all I had to do was walk there, help out, and that they'd give me a ride home."

He pauses, and his brows furrow. Meanwhile, my stomach picks itself off the floor and finds its way in my throat.

When he stays silent longer than I like, I finally release the whisk and dare to prod him on. "And?" I barely hear myself.

His jaw tightens. "There was no one in the field and he didn't come back. I was out there for three days."

*No.* My pulse flatlines. No one is that barbaric, to just leave someone—a child—alone to die. But I believe him, and the longer he talks, the more my heart sways toward him.

"He didn't even find me. Someone else on the property line did and rushed me to the emergency room." His usually broad shoulders deflate. "I had sunstroke, blistered skin, was dehydrated, and my arm was tangled in barbed wire. I thought it was a door, but I guess I passed out and fell in it." His throat bobs with a hard swallow while bringing his hand to the arm in question. "I almost lost it, but the doctors were able to save it. After years of therapy, I could use it again. And that's why you'll never see me in a jacket. I fucking hate the heat. I chase cool climates because of it."

*Damn.* I take a much-needed gulp of air. All my preconceived notions of him being a natural-born badass fade away and I'm thinking the Brett standing in front of me has earned and fought for every scrap he has.

I rub up and down my arm, hoping it comforts the sickness ravaging my body. "So, what happened after that? Did you get taken away?"

"Hardly." He rubs at the nape of his neck. "He showed up and said I got lost hiking. His name alone cleared him of any suspicion."

"That's disgusting." My face heats.

"It is." He nods, pressing his lips together in a grim line. "Thankfully, Connie stepped in after that. She sent me and Saber to a boarding school. Bless her." A gentle smile causes his eyes to glow. "I think we would have died without her. Sadly, she passed away last year." The soft glow snuffs out and he pulls his posture up high and tall. "He's why I'm here."

"Mr. DuBois?" My brows furrow when he nods. "I've never heard his name before. He doesn't live here, does he?"

"No." He backs away and ducks his tall frame to peek into the oven. "But he used to. It was way before my parents died, or before they knew him and Connie. They didn't meet him until after he'd left this town. However, he did live here and controlled half the damn city."

"So he's coming back?" I fold my batter into a square pan, preparing it for baking.

"In a way." Leaning against the stove, he props one leg over the other. "I caught wind he wants to buy a house north of town. It was passed down through the family, but they sold it suddenly one summer and moved away. He's been talking about that house for years. Growing up, all I heard was how he regretted selling it." A brow raises. "He wants to try to buy it to maintain the house and preserve the family name. I'm not going to let that happen." A smirk pulls up his mouth. "I'm going to buy it before he can. Maybe tear it down. Hell, even burn it. Either way, I can't wait for him to find out *I'm* the one who took it away from him. That's the land Monica's husband owns. That's the land I need."

*Wow.* Words fly away for a beat, and I'm not able to speak. When I finally do, it's one word. One I understand and know well, one that works down to my marrow. "Revenge." I shake my head in awe, understanding hitting me like lightning in a bottle.

His fingers tighten around the oven handle. "You probably think that's disgusting, don't you?"

"Not at all." Pressing a hand to my mouth, I allow the realization to settle in my sternum—the one that Brett and I aren't so different after all. I laugh while confessing the truth. "My whole career as a writer is based on revenge."

"Really." The smirk grows, climbing up in his eyes. I think he's impressed.

I nod. "Junior year in high school, Mom committed suicide because my dad was a drunk."

A frown steals the smart look away. "Well, that fucking sucks."

Something about the way he addresses it lessens the lump in my throat. He doesn't offer sympathy and soft coddles. Brett identifies it for what it was in his cut and dry way. The frankness tamps down the usual grief that tends to hit.

I continue, smoothing down the top of my brownies. "For a long time, I didn't realize how much Dad manipulated her. The reality that he caused her death happened once I'd broken away and went off to college."

"What did you originally study?"

"Law, and I hated it." Rolling my eyes, I finish working on dessert. "Dad always wanted me to go to law school. He said I was gifted for it. I excelled in debate classes in high school. Plus that's what Dad was. He wanted me to follow in his steps."

"Interesting." He tilts his head, amusement dancing in his observant gaze. "So tell me how a law student becomes a novelist?"

"I took a creative writing class and felt liberated from Dad's expectations." I turn to face him. Air tangles up in my lungs as I catch sight of the gentle look swimming in his eyes. It's totally disarming, forcing me to make a nervous shuffle on the balls of my feet. Clearing my throat, I look away. "Turns out my professors said I was gifted at it too. It came way easier than studying law." Thinking of Dad, I shake my head, smoothing back a flyaway hair. "Discovering something on my own made me realize that Mom never had a chance to delve into things that interested her. Dad always stripped her joy away. I decided I wasn't going to live my life like that, so I dropped all my law classes. The happiest day of my life was returning home for Christmas break and telling him I'd changed all my classes."

"Was he mad?" His brow arches.

"Livid." I nod.

He tilts his head and smirks.

Satisfaction zings across my chest, serving as a reminder that I made the right choice all those years back. "I did it out of spite, and I don't regret it. Disappointing my dad is the most rewarding thing I've ever done." Lifting my head, I look up and almost smile, something akin to a band-aid soothing over years of embedded pain as I connect with someone who finally gets it. "You won't hear any sermons from me. I know exactly what it's like to be fueled by someone you hate."

A gentle grin pulls at his mouth and a glow simmers in his eyes. "Well, what do you know about that?" He taps a long finger on the handle of my oven door and chuckles low. "Turns out we have more in common than we thought."

A cleansing swallow washes down my throat—one that takes dislike and hatred with it, casting it away to a dark place. Locking eyes with him has never been easier. Same goes for smiling. It's warm and sincere, unleashing a lightness in me I haven't had in years. I nod, accepting what feels like a silent olive branch of peace.

*Not so different after all.*

And we're not.

We cook and eat our steak dinner in peace, getting acquainted like normal, mature human beings, shocked when we discover we like the same foods, music, movies, and have almost the same travel bucket list.

By the time he's leaving for the night, my palms are clammy—from nervous attraction. All the layers of disdain that have been peeled back tonight allow me to feel the pent-up magnetism.

I'm shifting from side to side as he faces me from the front door.

"Good night, Bianca."

I grant him a stiff nod. "Night. Uhhh..." My nails dig into my palm, still not sure how to act. "Thanks for all your help."

"No problem." He says it softer than what I'm used to, and I want to choke on my own air. "Good luck finding a new car." His voice darkens. "And I meant what I said. If anyone offers to repair that thing, I'll smash their face into the hood. Don't get ripped off."

My throat tightens. "I promise to get a new car." The answer squeezes out of me as I fight not to twist my shoulders around at his intense stare.

"Good girl."

*Damn.* The heat in his voice zings up my spine. I push away a dirty thought about him—one of him whispering those words in my ear. I tug at my earlobe, hoping to hide the redness I'm sure that's showing in them.

"Thanks again." He turns his frame to leave, then stops, and there's something boyish winding in his features. His eyes flick to the ground and his mouth lightly presses up. "Hey, uh, maybe we could do this again sometime."

"Again?"

"Yeah. You know, like me come over and eat and we repeat this." He smirks. "That's what 'again' means."

My face deadpans. "I know what the word means."

"Didn't seem like it." The smirk stays affixed and I want to slap it off his face.

"Damn, you're annoying."

He widens his stance, staring down. "Same goes for you, little one."

"Don't call me that." I muffle back a grunt, irritation simmering at the base of my gut.

"I'll call you whatever I want." He winks, making sure any insult that could be attached to it washes away.

My cheeks flare. "Brett—"

"Night." He leaves, shutting the door firmly enough so my windows rattle. And while I want to be upset, the deep chuckle that I hear on the other side has me laughing too.

After his engine purrs away from the house and down the block, I stare at the door and sigh.

*Yeah. Not so different.* And right now, I'm convinced I find him a little endearing. I just don't want to tell him that yet.

Yet.

# Chapter 16

Standing on my tiptoes proves to be an insufficient way to reach the top shelf at the Nifty Dime grocery store. There's one remaining bag of my favorite popcorn flavor that I'm trying to snag, and of course it's the one that goes the quickest. Seems like I have the same taste as everyone else in this town.

Securing my foot on a lower shelf, I'm about to stand on it to get a better reach.

That is, until a large hand reaches above me and plucks up the bag.

"Excuse me—" I stop, and my fingers press into the shelf when I notice the swirling *A* tattoo accompanied by a clean, just-got-out-of-the-shower scent.

It's Brett, and his low voice raises a drove of goosebumps on my skin. "Needing this?" He hovers it down, dancing it in my face. "Or should I take it, eat it all, and then tell you how amazing it tasted afterwards?"

I spin around on my heel, nearly brushing against him. My toes curl in my shoes at the hot and smug smirk plastered on his face. "You would do that." Somehow I keep my voice steady, despite the quiver attempting to lie in it.

"I would." He hands off the bag. "But not to you."

I smile when his words hit.

It's been a week since he last helped me, and to say I've done a one-eighty toward this man would be the understatement of my life. I'll never admit it to anyone, but after he left my house, I found myself lonely, almost wondering if I should ask him over again. I haven't, of course, because that would be stupid on my part. Hope sparks too quickly and imaginations are wistful, slipping all too fast into the slippery pit of expecting things to last—whether that be amazing sex or something more. I'd hate for Brett to join the collection in my pile of disappointment.

However, our peace is nice. After our rough ride, it's relaxing to not exchange sneers from across the room.

My fingers curl around the packaging, and I tug it toward my chest. "Oh." I smile some. "How chivalrous of you." Eyeing my cart to the left, I make a sideways scoot. "Thank you for your help."

"I didn't say you could leave." Propping his hand on the lip of the shelf, he cuts off my exit. "Where do you think you're going?"

*Damn.* He's hot when his alpha comes out to play. Even if it's not intentional, I love his domineering ways. Always have. It makes me wonder how rough he is in bed. *Damn it. Window shopping.* But my body says otherwise as my stomach squeezes together. I hope a blush doesn't rise in my cheeks. "Did you need anything else?" Cold metal presses into my spine as I lean into the shelving.

"I'll say I do." He tilts his head. "I didn't see you at Lizzie's last night. So where were you? Did you get a new car?"

He's merely asking about my skipping out on a party and cars, but the way my body flares in temperature, and the way my stomach flips, you'd think he was asking me to go to bed with him. I nod. "Sure did get a new car. A nice one." My voice croaks. I hope he doesn't notice.

"And last night?" A brow arches. "Did you have a date?"

*Crap.* I was on a date. No one special, just a nice dude to pass the time with. Jake Goode. A friend of Lizzie's. Him and his family own this grocery store. Short, prone to pick out Converse to wear at a funeral. Definitely not Brett material. But how does he know I went out with someone? Narrowing my gaze, I stare at him hard and long. "What if I was on a date? Also, why would you ask that?"

He lowers his frame, encasing me more. Peppermint breath washes across my cheeks, cooling the heat in them. "Maybe *I* asked Lizzie because I didn't like *not* seeing you there."

I purse my mouth, not sure who's prey or predator at the moment, but I like it. "You mean you noticed?"

"I didn't *not* notice if that's what you're asking."

"Is that what I'm asking?"

"So are you going to tell me what you did or not?"

"Umm..." Taking in his face, a wry smile tugs up my mouth. He's only pushing because he's bossy, and I don't feel like following his orders today. "No." My grin widens when he scowls. "No, I don't think I will." I duck under his arm and return to my cart.

"Damn." He scoffs, then chuckles. "You're so difficult."

Flashing my teeth, I drop the bag of popcorn into my goodies. "Can't make it too easy."

"Ha." He picks up a handheld basket and catches stride with me as I go down the aisle. "Then neither can I. Expect company until you leave this store."

"Hmm." I round the corner, giggling as he keeps up. "Is that supposed to be some kind of punishment?"

"Possibly." He rubs at his nape with one hand and swings the basket in the other.

"You're failing then." Looking up, I wink. Lightness pulls me up to my tiptoes as he tilts his head back and laughs.

Reaching the baking area, I slow my pace. Thinking of Lizzie, I decide now is a good time to ask about her and Saber. She's still not saying a dang word and I wonder if he showed up, because if he did... oh boy. I'm sure that threw Lizzie for a loop. "How was last night anyway?"

"Fine." He shrugs, running a finger over a box of brownie batter. "It was the usual group you know."

"And Saber, was he there?"

"No." I don't miss the way his features darken or how his jawline tightens. "Why are you asking about him?"

Deep satisfaction ripples down my limbs. "Jealous?" I purr the question out.

"Ha." His brows lift, and some tension slides off his face. "You wish. Tell me why you're asking about him."

"Well, he seems to upset Lizzie, and I wasn't sure if you knew anything about them or if they had some kind of past."

"Not that I'm aware of. He's never mentioned her." The answer sounds honest and steady. "I can ask him if you want."

"Oh, no." I shake my head, regretting I asked anything at all. Lizzie would probably be upset if she knew I tried to pry. "Don't worry about it. I was just curious. I'll talk to Lizzie about it." *Again.*

"All right."

With the subject dropped, we say very little, completing our shopping in major waves of silence. I won't even lie. The company is nice. And being with someone who lays on zero pressure for conversation is welcomed as well.

Talking only resumes after he's helped me load my groceries and is walking me over to my car door.

"Hey." I smile. "Thanks for your help today." Pointing to the trunk of my new car, I curl my shoulders inward. "I appreciate it."

He pauses for far too long, and his eyes pinch together. "My pleasure." The words sound forced, and I can't figure out what's changed.

I shift on the balls of my feet, try to smile once more, then swivel on my heel. "See you later."

"Who was it, Bianca?"

I stop dead in my tracks, confused by the question. "Wh-what?" Twisting my neck, I turn my ear toward him.

"Your date."

My pulse rings in my ears. He's not going to let it go, and I can't figure out why he wants to know. He was adamant about not finding me attractive on our second night at the cabin. I don't know what this is, but either way, I won't entertain it.

Shaking my head, my lips purse into a hard line. "No one."

"No one," he echoes in a skeptical tone. "Kind of hard to go out with no one."

My pulse taps harder at my neck. "Why do you want to know?"

His shoes drag on asphalt, and my breath sucks in when his warm chest presses into my back.

My eyes squeeze closed, unable to stay open as I fight the urge to sink against him. He feels so damn good hugging against my body.

"Because..." His voice fades away and he inhales deep, the span of his chest growing against me, and God, how I want to turn around and just rub against him. "Just tell me."

"Again." I strengthen my voice while saying it, trying hard to force away the magnetism which makes my head swim. "It was no one." I take a stumbling step forward.

He stops me by wrapping fingers around my shoulder. "You're frustrating." His voice is low...dangerous. "Do you know that?"

I'm biting my teeth into my lip, almost drawing blood as he drags his hand down the length of my arm. "Am I?" It's all I can think to say, he's taking everything else away from me.

"Yes." I swear he's panting, and it's causing my knees to wobble. "So fucking frustrating. I..." His voice fades away and I wish I knew what he was going to say.

I drown out the idea of him kissing me, holding me. Because now, that's what I want—more than ever that's what I want. He's finally repositioned himself to my top obsession.

I just don't want him to know that.

After everything we've been through, we'll be too muddy and messy. So I'll keep him at bay.

*But for how long?* The question mocks me the longer I stand here, because I know that the more I'm around him, the more I'll weaken. But if he ever decides to make a definite move on me, then it's endgame.

Not facing him gives me more courage than I should have. Straightening my spine, I pull out from his hold. "Have a nice day, Brett."

"Yeah." He sighs, his hand plopping against his pants as he lets it fall. "You too. See you around."

There's the crunch of gravel and I hear him twist on his heel. He's leaving, and thank God.

My shoulders round, and with our distance, something compels me to turn around and watch him.

His posture's a little lower and his pace is slower as he makes his way. Guilt plucks at my insides for shutting him out, and when he's halfway across the parking lot, I decide I can't keep it inside.

"I went out with Jake Goode."

He freezes. Then he laughs. So hard, I can almost feel his shoulders shake for myself. His gaze locks with mine and he smirks. "Is that your type?"

Heat slithers up my cheeks and I'm sure they're crimson. I shoot him a coy smile. "No." I twist one of my shoes inward while saying it.

Pocketing his hands, he stares at me from across the parking lot. I swear I could float away as I see a glimmer twinkling in his gaze.

"Good," he says, winks, and resumes his course. "See you."

*Good?*

Good because he wants to be my type, or good because he thinks I could do better than Jake?

I'm not sure.

All I know is that I'm loving the answer. I manage a weak finger-wave goodbye and finally return his final words. "See you."

But he can't hear it.

He's already gone, zooming out of the parking lot. I wish he wasn't. I wish he was still here.

*Shit.* Sucking in air through my teeth, I gaze at his abandoned parking spot and sigh. "I am so screwed."

# Chapter 17

It's Thanksgiving, and a frosty chill wraps up my body as I climb out of Cora's car. Carpooling is the norm when we meet up at her cousin Donnie's house. He's a nice guy, married with a few kids. Every year, his place is the spot we congregate before taking part in a pool tournament to raise funds for the local shelter, Margaret's Hope.

Basically, a ton of people decide to ditch the usual holiday tradition of "gobble till you wobble" and instead spend several hours around cigar smoke, playing billiards until everyone wants to drop from exhaustion. The price for a game is met dollar for dollar by the pool hall, and all the proceeds go to the shelter.

Me, Cora, and Lizzie have been spending our Thanksgiving nights there and drumming up proceeds for years now. Over time, more people have begun participating, and somewhere along the way Donnie's house became the place to round up and then depart after having a few snacks.

Lizzie won't be here this year. She's still laying low, but I've heard there will be more people than ever going tonight.

The comforting scent of warm bread swirls up my nostrils once I step in. That's good. I'll be pounding down more snacks than normal. I skipped lunch earlier, trying hard to outline a new book idea. My stomach is reminding me of the occurrence too. It grumbles as I drape my coat over the living room chair.

"Damn." Cora peers into the kitchen a few feet away and her brows raise. "Don wasn't kidding about how many people turned out this year."

"So that means I can go home?" I try to infuse humor in my voice, but I'm only half joking. Billiards makes me think of Dad. He loved it, more than me or Mom, and the times he came home from a long night at the pool hall were always hell.I dread this event every year.

Cora knocks me on the arm and snorts. "Stop. You can't hide in your house all the dang time."

My lips fold backward. "I'm not always at home."

"Uh..." Her face deadpans. "This is the first time I've seen you since poker night."

*Pfft.* I stroll past her. "Whatever. No it's not. Besides, you were gone for a little last week."

"So I was." She's following right behind me, her thick boots thudding on the floor. "But I wasn't gone for two weeks. That's how long it's been."

"Oh, shut it." Passing into the kitchen, I fail to hit up my usual route—plate, food, drink. My eyes immediately pull to the corner of the room. To Brett, and the look is mutual.

I feel like he's drinking me in, pulling every ounce of moisture from my mouth, taking it as his own as his vision climbs up my body. He hits my eyes and toasts his Solo cup to me.

Raising a hand, I manage a meek finger wave, and my heart thumps so hard I feel its thrumming in my kitten heels. *Shit.* Even when I want to be strong around him, I'm weak. Brett Walker has my inner resolve hacked away. It's no different at home. I'm getting off on him more than I'd like to admit and saying his name each time I spill over the edge. It's pathetic, really.

Replaying my actions from last night, a fire pools in my cheeks and my smile goes sheepish.

Brett's brows come together in a playful observation, like he knows something indecent flashes through my brain.

I turn my head away, grab a plate, and eat, keeping far away from my baffling obsession who seems to stick with me regardless how I feel about him.

As more time passes, I think he's going to come over. Lord knows he's staring at me enough to make it happen. He stays locked on me almost the entire time, not really even bothering to look at the people talking to him. Instead, he's lingering on my breasts, waist, and hips before bouncing back to my eyes. Each time our gazes lock for more than a second, he smiles—each one steals my breath away.

By the time Donnie announces that we're about to leave, I'm wondering if I'm breathing at all.

Cora walks up to me, breaking my attention. "You ready, Bee?"

"Almost." I take a drink of water. Not that it helps. "I'm going to pee and I'll be right out."

"Well, hurry." She jerks her head to the bathroom. "You know how Donnie is about all of us leaving on time."

"I won't be a moment." Ditching my plate, I slink out of the kitchen and go down the hall.

Taking care of business, I try to make fast work, but also take time to cool off. Brett's wound me tight. I already know I'll be rubbing out built-up steam tonight after I get home. I need a few breaths to not act like a hot and bothered mess in public tonight.

After I *think* I'm composed enough I stroll out the bathroom, returning to the hall.

I'm blinking in shock when I don't hear a peep. "Hello?"

Not a soul responds. The house sounds empty. Irritation flickers in my veins at being abandoned. "Great." I meander out into the half-lit kitchen and sigh. "They left me."

"They didn't leave you." Brett's deep voice sounds from where I last left him, and a thrill coils up my spine. I didn't see him right away because he's in the shadows of the kitchen. Shoving off the wall, he draws closer. "I told them to go ahead. I waited for you."

*Damn.* I love how all of that sounds, but I try not to let that show. Cocking a brow, I pucker my lips out to one side. "You didn't want to carpool with a third or fourth person? That's what most people do."

"Please." His tone drops and he rolls his eyes. "Do I look like a guy who *carpools* with someone?" He widens his stance and folds his arms. "Hell no. I bring my own damn car. You won't catch me not going home when I want because I'm waiting on someone's ass."

I snort, then smirk. "But you'll wait on my ass."

He tilts his head back, indecency flickering in his eyes. "It's a nice ass. I'm parked out back."

A heaviness forms in my chest. It travels down, landing in my core, making it squeeze together. I try to ignore the sensation and wave my hand in dismissal. "Like you've noticed."

"Oh, trust me, I have." The words roll off his tongue, reaching out and slapping me with a heavy dose of wanting him.

The flirtation breaks a smile across my face and I tuck a stray hair behind my ear.

A softness rounds out his features. "Not as nice as that smile, but it's nice."

I stare at him for a beat, allowing my body to tremble under his attention—then I force it all away by pushing myself for the exit. I stride for the side door that's a little beyond him. "Let's go."

I'm passing by when he stops me with his voice. "Do you want to go?"

My feet fasten themselves to the floor. Craning my head back, I glance at him past my shoulder. "Sure I do." I shrug, knowing how weak it sounds. "I mean...it's the right thing to do, isn't it?"

"I didn't ask that." He shuffles closer. "Of course it's the right thing to do. I asked if you wanted to go. I sure as hell don't."

The blunt confession steals my words, and my brows pull together. I try to decide if I'm brave enough to voice the same sentiment. Admitting I don't want to help and raise money for people in need would riddle me with guilt.

I think he sees that.

"This might seem random, but I actually don't like billiards. I know it's for charity, but Saber's dad played all the time." He pockets one hand. "He gave me the lashing of my life one time when he caught me playing. I used his Italian cue stick as a cane." He takes a deep breath, and I swear he even shivers. "I never play unless I *have* to."

His words hit a verbal bullseye and vibrate through me. I wring the bottom of my sweater in my hands and mirror his frown. "I don't like going either." Surprisingly, there's no guilt when I say it. Just a sadness waving across my chest.

He nods, urging me to continue.

"Dad played too. Actually, what happened the night Mom died was after he'd gotten home from a long tournament." I end up shuddering even though I'm not cold. "I hate going and I always feel uncomfortable." The strength in my voice wanes away, dragging my eyes with it. I end up staring at the floor with a glossy haze clouding my vision.

"Well, shit, that settles it." Brett lifts and drops his shoulder. "We're not going."

My lashes flutter in disbelief and I almost laugh. Us *not* showing up won't go unnoticed. He has to realize this. "Then what will we tell everyone?"

"A few options. One, we can say we got caught up talking." There's a pause.

Oxygen expands in my chest and sticks in my lungs when he dips his line of vision to my mouth. I can only exhale when he speaks.

"Two, we can tell everyone I lost my key fob." He yanks it out of his pocket and dangles it in the air. "Or three, we tell them the truth. We didn't want to go. We'll look like assholes, but we'll be honest assholes."

I snicker, sliding forward a step. "I like number two." My fingers grasp around the opposite end of the fob and playfully, I try to pull it from his hands.

It doesn't go as planned.

He resists the tug and pulls me closer. My shoes slide along the wood, obeying his strength. Blood stops, reversing its flow and dumping into my stomach. *Shit.* I might be in trouble.

I know I am when heat washes through his gaze and he loses his breath. It rags out, hitting the air in uneven waves.

"I like option one." His words rasp out, and he fixates on my mouth.

When he draws another breath, it's shallow, yet it siphons all the supply out of me. My senses go heady and clouded. The room vortexes around me and my heart plummets into my heels. I think he's going to kiss me and I'm going to let it happen.

"I like you." He's inched closer—close enough to where his minty breath wisps against my cheeks.

A whimper travels out my throat, forcing a confession with it. "I like you too." My hands raise, fingertips ravenous to claw down the front of his shirt. "Brett..."

His eyes darken, dilating under the light. "Fuck, Bianca." He yanks me snug into his arms, air depleting out my lungs as I collide against his marbled frame. Our lips meet and we gasp together.One large heavy hand tangles in my hair, gripping hard into my wavy locks. There's a tug of discomfort at the roots, but it fuels the thrill pulsing between my thighs—making me thirsty for more of the strange marriage of pain and pleasure.

I sink into it, composure ripping away, leaving my nerves raw while our pent-up push and pull busts apart. We nip at each other's mouths and grind into each other so hard the fabric of my jeans scrapes at my skin. Threading from my blouse snaps, giving way to Brett's tugs. Fire shoots down my body when he slips underneath and connects with my skin.

*Shit.* I need more. *Demand* more. Compounded need for him overpowers me and my fingers rake down his shirt front, fist and twisting the fabric till I think it will tear. A tremor rattles down my body when he groans—deep and resonating as it mixes with the blood ringing in my ears, blackening out time and space.

In sync, our mouths open wide, and our tongues take turns stealing tastes between muffled pants and huffs.

My heart slams against my ribs when I successfully unpluck a button on his shirt. I run my hand underneath the clothing, groaning at the ripple of abs, loving how his torso tightens. Scraping down his skin—his dick swells against my stomach and he thrusts.

He breaks the kiss, gripping his hands at my temples, and I wonder if he can feel my heartbeat in his palms.

"Keep that up and you might regret it." One hand slinks down my back, and strong fingers bite into the round of my ass cheek.

The authority of it works through the layer of my jeans, and I crumble to the command of his touch. I grind against him, rubbing my clothed tits against his body. My thighs tighten when he falls against the wall and lowers his frame.

He spreads his legs, using well-built muscle to keep him upright, and guides me inside his thighs. Staring deep into my eyes, he doesn't miss a beat even though he's winded. "Fuck, kitten. Keep rubbing against me like that. Let me *feel* you, Bianca."

Obeying is too simple. Using my body like a paint brush, I stroke up and down this beautiful creation, whispering his name while I do it.

"Shit." A thud shakes the windows as his frame lifts and falls to the rhythm of my body. He tilts his head back, cusses, and palms my ass with both hands, somehow forcing me closer. "So fucking frustrating." He yanks at the waistband of my jeans, hooking his index finger through a belt loop. "Do you have any idea how long I've waited for this?"

Palming his cock through his pants, I ghost my mouth against his. "Not long, I imagine."

"Bullshit." His voice is dry heat. "So fucking long. Since we first laid eyes on each other."

My stomach bottoms out, forcing me to go completely still as he holds me in his arms. "That's impossible." Tracing my fingers along his collar, my brows furrow. "You said you didn't find me attractive."

*"I'd have to find you attractive to want to touch you."* I haven't forgotten those words or the way they stung.

Hooking my chin with his finger, he forces our gazes. "You're right. I don't find you attractive."

A quiver of rejection plucks at my heart. I try to hide a frown.

"I think you're the sexiest fucking thing I've ever laid eyes on."

Goosebumps pluck at my skin and my eyes widen. "Brett—"

"And when I saw you, I was angry." Scanning my face, his throat bobs with a swallow. He presses a finger to my bottom lip and scowls. "Angry it wasn't your gorgeous mouth around my cock. I was with the wrong person that night."

I can't breathe as I soak in his words.

Gripping my hips, he makes us flush, brows lowering along with his voice. "Who told you to stop grinding up against me?"

The words act like a whip, spurring me to action. Determined to please, I grind my clit against his length, relishing the way it throbs at the feel of him.

He gropes my breasts, forcing them high and tight together. With the mounds of them pushing out my shirt, a brief smirk presses up his mouth and he lowers his head, his tongue laving my skin.

The wetness dances across my flesh with electricity. "God." A shiver rips downward as he works the other side, all while holding deep eye contact. I love how dirty he is and how unapologetically grimy he makes me feel. My fingers stroke through the front of his hair. "You're just as sinful as I imagined."

He grunts. It sounds like approval. "And you're just as delicious as I thought you'd be." He glances down and sighs. "Look at these gorgeous tits." His eyes float up to me, and they soften. "Look at *you.*"

Air captures in my throat—I press more weight into him.

His right hand releases my tit, only to snake down and find my nipple through the bulk of my sweater. He pinches hard.

The painful bundling of nerves releases a whimper out of me. I melt into him and pant. "Do it again." He does it harder. My teeth clench and I hiss through them, eyes squeezing shut. "Oh, fuck me."

"I intend to, little one." The pleasure in his voice rumbles off in my ear. "By the time I'm done with you, there won't be one part of your body I don't know."

"Yes. Brett. Yes." My pulse pounds in my stomach, and I can't stop my hands from biting into him.

"The question I have is..." His calloused thumb smooths over my cheek, forcing my eyes open. "How hard?" A darkness builds up in his voice, and his jawline ticks, making a vein pop out. "I have a lot of pent-up frustration with you, and I need to work it out. After a good, hard, proper fucking, I can be gentle the way I want to be with you, but right now I can't."

I dig my fingers into his skin. He's speaking a promise to me—one I'm dying to have. Chewing down on my lip, I stare at his perfect mouth, preparing to follow and give myself to whatever he wants.

I want Brett.

Untamed. Unhindered. Unmanned. And I'll do whatever I can to experience it.

"So how hard, Bianca? How hard do you want me to fuck you?"

He's octane to my desires, making me desperate. I yank at the collar of his shirt, nipping at his mouth. "I want you to fuck me harder than you've ever fucked in your whole life."

"Shit." It comes out breathless and he collapses into the wall. "Like a little bit of danger, do you?"

"With you?" I moan as he stands upright and adjusts me in his arms. "Yes."

"Then I'll give it to you." He hoists me over his shoulder in one fluid motion with a single arm.

Hair dangles over me. I get a clear view of the floor rolling by while dangling upside down. Blood rushes in my head, building in pressure as he goes up the stairs. His intention is to have me in this house. *Shit.* Panic ricochets through my limbs and I clutch at his shirt. "Here? Brett we could always go—"

"I can't wait." His voice is gruff and he takes the steps two by two. "That's what you do to me, Bianca. I can't fucking wait for you."

Butterflies alight in me and I giggle. Fuck yes. I make Brett Walker desperate, and that's the best thing I've heard all year.

He enters another room. My surroundings blur and whiz in a wild spin. I'm tossed like a ragdoll onto a soft bed.

I do a slow blink to gather myself. A sea of faded blue comforter spans around me and a popcorn ceiling comes into focus.

"Lose the damn sweater." He's towering over me, pure black racing through his pupils.

My chest drops into my heels, hitting a swirl of flutters on the way down. I peel my sweater off fast as I can, anticipation forcing my ass off the edge so my toe tips touch the ground.

He grips around my jeans, hooks, and flicks his thumb to undo the button. His jaw tightens as he flays the front of my jeans open. He looks dark and lost, like he's waiting to devour me whole, but when his knuckle brushes with the lowest part of my bare stomach, it's light, almost reverent in feeling.

I whimper, arching at the wild currents he sparks in me.

"Fuck, Bianca." He tugs at the fabric. "Why didn't you tell me you wanted me this bad?"

"Because I didn't think you wanted me." A tremble whispers in my body as his fingers coast along the front of my stomach. I roll into it, wanting a firmer touch.

"My hard-on at the restaurant wasn't proof?" He strokes the top of my hair. "You had me. All you had to do was ask." Floating his hand down, he presses his thumb against the front of my neck. "Were you bad, baby?" One side of his mouth perks up. "Did you ever get off on me?"

The question is a soft droll of carnality, making me sink into the mattress, pulling out an easy confession. "Yes."

He grits his teeth, the kind expression vanishing and transforming. "Bad girl," he growls, yanking my pants off in a lighting motion. He forces them off me, pulling my heels off at the same time. "Always come to me. Only *cum* to me."

I shudder at his dangerous tone. The loud thunk of my shoes and jeans hitting the wood floor grounds me harder into the moment. I'm nearly naked in front of Brett.

All that remains of my garments are my sheer white balconette bra and a *V* thong. His gaze drinks me in. I twist under it, my clit aching and heavy.

He stumbles back a step, gives me another keen pass, and runs his fingers through the sides of his hair. "Fuck." He scrambles through the buttons on his shirt. "This is going to be fast." Undoing his belt buckle, he tosses off his shirt, standing in his white undershirt. His dark voice rumbles out, working my stomach into a kinky knot. "Turn around. Ass in the air. Feet balancing on the side of the bed rail."

I nod, dry saliva catching in my swallow. My heart beats in my fingertips while I lay my stomach flush to the mattress. This moment is like redirected deja vu. I've heard that voice before, but tonight it's mine. All mine, and I'm loving the monumental ache he's stoking in me. *Damn.* He's so hot it should be a sin...maybe it is.

I flinch when the string of my thong bites and buries into the side of my hip. Brett's fingers lie against my skin. A snap occurs, the thong falls away. I scowl at the loss of expensive lingerie. "Brett—"

"It was in the way."

My mouth snaps shut. So do my eyes when his palm trails over my ass cheek and his groan reverberates in the air, making it grow thick and heavy. My pulse explodes. Then—

*SMACK*

I cry out at the descent of his hand on my skin—the yelp cracks in the silent room but pleasure ignites in my veins. My hands claw into the fabric.

"That's for watching me get that blow job." His low voice fills my head, causing it to swim.

His hand finds my ass again, in a different place, and I moan—his name spilling off my lips. "Yes. Brett."

"That's for all the times you made me feel bad for saying mean things to you."

My clit screams out for his cock, for him to fill me and own me—dominate me the way I first hungered for. The wait he's forcing builds up expected pleasure, and slickness already resides in my thighs. My legs shake when he takes note, grazing over my opening.

"So deliciously fucking wet. Remind me to taste you someday."

A muffled groan slips out. *This is insane.* It's a muddled thought, but it's there. We've hardly kissed, yet I'm wetter than I've ever been—burning desperate in pure overload for Brett.

When he strikes me a third time, I mewl in ecstasy. His raspy voice stroking my desires.

"That's for all the times I thought about fucking you when I should have been asleep."

There's a pause...nothing. But I can't bring myself to glance behind. Not when his hard and battered breaths collide in my ears.

"Ahh!" I lurch with another descent of his hand. This smack is louder, the strike harder than the others. My back sways, making my butt wiggle.

The skin on my ass is flaring and heated, but I want more. Need more. I thought one experience of Brett would be enough. So far every little taste of him leaves me dehydrated and I *need* more. The scary part is we're only just starting.

"And that..." His voice softens and he soothes over the area he struck. "That," he repeats after a moan, "is because you feel too fucking good in my hands."

There's no time for me to respond. My next sound is a shout.

He slams his length into me and cusses. Bundling my hair into a low pony, he pulls out and does it again, almost pushing me to my limit in the process.

He's thick, wide, long. Perfect. My walls clench around him, but my knees shake. When my ass starts to fall, he spanks me again.

"Keep it up, Bianca." He can barely speak. "You feel perfect. Don't move...please."

"Please" does the trick. I'll do anything to keep my ass up for that sweet word. My obedience seems like an open invitation for him to unleash.

He picks up the tempo and his thrusts go manic. The bed shakes and drums in a steady rhythm, and he freely ravages me. My shins thud against the box spring, my toes curl around the bed railing, my breasts chafe against the worn fabric, and his repeated slams have me grasping for anything I can find. Our skin claps with each rough connection. I pant and, fully adjusted to his girth, I back myself up to the beat of his pushes.

"Fuck." His fingers bite into my hips. "Fuck, you ride good baby. Take me. Take me just like that." I don't recognize his voice. It's too gruff. Too lost—and my body doesn't feel like mine. It feels like his. He pulls me in deeper, and races us to the finish line of undoing and spillage.

"Yes, Brett. Fuck. I'm about to come."

He grunts. "Only if you say my name when you cum."

"I...will." I groan as he expands in me. "I'll say your name."

"Then cum. Take me with you."

We release at the same time, moaning, shouting, echoing each other's names.

When he draws out and collapses onto his back next to me, I'm already loathing the emptiness. Whatever frown I want to make rubs out at his breathless chuckle.

"Holy shit." He wipes sweat off his forehead, looks at me, and smiles. "I'd say that was overdue."

My legs finally give out, losing the last bit of their endurance. I bury my head into the bedding, and doing that reminds me we're in someone else's house. I examine the tousled comforter wide eyed. "Whose bed is this?"

"I don't know." He's still panting, raking through the front strands of his hair. "But I need to thank them. I've never been ridden that hard. Ever."

A giggle works its way up, but it halts and my heart sinks. "Brett, we didn't use a condom."

"We sure as hell didn't."

"But, but—"

"It's not like I had one anyway."

My eyes widen. "Really? I thought—"

"That I carried them around in my pocket for randos?" His eyelids lower. "I should spank you again for that lewd thought."

"Please do," I purr, still loving the way my ass stings.

"Dangerous words, kitten." Peeling himself off the bed, he stands and refixes himself, setting his hair straight and tucking his shirt in his pants. "But if you're serious, gather up your things and I'll take you home."

*Hell yes.* My pulse sings at the words. Too bad my body groans as I try to stand. "Well, if you're taking me home, then I hope you like teal and purple flowers." Collecting my broken panties, I wad them in my hand. "That's the color of my room."

"Your room?" He scoffs. "Who said anything about your room?" Waggling his brows, he observes my half-clothed body. "You sure do assume a lot."

"Your place, then?" I poke my head through my sweater.

"Yes, my place." Wrapping a tendril of my hair around his fingers, he lowers his head. "I'm tying you to my bedpost with my belts. No one is going to see you all weekend."

I clamp down on my lip at those words.

He smirks. "Think you can handle it? I told you our start would be a little rough and ready."

Shimmying up to his build, I brush my tits against his torso. I grin when he bites back a moan. "I think I like you rough and ready."

"I like you."

"You said that already." I toy with him, hooking a finger in the pocket of his jeans to tug him closer.

"I sure did." He stumbles my way, bringing our bodies close together. Reaching behind, he wraps a hand around my back. "I'll keep saying it too. Now, get those shoes on so we can leave."

"Yes sir." After a quick clean up, I slide into my jeans and shoes faster than I can comprehend.

We leave, our arms slung around each other, wide grins splashing across our faces, and my body aching for more. We leave with me thoroughly, completely happy and wishing on my lucky stars that he makes good on that bedpost threat. Because I need it. Damn, I need it, and I think he does too.

# Chapter 18

"Hot damn." Brett smacks my thigh and chuckles before rolling off me.

This morning, he's served me via good old-fashioned missionary style. The most normal and subdued method we've tried yet since last night. Well, minus the fact that I'm certain I almost broke him when I begged him to choke me harder. That riled up some breathtaking slams out of him. Not that I'm complaining.

After tucking the sheets around his torso, he props himself sideways, rolling closer to me. "You should have come with a warning label." Hunger glistens in his gaze while he brushes his fingers over the sheets, right between the area of my tits. "I didn't know you'd fuck me till my cock wanted to break off."

I glance down and giggle as said member pokes me in the thigh. Brett's staying semi-hard after each round. Impressive really. "Seems to be holding up okay to me." I sigh. "Are you sure you have to leave?"

Scooting toward him, I provide enough bodily connection to stir up a darkening across his face but nothing more. "We're just starting. Surely you could put off this business trip."

"Sorry." He sweeps a stray hair away from my forehead. "Saber is pulling the order on this one. I guess we need to go back and get some paperwork. Monica's husband still doesn't want to sell the property. Saber thinks if we show him it used to be in the family that he'd be willing to part with it."

My brow arches. "You really think that's going to work?"

"Shit, it's worth a try." He adjusts to be flat on his back. "But I guarantee you that if we can't get our hands on it, Saber's father will. He's persuasive."

"And Saber doesn't care that you're trying to screw his dad over?" Sheets smelling of our mingled scents of soap and strawberry tangle around me while I nestle closer to Brett.

"Hardly." He laughs, propping his hands behind his head. "Saber would let his dad rot if he could. The man didn't spare him either. Whatever beatings I got, Saber did too."

"God, that's just awful." I shake my head, clutching part of the bedding in my fist. Each time I hear about it, more guilt rubs at me for the things I said outside the bar. Like salt in a wound, causing a sting I wish to erase. I hurt for him. My brows wrinkle till a crease forms in the middle. "Why was he like that? Didn't people try and help you?"

"He was a drunk behind closed doors. The kind that keeps their shit together in public, but is a monster in secret."

A bitter taste pops up in my mouth, souring my face along the way. "The worst kind of drunk. That's what my dad was."

"Then I don't need to say more about that. As for the beatings, no one really knew." His fingers trace up and down my arm, but I feel like it's a mindless action as he continues. "Saber and I were usually too nervous to talk about what happened. And his dad knew what was too far even when he was pumped full of drinks. He knew to avoid our face and hands. Even our legs during the summer."

I gasp, hating the way my insides tumble downward. All of that is flat-out sickening. "God, Brett—"

"No one knew." A darkness splays across his carved features, and his grip around me tightens. "We'd go to church, all dressed up and shit, proper and prim in our fancy-ass clothes. But from the collars down?" His throat bobs. "Covered, purple and bruised." His jaw tightens. "It was a Godsend Connie enrolled us in that boarding school the summer after I almost lost my arm."

My heart aches at the thought of all that, of envisioning their broken little bodies, hurting and sore. I think of the instances that caused it, the beatings. Brett and Saber—children—probably scared, hiding and crying, probably begging for it all to stop. *Shit.* A hard lurch carries my stomach into my throat and I cover my hand with my mouth, bile threatening to creep up.

"Bianca." Brett's soft voice catches my attention, and he gathers my hand in his, bringing it to his mouth for the gentlest of kisses. "Saber and I are alright. We no longer have to live like that."

"But still." I stroke my fingers through his hair, relishing how the day-old gel cooperates to my touch. It fought me last night. "That must have been awful. Why would your parents leave you with someone like him?" Anger bubbles up, boiling in my sternum when I realize they had to give legal custody for someone to provide care to Brett. And they picked a person who abused him. *Screw them.*

He shrugs, obviously not feeling the same anger I do. "Because they didn't know him. My parents were amazing, and while they were friends with him, they only saw the good side...that's what Mr. DuBois does. Lies to everyone except the ones that live with him and uses his money to silence the ones that know wiser."

I bring my ear to his chest and sigh. "Shit, Brett that's just awful."

"Hey." He props himself up on his elbows. "Don't upset yourself on my account."

I blink, aware of the film of tears glazing over my eyes. Until now, I didn't even know they were there. "I'm sorry. I just hate that you went through all of that." My shoulders deflate. "It makes me think of Dad, and I know how evil drunks can be. I mean, Mom—" My voice fades away. *She died because of him.* I can't say it. Talking about her will never be easy.

"Precisely why I just told you all that." He smiles some. "Is that why you don't do serious relationships?"

My head pulls back, brows folding together. "How did you know that?"

His brows lift, and his words come out slow, gentle. "Lizzie told me. She mentioned after our time in the cabin that you gave up dating."

"Of course." My eyes roll. Lizzie's had me set up with Brett from the start. I huff out a blast of frustrated air. "I think it is." The confession is a mumble. *Damn.* Working out the truth is hard. "Whatever my reasons are, I'm sure Dad didn't help."

"I'm sure he didn't." A softness that I haven't heard until this morning overtakes his tone.

*Shit.* It's so gentle, my frame melts into the sheets. I love it and loathe it all at once, and my pulse bangs at my throat while he slides over to me.

He's no longer lying down. Brett's powerful body blankets over me, a smirk on his face. "Whatever your reasons are, maybe I can help you forget that you don't do serious."

*No.* Ice plummets through my stomach. "Brett—"

His mouth collides over mine. A pass of his tongue across my lips seems like a silent plea for me to open. At first my lips seal themselves tighter, then he moans while gripping both my tits in his strong hands. Massaging my mounds, calloused thumbs circle around my nipples till they pebble.

I whimper, peeling my spine off the sheets, so that I erase all needless space between us. My mouth widens, and his tongue dives in. Peppermint floods my mouth, lungs, and head, intoxicating me, making me dizzy with a need to be consumed while his threatening words from moments ago wash away. My fingers yank at the roots of his hair. His arms wrap around my back, drawing me closer to him. A wicked ache vibrates in me and I writhe, mewling in gratitude as he senses my need and wedges his knee against my drenched opening.

*Shit.* Ever since I experienced him last night, it's like he understands my needs better than I do. My climax rests ready between my thighs, needing only a few attentive strokes from Brett. That's how well he commands me. The release I seek dangles on a cliff's edge—

It shatters due to the shrill of his phone. The trill is ear piercing and I flinch and groan, plugging my ears, pissed that the excitement in my clit ebbs away at the sound.

"Fuck." Brett punches his pillow and glances at the phone. "It's Saber." He tries to reach for it, I claw at his arms.

"Brett, no."

"It will only be a sec. He's not big on chat." He rolls off me, answering the call before I can make any objections. "Yeah? Make it fast."

A grumble slips out of me. Him abandoning my hot and twisted needs for a damn phone call is so wrong, and I scowl at him the whole time.

It's not until the conversation is winding down that I realize I need to make a text of my own. *Cora.* I rub my hand over my face. *Crap.* I never told her where I was going last night, and I need to fix that.

I'm sitting up and peeling off the sheets when Brett ends his call and raises both brows.

"I don't recall giving you permission to leave my bed." He reaches out. His hand wraps around my throat, his thumb dangerously stroking the front area of my neck.

The ticking of my heart skyrockets with the desire for him to take me, but I can't make it so easy. He'll get cocky. Boring my eyes into his, I arch a brow. "And I don't remember saying you could answer that phone call." Wrapping my fingers around his, which still toy with my neck, I dare him to choke me.

All I get is a dark chuckle.

"You're frustrating. You know that?" He smiles wide as he says it, encouraging me more.

"Hmm." I lick my lips, going wild with anticipation when his eyes dip to watch. "Maybe I like pushing your buttons."

"Well, you do a fucking good job at it." He applies the smallest amount of pressure, just enough to test the integrity of my windpipe and pump up my need for more, teasing me to where I want to beg for it. My skin waves with goosebumps when he ducks his head for my ear. "Stay in bed and push them all. See what happens, little one."

The delightful threat sends my eyes to the back of my head, but after that happens, I remove his hand and slide away, the sheets whooshing underneath my skin. "After I text Cora and tell her where I am."

"You think she hasn't figured it out?"

"I'm sure she has." I wrinkle my nose in response. "But if she hasn't, she might be worried, and since I was with you last, she might think you kidnapped me."

He smooths over the back of his neck and smirks. "Technically, I have, and I'm not done."

"And I didn't say I wanted you to be." My fingers sink down, stroking once over his semi-hard cock. I bite my lip in delight when a growl slips out from the back of his throat. "However..." I take my hand away. "If you don't want a SWAT team breaking down your door, you'll let me go text her. She's extreme like that."

"Let them come." His voice dips lower, and he captures my chin between his thumb and index finger. "They'll leave in a heartbeat after they see you twisted up like a fucking pretzel, screaming my name... because that's how I'm going to have you next. On your side, spread for me. One leg around my torso, the other draped around my neck, my cock mercilessly slamming into you, and you loving every second of it."

"Someone's confident." I fake a disinterested, unimpressed voice despite that fact my body aches in total desperation.

"Someone *wants* it." He leans forward, brushing my mouth to his. "I see it in your eyes."

I stay silent and my eyes flutter closed. The only sound that manages to escape is a whimper when he nips my lower lip between his teeth, rolling it till the skin nearly splits. It's a skill he's damn good at, and it's managed to steal my breath away each time he does it. This time is no exception. My eyes remained sealed closed well after he's done.

"Go text her."

His raspy voice shoots an arsenal of beautiful expectation up each vertebrae in my spine. It's hot, consuming me from the inside out.

"Tell her you're with me, getting your brains fucked out, because you made me wait too long for you. Do that and hurry back. Understand?"

My eyes fly open and I nod, sliding backward off the bed.

I'm padding down the hall, quickly—not sure how long I can stand to be away. Even leaving to ensure Cora I'm safe seems like lost time, so I'm rushing.

The phone is grazing my fingertips when it happens.

A small appearance behind both eyes. *Damn it.* I attempt to shake it away, physically—jostling my head back and forth, fighting it anyway I can. It doesn't leave, but at least it's not knee-buckling when I lift my phone.

"Shit." Cora's lit up my phone more than the tree they use at Rockefeller Center. I push one of the notifications and call her back. It rings once.

She doesn't even say hello, and that only happens when something's up. I grind my teeth together in semi-enervation and suck in a deep breath. "Hey." My voice shakes. "I'm at—"

"I know where you are, Bee."

"Oh." A half-confused smile affixes to my face. She must have really been in tune to what Brett and I were feeling last night.

She sighs. "So does everyone else in this damn town."

"What?" I dig my fingers around the case of my phone. Not sure if I'm mortified or shocked that word of us circulated so fast. "But, but, how?"

"You two had a visitor last night while you were, *ahem*, how did Monica put it?"

"Monica?" My face goes clammy, all the blood in it pooling in my sick stomach. Of all the people in the world, she had to be the one to see us.

"Ah, yes." She ignores my question. "Defiling a child's bedroom."

"Fuck." I sink my ass on the couch and sigh, my shoulders deflating like an old balloon.

"Yeah, I'd say that's what you were doing alright. Good and hard from the sound of it, and in my nephew's bedroom too."

Guilt knots in my stomach, I bow over from the tidal waving sensation. "Oh, Cora—"

"Oh, Bee, come on. You know I'm gonna be the last one to judge you. It's not like anyone cares that you're together. You're both single adults."

I hug an arm around my stomach. "But you don't sound happy with me."

"About using sweet Wesley's room, no. However, you fucked the hottest dude in this town. One that every sane woman's been trying to get her claws in. So props to you for that."

That makes a giggle shake out of me. "Thanks. What was she doing there, anyway?"

"Eh, I guess she missed the memo on the time *again.*" Her hard laugh grates into the phone. "You should have seen how pissed Monica was. Stupid slut. Serves her right."

But I can't laugh at that. *Shit.* My hand squeezes around my throat in a panic. If she was upset, then there's every reason that she could retaliate and talk about Brett. "Did she say anything to her husband?"

"Husband? Why are you so weird? What kind of a question is that? I'm sure she told him about seeing you guys."

A queasy gulp washes down my throat. "What did he say?"

"The shit if I know." I can hear the confusion and curiosity in her voice. "He wasn't with us last night. I think he left town the night before on a business trip."

"Oh." That's all I can manage to say as I think about the situation that could cause Brett some problems. I don't know if Monica is vindictive, or if she's still upset about Brett walking out on her when he found out she was married. And if she tries to compromise him in any way with retaliation? Well. That's a whole slew of problems. I'm sure Brett doesn't want his deal blown to hell over me.

"Bee?"

I leap at the voice of Cora, forgetting I was on the phone with her. "What's going through that head of yours?"

"Uhh..." My voice quivers. "Nothing." I don't feel comfortable telling Cora about Brett and Monica, that's his business. Poking at a coaster on the coffee table, I use it to funnel out the anxiety clawing at my chest.

"Bianca?" The warning tone says she doesn't believe me.

I shake my head, pinching my lips closed. "Really, it's nothing."

"What's nothing, little one?"

The phone fumbles in my hands at the voice of Brett. He's emerged, stark naked, full hard-on bobbing between his corded thighs.

Leaning one shoulder into the wall, he points down to his cock and smirks. "You're taking too long."

I can't even be mad about him forcing me back to bed. I shift my weight around from hip bone to hip bone, fully aware of my throbbing middle. It hurts not having him in me. Securing the phone to my ear, I keep my eyes locked on Brett. "I have to go, Cora. I'll call you later."

She laughs. Probably realizing why I'm ending our conversation. "Have fun."

The call ends, and I toss my phone onto the couch, letting it land with a soft plop.

He curls his finger, motioning me close to him. "Shame on you for taking so long."

"Sorry." I pull to my feet and slowly saunter toward him, letting my hips sway and my breasts rock and bounce with each step. I don't miss the way his jaw tightens to the rhythm of my body—I also can't shake away the ache behind my eyes, but oh well. I guess it's here to stay. "Cora had some news."

"About what?"

My pulse flatlines. I don't want to tell him. I don't want to ruin this. There's no telling how long my fling with Brett will last and I'll be damned if we're over the day after. A discussion about Monica will be a real mood killer. I plaster on a half-smile and step closer. "It was about nothing."

"I doubt that—" His objections die and he hisses through his teeth while I scrape my nails down his abs.

Excitement catches in my blood and I take it a step further. I dig into his shoulders, knocking and crushing my body hard against his, shifting his weight. Broad shoulders align with the wall as I shove him against it, grinding my breast against his torso, purring when he grabs hold of his dick and paints the tip of it across my hips. I nip at his chest and his head falls back.

"Fuck, do that again, Bianca." I obey, happy this was all it took to make him forget about pressing the issue of Monica. A few passes later, and he has me hoisted over his shoulder, carrying me back to bed. Keeping his promises to me.

The pretzel, the screaming, the way he makes me say his name...he makes it all happen, and pretty soon I don't care about my headache at all. I don't care about Monica. The one thing on my mind is chasing the high that can only come from Brett.

I chase it all day long. I chase it till he leaves town a few days later. Monica can wait.

# Chapter 19

"**W**hat do you mean, you're moving?" Cora's voice overtakes and shatters the usually tranquil serenity of Tanka's Coffee and Tea. Her eyes widen until the natural brown underneath her purple lenses seeps through.

The same shock Cora's showing shoots hard down my body, snapping my frame upright. The only reason why I didn't have an outburst is because I have a mouthful of hot coffee.

I force the hot liquid down so I don't spew it anywhere and stare open-mouthed at Lizzie—who's just informed us she's moving.

Poof.

Gone.

No longer a part of this town in T-minus four weeks.

After staying tucked away, and hardly contacting us, the first words out of her mouth are to inform us that she's moving away from the only place she's ever known.

"And what about your Aunt?" Cora asks, her brows knitted tight together.

"She'll be fine." Lizzie's voice is small, and it doesn't sound like a response she'd make. Her Aunt is someone she worries about all the time.

I'm ignoring the scalding of my esophagus from my fast gulp as I observe her. She's withdrawn, shrinking into the seat, and she looks small and out of sorts. Too thin and sleep deprived with darkness hugging under her eyes. It has me worried.

My brows pinch together, mirroring the concern tingling through my spine. "Lizzie. You can't mean that."

"I do." Her voice barely rises above the natural bustle of the shop. "I'm leaving." She pushes away her teacup, almost like she's disgusted, and bores her vision into the floor. "I found another job in Boston. That's where my dad was born, you know. I'll be moving in with my cousin, John." Large blue eyes lift from looking at the table by a hair. "It's simple as that."

"Simple as mud," Cora spits out. Shoving to her feet, white knuckles grind against her hips. "You can't just come back here after being away and give some lame ass excuses all while looking pathetic, weak, and—"

Lizzie's eyes round. The sight acts like a whip, spurring me to action.

"Enough, Cora." The legs of my chair scrape against the tile, and I'm on my feet, bouncing off my toe tips as a way to contain the perturbed energy growing in me.

Cora can't see it, because she's too dang tall, but when the word "pathetic" hit the air, Lizzie's lips trembled, and her eyes went glassy with wet tears. A few more verbal lashings from Cora and they'll fall. I know they will.

Making Lizzie cry should come with corporal punishment, because the sight of her heartbreak is downright sad. Her grief is quiet. Suppressed. Like you know her heart is probably shredding in half, but she won't let you see it. Lizzie doesn't need a hard word today. For once, the person who straightens everyone else's crown needs help, because I think hers fell off a few weeks back. I'll do everything I can to glue it back together and replace it where it needs to be. Lizzie deserves that much from us.

Cora's nose screws up and she tries to recoil out of my grasp when I grab hold of her arm. "Bee, stop. We can't let her—"

"Sit down and be quiet." My fingers bite around Cora's skin, and I yank at her, forcing her ass into her seat.

Knives poke at me with Cora's squinted gaze, but I've never been scared of her.

Instead of shying away from the look, I plant my hip bone against the lip of the table and return the glare. "You're upset. Understandably so," I add after her grumbling sigh. "But you're about to say something stupid and reckless. *Don't* fuck things up forever with your best friend because you lost your head for a moment."

Cora knits her fingers together, lacing them through each other and squeezing. After taking a deep breath, she flicks her gaze to Lizzie, who hasn't made a peep since shit hit the fan. She slowly trails out the air she's holding then looks to me. "Fine, Confucius. You win." Collecting her book bag off the floor, she slings it over her shoulders and stands— like a normal calm person this time around. "Sorry, Liz."

Lizzie smoothly strokes fingers down her long neck, keeping her eyes averted. A slight nod is her sign of acknowledgment.

Cora's spine slouches, and she digs a toe of her boot into the floor, a sure sign she knows she went too far. Her eyes dart and flick around the room and she ruffles the back of her hair. "Call me later. I'm gonna leave now so I don't shoot myself in the foot, okay?"

"Sure thing." Lizzie ducks her head lower, making the shiny crown of her head the only thing we see.

"Cool. See ya." Cora glides past and pats my shoulder on the way out—her subdued way of thanking me for stopping her. Cora has the crappiest way of showing she cares sometimes, but at least we understand her well enough to read between the lines.

I think Lizzie knows it too as she looks up and lifts the right corner of her mouth. "Thanks for that. You know how she can be."

"Oh man, do I." Returning to my chair, I extend my legs under the table. "She only said all that because she's hurt."

"I know."

We exchange a docile stare, one not accompanied by words. After that blowup, I want to give Lizzie a moment to resettle. I'm sure she needs it, and I only dive in after her shoulders have loosened up and she's reaching for her teacup.

"Lizzie, you know you can talk to me and Cora about what's happening." Shit, I might not be able to get her spill her guts but I'm sure as hell going to try. She's moving away. To say there's something major troubling her is an understatement.

"Oh, I know." She twiddles with her long fingers in her lap. "I just...I just..."

Tentatively, I try to dive into the only topic I can identify. The one that made her change basically overnight. "Is this about Saber?" I say his name in a hushed tone, hoping it doesn't scare her away.

*Bingo.*

I know I'm right when she nibbles at her lower lip and shifts in her seat like it's made of thumb tacks.

"Lizzie," I make sure my voice is soft. "Who is he?"

"We went to school together." A mask of distance slides onto her slim face, walling off any discernible emotions from me. Her eyes glaze over while focusing on the wall past my shoulder. "He was the boy everyone knew, and I was the wallflower."

"So." I tilt my head, desperate for understanding. "He hurt you?"

"Hurt?" A bitter cackle leaves her lungs, making my heart twist into a knot from its disturbed sound. "*He* never even knew who I was."

"Doesn't sound that way to me." From the noise I just heard, it sounded like he destroyed her. My brows hit my hairline in disbelief when she shakes her head.

"I'm serious. Growing up, we never had one moment of interaction." Her shoulders slump, taking the strength of her voice with it. "One summer his family packed and that was that."

I rub at my forehead, more baffled than before as I rummage through her dodgy time frame and meanings. Pretty sure I'm clutching for water as I try to learn more. "And Cora? Why doesn't she know him?"

"Because he left the summer before she got here."

A lightbulb pops off in my head, blinding me in realization. *The summer before.* Meaning the summer after Lizzie's parents died. She doesn't talk about it, all I know is their ends were grizzly. Instinctively, I touch my necklace, smoothing over the worn *K*. I'm stroking it like a genie's lamp, wondering if some part of me believes that if I wish hard enough, Mom will hear my wish and grant Lizzie's parents back to her.

From what I understand, she was young and her circumstances didn't improve. I frown, being grateful that I at least had Mom for as long as I did. Lizzie was robbed of too much too soon. Now I'm wondering if Saber's more deeply connected to her than she wants to admit.

Clutching around the charm, I force back a swallow. "Does he have anything to do with your parents—"

"Bianca..." The usage of my name is so soft and I wonder if she's going to crack. When she speaks again, I think she's gluing herself together just enough to finish our discussion. "Please. I know you're trying to help, but I don't want to talk about it."

My hand falls away, leaving the indentions of the letter in my palm. I nod in full acceptance. "Just know that I understand."

"I know you do." A small lightness turns up a corner of her mouth. "You more than anyone." She sighs. "I just think—"

The bell to the shop catches on the door and chimes.

The man himself steps in.

Saber DuBois. Tall. Other-worldly handsome with his high cheekbones and opaque eyes of green. He's dressed in a tailored wool dress coat, expensive-looking slacks, and patented leather shoes. He instantly captivates the air, making the room hush. My eyes dare to flick around, and I notice each head is turned to observe him.

If he's aware of the spell he puts us under, he doesn't give it any credence. He keeps his head down, dusting off a powdering of snow from his broad shoulders with his gloved hand. It's not until his eyes pull up that he seems bewitched as well...but his spell is different from ours.

It happens when he spots Lizzie—eyes pinpoint to her and don't move. I can't even see his chest pulling up for air, and frankly from the heavy way he looks at her, I doubt there's any oxygen left in the atmosphere. I think he's killing it all.

I'm having a hard time breathing myself.

The moment fractures apart when Lizzie scrambles to her feet. "I have to go." Panic rings in her voice, and she's darting away, already crossing part of the room.

"Lizzie, wait." I clamor out my seat, following after as fast as my legs can carry me, abandoning my purse and phone on the table.

I'm almost caught up when Saber cuts off our route, stepping out in front of us.

My feet freeze in place and my head cranes back, struggling to tilt all the way to accommodate his towering height. He's taller than Brett, and not paying me any mind as he keeps his line of sight affixed to Lizzie.

Swooping back part of his coat, he gives us a peek at his custom suit underneath. He ducks his head in a greeting, reminding me of an old-fashioned gesture. "Good morning, Eliza."

"It's Lizzie." She spits it out and her shoes shuffle on the floor while she retreats a step.

"Not to me, *il fiore*." The ending word is smooth and flowy—too soft and sensual for anything casual. I mean damn, it even works through his eyes, lessening the shrewdness that lives inside of them. His gaze streaks with tenderness, but only when he stares at her. And I swear it's like watching two magnets dance around each other as he steps closer and his chest strains for air. "Eliza—"

"Stop it." Ice coats over her vocal cords and the reply is cold when she pulls away. Not like her at all. "My name isn't '*Eliza*' and I'm not your...your '*fliolire*.'"

"*Fiore*," he corrects.

"Please, just..." Lizzie raises her hand in the air and shakes it. "Stop."

He flinches at the word and his eyes pinch together while he extends his hand. "Eliza. Please—"

"Go away, Saber." With expert litheness, Lizzie hops to the right, ducks past Saber, and floats out the door.

"Eliza!" But it's too late. His muse is long gone and finally his eyes rest on me, telling me that he's aware there are other people on the planet besides Lizzie. A blankness seizes over his features, and he sighs.

Folding my arms across my chest, I scowl. I've known Lizzie for ten years, and if you would have told me I'd see her react like this toward anyone, I would have declared you a liar. Lizzie's always been so composed and calm, but in front of me stands a person who strips all that composure away. I chew the inside of my cheek in disturbance while sizing him up and down.

A groomed brow arches and when he speaks, it lacks the softness from a moment ago. "Is there a problem?"

"You seem to upset her, *a lot*. I'm not sure I like that."

He closes his hand around one of his hips and spreads out his build. It's hella intimidating, especially as he peers down at me past the end of his straight nose. I wish the floor would swallow me whole. "That's your introduction to me?" He's all calm and controlled. "Not a hello or anything? Hardly cordial, Bianca."

"I...um..."

"Bianca isn't *cordial*, Saber." A large hand traverses down my back and I'm already familiar with the touch.

Brett. He's entered the coffee shop without me even realizing it. "She's difficult and stubborn. I told you that."

My eyes want to roll to the back of my head at the sexy wicked way he utters each word. They eventually give in when he wraps his arms around me, his heated chest to my back, and hooks his thumb in the pocket of my jeans.

"Hey, sexy." The low rumble of his voice reverberates down my spine like a gong, working its way into my core, convincing me I need to get him home with me immediately.

I tilt my head back, straining it backward so I'm staring up at him. "Hi." The reply is low and sultry, and I'm certain he wants to rip my clothes off when he tugs at my pants and groans.

He plants a gentle kiss on my mouth. My skin lights up with a thousand electric currents. Tingling head to toe, I'm wondering how

I went two days without him—regretting fighting him so hard in the beginning. We could have been enjoying each other from the start.

A plea for him to take me home and fuck me hard is on the tip of my tongue when it gets interrupted by Saber.

"I remember you telling me she's stubborn. What you didn't tell me is how amply she comes to the aid of her friends."

Nestling into Brett, I tilt my head. "I'd defend Lizzie with my last breath if I had to." My shoulders slump when I think of how she'll be leaving. "Pointless, however, since she's moving."

Saber's head snaps up, eyes dilated. "What?" His question cracks at the air, reminding me of a whip.

I retreat further against Brett. "You didn't know?"

"Certainly not." His inhale seems alarmed and he takes a step back. "When is she leaving?"

*Damn.* He's staring at me so hard I think I'll rupture into flames. It's hard not to stammer over my own words. "She said in a month."

"*Shit.*" The word mutters out low and dark. A sharp hardness spirals through his vision, making the hair on my arms rise. I'm glad when he directs it to Brett. "Go home with her. I have to leave." He points to me, turns on his heel, and flashes out the door—his coat flapping in the air behind him like it's struggling to keep up with his pace.

I can only assume he's chasing after Lizzie, and I'm not sure how she's going to feel about that. Hell, I'm not even sure how I feel about it. My lips pull down. "Should he be bothering her?" My heart flutters, rapid against my ribs when Brett chuckles and pulls me in closer.

"Leave them, little one. They're adults. Let them solve their differences."

"You're right." The advice settles right in my stomach, even though I don't like it. What I do like however is how he turns me around and holds me in his arms. His large, calloused hand coasts down my torso, kneading hard through the fabric of my sweater.

"And I like what Saber said." He winks, washing away some of this morning's turmoil. "Take me home with you."

Shimmying closer, I dare to gently push my tits against his chest, just enough so he feels it, and so we don't get pointed stares in public. "Don't you want coffee first?"

My plans for discretion crash out the window when he threads a finger through a loop of my jeans and yanks me toward him, making us connect.

We both grunt and his cock digs into my belly. I squirm, desperate to crumble around it.

"I came because I knew you were here. Now, take me home." He lowers his head, hushing his voice so only I can hear him. "I'm sick of having to jerk myself off to you. It doesn't work well ever since I've been buried inside of you."

My hand trails down and I find his. Interlinking our fingers, I pull us to the table to gather my things and then I'm yanking us for the door. "Let's go. I hope you're ready to be holed up for the weekend."

"More than ready."

My blood hums in my ears when he unlinks our fingers and catches me in his arm, grabbing around my hip.

"The real question is, are you, because three days without you is too long. It's going to be like we're starting all over again."

"Then," I say, poking my finger into his arm, "why are we wasting time here?"

"True." He shoves me out the door, pushing me toward the direction of my car. "You better speed home."

"Yes, sir." I squeal and jump when he spanks my ass. Hard enough to make it sting through my jeans.

"Good girl."

*Damn.* He wasn't kidding about us restarting. We're not even in private and he's rough and ready to go. It's every indication that this weekend is going to be just as wild as the last...I'm ready for it.

*Dirty.* The word rings in my head as I keep my word by speeding home. *Dirty.*

But only for him—just the way I like it.

# Chapter 20

"And you're sure she saw us?" Brett pauses mid-motion while reaching for his glass of whiskey over the rocks.

"Trust me, she did. You should have heard Cora when she broke the news. She wouldn't lie about Monica seeing us." I shake more salt into the pasta that's bubbling on the stove, partially regretting my choice about coming clean regarding Monica catching us.

It's not a topic I want to discuss, but I've gotten plenty of pointed stares and even more innuendos since Brett's been gone. Now that he's back, things are bound to heat up. Keeping it under the rug and pushing things aside isn't going to work, so I'm coming clean before he goes out and faces the town. I decided telling him over a meal would be best.

Casting my eyes to Brett, I expect to find him frustrated, but I don't see that. All he does is hum and scrape the back of his hand along his jaw stubble.

I can't say I'm able to mirror the same calm he projects. In contrast, my grip around the salt container tightens and after a few solid squeezes, I opt to place it down. "Do you think she'll say something about you guys, or you know...try to make it sound like you forced her?"

"She might." His shoulders rise, then fall. "I don't know her. Only how pissed she was when I blew up about her being married and ended our session early. I don't think she was ready to stop."

My nose turns up in disgust. "But how? How can she be the one that's upset?"

"Oh, I don't know." He slowly shakes his head, then brings the rim of his glass to his mouth, partaking in a lazy sip. The amber liquid splashes against his lips before washing down his throat. He even makes taking sips look sexy. "Some people have skewed viewpoints on life, you know? Always claiming to be the victim or whatever. I've seen it plenty."

He's not lying. My dad did that all the time. It was always Mom's fault that she picked her end, not his. Never his. I still hate him for that. *Damn.* My frame sags, something I combat by swirling through our pasta noodles and focusing on Monica. "So what happens if she goes to her husband?"

He shrugs, a half-cocked grin on his face. "Then she goes to her husband. What the hell am I supposed to do about that?"

"Is that all you have to say?" My eyes widen a fraction, barely showing the surprise coursing through me. "Won't you be upset? Surely her husband won't sell you the land."

"Probably not, but why worry about it before it happens? We still don't know if she'll say anything."

Shock at his easy dismissal sends my jaw to the floor. "Brett, you've been fighting for this. Aren't you mad or concerned?"

"Some of my priorities have changed." A glimmer takes over his gaze and he stares at my breasts. "And besides, sometimes there are more important things to worry about."

The air thins, my blood thickens, making me aware of how hard it pumps from the look on his face. He looks starved, and dark, like he wants to eat me alive—which I'm too happy to oblige.

I release the spoon, placing it on the stove, eagerness driving me to tease and prod him until he shatters and consumes me. "Really? And what concern could be more important?"

My core tightens as he picks up his glass and reaches me in three solid strides. Craning my head back, I want to sway forward, lean into him, and I'm licking my lips expecting the most sin-filled words as he gently wraps his fingers around my throat, lowering his head for my ear.

A rumble comes up from the back of his throat and he strokes his thumb against the front of my neck. "I'm worried you're not adding enough salt to the water and that you're overcooking our noodles."

Stillness drapes over me and my want smashes to the floor, swiping down all the sweltering heat swirling in me. A sense of disbelief floods downward when he drops his hand, and his broad body shakes with a laugh.

I snap into action, swatting at his buff arm when he laughs harder. "Awful." My brows come together, but a giggle slips out. One I try to hide. "You're awful."

"What?" Leaning his backside onto one of my counters, he grins. "Were you expecting something else?" He *tsk*'s. "God, you're dirty."

"I am not." Defensiveness seeps through my voice as I snatch up my spoon. "Besides, how much can you expect out of me if you're going to stand there and get me excited?"

"Excited?" He snorts. "You want to talk about someone getting excited, then why don't we talk about me? Last time I checked, you were the one leaving me with not *one,* but *two* hard-ons at a restaurant."

"Two?" My nose wrinkles up when he nods. "Giuseppe's?"

"That was the second one."

The statement has my head jerking back, because I can't think of how I would have missed the first one. "And the first time?"

"During the cabin retreat with Cora and Lizzie." He rakes through one side of his hair, biting on his lip in a way that has me mad he's not rolling my lips through his teeth. "The moment you said you were going to kill me in your book and then looked up at me with those innocent eyes, asking me if I'd read it, was the sexiest fucking thing I've ever seen."

I choke in total surprise as my mouth hinges open. "You liked me talking about killing you?"

"I told you." He shifts one shoulder up and drops it. "I like a little bit of pain. Either way, that's when I understood how fucking screwed I was with you. I already couldn't stop watching you, but that's when I knew I wanted more, even though it pissed me off."

"Did it now?" I cock a brow, loving the smugness in my tone, adoring the way his confession sounds.

"Of course it did." He twirls the tumbler, letting ice mingle in with his drink of choice. "I wanted a little fun with someone, no doubt about that, but I didn't come here to get tangled up with a smartass author who always mouthed off to me." He raises his glass up in a toast, smiling. "I'd read that book by the way. You made it sound good." He lifts the edge to his lips and begins to drain the remaining whiskey.

All the happy feelings welling up inside puff out and die—Brett's meaning to compliment me, but he's accidentally served up a sad reminder that I can't write, and that I wasted many hours *trying* to write while he was away.

Whipping out a hot glove, I tug it on, ignoring the sting festering in my chest, and throw the oven door open.

With my back to him, I sigh. "Then you'll be waiting a while."

I set the pan down hard on the stove top, letting the loud bang of the pan voice my brewing frustration and spill out the sad facts. "My last bestseller was years ago, and after its success, all my good ideas dried up with it." Losing the glove, I grab at my pendant and give it a firm squeeze.

"Are you talking about *Play Me, Love Me?*"

My blood stops and the air captures my limbs, making my one arm dangle out in the open while I reach to turn off the oven. He's just named my top bestseller like it was resting on the top of his head. Slowly, I swivel on my heel, eyes wanting to bug out of my head. "How did you..."

"I read your books." He rubs at his nape, a slight redness pooling in his cheeks.

"You... you what?"

"All of them." He shifts his weight to the opposite foot, maintaining eye contact. But his stare is void of the usual sinful flames. Soft embers smolder instead.

The look, knowing he sought out all my books. It sears right through me, charring through every fiber of my being, creating an ache for more than all the hardcore sessions. It leaves me with a desperation for something lasting. Permanent—and that's dangerous. Dangerous since I know Brett has no intentions of staying here. I douse out my own desires, while trying to wrap my head around the notion that he's read every single one of my books. That he's learned about *me*. Because that's what my writing is. Pieces of me strewn out in broken fragments for everyone to see.

Arid breath collects and holds in my lungs. When I finally speak, it's one word, croaking out from the deepest part of my throat. "Why?" I wish I could sound sexier when I say it, but I can't—not when I'm starting to crave more and refraining from testing how deep our connection can go. *Also dangerous.*

"Why?" He repeats the question I'd almost forgotten I asked. "Because I couldn't stop thinking about you after I left. I tried." He lightly taps the base of his glass on the counter in steady beats. "Trust me, I tried. But it wouldn't fucking happen. I didn't know how to get you out of my system, so I picked getting you into it instead."

I want to swallow but I can't. I want to cry. Nothing. A head shake that almost doesn't exist happens, but that's it. Something in my chest collapses, concaving against my heart as he stares into my eyes—into my depths.

"You *can* write, Bianca." Cradling his glass in one hand, he strides toward me. Steady. Slow. Each step matching the slams of my heavy pulse. His touch is pure fire as he skims the back of his knuckles across my cheek. "I don't know what this road block is. Mental? Emotional? But you *can* write. I read your stuff, Bianca, and I'm sorry for all the shitty things I said." His voice dips low, flaring up the most carnal needs which begin to bloom in the lowest parts of my stomach. "You can do it again. We'll get you through it."

*"We'll get you through it."*

Words no one man has ever said to me before—and there's no way for me to respond. The phrase breaks me, churning my mind into a whirlpool of blankness. I blink several times, unsure if I've heard anything right. Asking for a repeat isn't out of the question either. I find a way to steady my voice. "Brett—"

The question is stolen away when he pulls up one brow, a slyness tugging at every feature of his handsome face. "Maybe you need a little inspiration."

"Inspiration?" My head tilts.

"Yeah. Like something to fire up your imagination?" He studies me for a moment before one silent chuckle animates his shoulders.

"What?" There's a tease streaking across his gaze, one I'm not sure I want to open, but still, I have to know.

"I was thinking about one of your implied scenes. The one with Shane and Julia in *Play Me, Love Me*."

"Oh gosh." I cover my hand with my mouth, wondering which scene he's referring to. Most of my stuff is PG in writing, rated R in implication—and I'm sure laughable to someone like Brett. I prepare myself for some serious teasing. "Don't keep me in suspense. Tell me which one."

"The one where Shane puts an ice cube in his mouth and tells her to lie down on the table." The joke I saw dancing in his vision a moment ago diminishes as he closes the statement.

I cinch my arms across my chest and throw the verbal ball back in his court. "What about it?"

A ghost of a smirk presses up his mouth and he brings the tumbler to his lips once more, pausing just long enough to ask his question before taking a drink of whiskey that's no longer there. "Have you ever had that done to you?"

"Well, um..." I haven't, but my answer delays at the sound of rattling ice as Brett tilts his glass back almost all the way. Shaking the sound away, I briefly flick my eyes to the floor and finish the reply. "No, I haven't. But I thought it would...be..." Looking up, the words die in my throat when he pokes his tongue out, displaying a cube of ice on it.

With a sly curl of sin and heat mixing across his face, he pulls it back in, flicks off the burner to the stove and speaks through a voice that sounds parched. "Perfect. Go lie on the table. Spread your legs."

*Holy shit.* My hands go limp and the spoon slips from my grasp, falling to the floor. I love it when he goes alpha, and it's just what I need to stamp out the useless remaining feelings of wanting a deeper connection. Of wanting something to last. I'm realizing how twisted my thought process was moments ago. I don't need more of him. All I'm in need of is a hard and proper lay—which I'm obediently going to give in to.

Starting now.

Scuffling backward, my heart pulses so hard my knees vibrate against each other.

Brett wastes no time stalking after my steps in slow, methodical strides, primal hunger shooting from him and crashing over me like a tidal wave. It's lessening the oxygen in my already spinning head, and I'm dying for him to kiss me and deplete the supply even more.

I squirm when my backside hits the table. My fingertips rotate, clenching into the lip of it as he stands a few feet away and stares with an intensity that makes me want to crumble. It's like the old days. He almost looks pissed. A hard swallow captures in the middle of my throat and I can hardly speak. "Why are you looking at me like that?"

"Like what?" His reply reverberates low in the room.

"Like you're irritated." Pulling back my shoulders, I try to straighten my spine while saying it. If anything, for my own resolve.

"Because I can't fucking look away." His eyes hood over, covering all the browns, and I'm already panting from the pressure in his voice. "Even when I want to, I can't look away and sometimes that annoys me. You have me, Bianca. Did from the start. Now..." The white T-shirt hugging his body conforms to each muscle as he takes a deep breath. "Lose the top. Lie on the table."

Peeling my sweater off, the room circles around me, going black in my peripherals like a tunnel, forcing my eyes to stay locked on the man watching me strip. He licks his lips, and except for the frantic beat of my heart and his staggered breaths, sound hones out. Goosebumps trail from my arms to my tits, pebbling my nipples at the upward sweep of his scorching gaze.

He tilts his head and cocks a brow. "Ass on the table and lie down. Now."

Obeying, I use my hands to shove off my feet and prop myself on the glass table top. A chill pricks at my ass cheeks. I know damn well it's a small prelude to what's coming—my lungs hold, air weighing my sternum down with torrid anticipation. As I relax my spine, shivers roll down my vertebrae where my back kisses the glass. Suppressing a squeal, I arch, seeking relief.

"Don't fucking move."

My eyelids roll to a close and at his voice, my body glues itself in place. I can't move, even if I wanted to. "Yes, sir."

"Good girl." He purrs it in the way only he can.

I moan as his large and powerful hands coast up my thighs and grab at the waist of my clothes—I rock my hips to aid him in deftly removing the lower contents of my garments, and I smile at the sound of denim from my loose-fitting jeans brushing to the floor.

With my eyes still sealed shut, both ears perk up at the singing of glass and the gentle clanking of more ice being removed.

"Ahh!" My once-settled spine lurches off the table and my eyes flick open at the sting encasing my nipples. I look, and Brett rests a cube over each one. Slowly melting, chilling me, yet stoking each nerve ending on fire. A gasp slips out when they linger against my flesh longer—their frosty nibble growing into a bite. "Brett..."

He guides my hands one at a time, securing the small squares against my breasts, then brings a finger to his mouth. "*Shh,* kitten." He's Sin. "Don't let them slide off. Understand?"

An unsteadiness strikes at my vocal cords. "Brett, it's cold."

"Yes it is." He grazes a long index finger along the inside of my thigh, then his zipper drags down. Unleashing himself, his cock springs out in attention.

I gyrate my body, desperate for him to fill me, even though I know he has other ideas in mind.

Resting his knuckles on the table top, he licks at his mouth. "And it's about to get colder." That's a promise—a beautifully delicious one. "Remember how I told you I love the cold?"

I nod.

"I chase it, Bianca. I only live in cool climates. It's what I love." He laughs once, deep and husky. "Lucky for you I'm about to show you how fucking hot the cold is."

The urge to speak is there, but the glass clinks again. More ice is being removed.

"Shit, Brett." Ice cubes descend on my inner thighs. I buck one time, then my hips snap down with a slam from Brett's heavy-handed strength. His fingers enclose around my thighs, the only barrier between his palm and my flesh being the chunks of ice which press harder into my skin as his grip tightens.

"Stay still, little one," he grunts. "It's hard to control you when wet."

I gulp back a moan. "You seem to be doing just fine."

Those are my last coherent words. His head ducks in between my legs, his chilled tongue finds my clit.

"Oh, shiiit!" I'd move, if I could to recoil from the freeze. Yet the cold from the ice and the heat of his breath creates a beautiful, twisted marriage. One pass of his tongue, and my eyes roll to the back of my head.

My hips lift, he shoves them down, confirming the thought I had in the lounge that night. He can hold me down with his hands. Stars flash behind my vision as I willingly become a slave to this man, letting him devour me however he pleases.

He sucks me, drawing my tender flesh between his teeth. My thighs clench around his head, squeezing tighter than a vice while I holler his name. More flicks send me writhing against the table. His unshaven stubble rasps against my skin, unleashing a delicious volley that travels up my thighs to land in my pleasured center. My nails pinch into my breasts, my teeth gritting in euphoric overload.

"Holy...Brett." I buck, successfully this time, not recognizing my own voice. It's too dark and raspy.

He comes up, breath stolen, panting hard and fast. "Fuck, kitten, you're sweet." He lays a half-melted ice cube on my clit, ignoring my shrill. "Next time I do this, I'll use my fingers. I'm going to pump you so hard, and make you feel so fucking good, your neighbors will call the police."

"Holy fuck," I say it raw—his dirty, grimy words undoing me, breaking me of obedience. I toss my arms overhead, dropping the ice cubes from my breasts. My spine arches when he smacks the inside of my thigh.

"Bad. I told you to keep the ice in place."

For once, I don't fucking care. "Brett." My voice whimpers out. "Brett, please. Please?"

"Fuck." He rips away, dropping the remaining ice from his palm, spitting the mostly melted one from his mouth. "You only have to ask once."

He lines up, stroking my drenched opening, and slams into me. Backing out, he slams in again, making breathing an impossibility as I gasp with each stretch of my walls.

"Shit." His voice is gruff. "I need you closer." Securing his elbows under my knees, he yanks me further down. We're flush, skin to skin, and he growls, unraveling before me. I relish the sight, at the way emotions play openly on his features.

His brows pull together, his face straining, changing color, and when I think he's about to combust, a string of words roll off his lips. "Inspiration, Bianca."

*Inspiration.* My eyes widen and while I want to echo him, I can't. Instead, I listen to a speech that comes out broken in between huffs, puffs, my shouts, his groans, and the table that's starting to scrape across the floor. A fresh assault unleashes on my heart and I can't stop it.

"Mine." He breathes. "God, Bianca, you're..." He drives himself deeper, to my breaking point.

"Brett!" I shift my hips up, aligning to better clench around him, which forces his head back.

"Fuck," he growls, expanding in me. "So good." A deep breath sucks in, and he pushes it out through rounded cheeks, increasing the fortitude of his stance by widening his legs out. "Like you're made for me."

"Oh my God..." I prop up on my elbows, my heart thumping so fast I wonder how it remains encased inside. Tears spill out the corners of my eyes as my head dangles backward, accepting the way my body surrenders to his thrusts. My nails screech against the glass as I dig for something, anything to ground me.

Because I need it. Demand it as he plucks at the closed seams of my scarred up, disbelieving heart.

My head snaps up when he stops thrusting, eyes opening.

"Bianca." He's staring straight at me but the burn in his gaze is still present, his chest rising and falling in rapid beats. His voice is calm when he speaks, and it's laced with fire. "You're going to put me in your next novel, and it's going to be your new bestseller."

My pulse beats out of sync, hammering in shortened tempo even as he resumes pumping in me, and this round he serves is hard—our skin clapping each time he fills me, my legs trembling as he lifts them so they're straight up, resting against his chest. When I try to close my eyes, I can't.

*Fuck.* Like he said earlier, I can't look away, even though I want to. Now there's a connection, a string binding me to him—knitting me to his body, his soul...to *him.* The link creeps into my chest, threatening to snatch my heart right out of its cavity before passing it to him. The only way I can stifle the overwhelming sensation is by slapping my hand over my ribs. It only releases me when Brett's eyes darken and an order barks out.

"Cum, baby. Say my name louder than ever before."

I do it, triggered by his order, eyes sealed shut—spasming in waves. A limpness trails through me, clouding my mind and words to where I can't even grasp what I'm saying. And I barely comprehend his own shout of release when it happens.

It takes me several moments to gather my surroundings and find the bottom of my swimming head when it's all said and done.

"Holy shit." Brett pulls out, panting. He smirks, looking far too happy with himself. He leaves his jeans pooled around his ankles and comes over to the side of the table. Bending down, he kisses me, just grazing his tongue against my teeth, and I realize we haven't exchanged a kiss this whole time.

"Inspiration," he repeats. "I hope it helps, because, fuck..." Cupping my cheek, he plants a gentle kiss on my forehead. Breaking it, his lips rest on my skin and my senses sink, falling into him as he murmurs. "If you knew the ways you inspire me, you'd never doubt yourself again."

"Me?" My brows knit together. "I'm not inspiring."

"Yes." He threads his fingers through the back of my hair, forcing our eyes to meet,his powerful grip matching the intensity in his voice. "Yes you are. Now, write a fucking book and use this for some direction."

"I...I will." My heart flutters in uneven beats.

"Good girl." Backing away, he winks. "I'm going to clean up. Join me if you'd like, for a shower."

He's a few steps away, swaggering as he heads off for my bathroom, when the connection from moments ago reawakens, surging up and down my skin.

"Brett?" Goosebumps rise on my arms, trailing into my nipples while he turns around.

He wipes a bead of sweat away and softly smiles. "What?"

"What was that?" The question sounds so vague, but his eyes round. The tenderness in them reaches out, drowning me in a riptide that renders me lightheaded—feeling like I haven't come up for oxygen in a lifetime.

"*That,*" he says, in a tone much too gentle "Was me helping you forget you don't do *serious.*"

# Chapter 21

"Are you sure you want some of your things here?" My voice wavers toward the end of the question as I smooth my finger over the edge of my mother's initial.

"Absolutely."

*Crap.* I wasn't expecting his response to fire back so fast. The further Brett strolls into my house, the more I clutch at my necklace. By the time he's walked past me, I'm twisting it so much it's a wonder the chain doesn't snap.

Two weeks have passed since he blew my mind with the ice cubes, and damn if he hasn't changed my mind about a lot of things. Last week I was ludicrous enough to suggest him keeping a few items here, a thing I've never allowed for any guy, and it's catching up with me now. At first he hesitated, but now I can't see any of that. His steps are confident and bold as he walks across my house.

A pit rips open in my stomach the closer he draws to my bedroom.

The sickness inside corrodes any remaining confidence, eating through my calmness till my palms are clammy.

Watching him, I realize that for the first time since hooking up, we won't be going in there to screw around. He's using my room to unpack his things. *Shit. His things.* My joints are rigid, taking over my feet, tacking them to the floor.

It's like he senses what's come over me. He slows his pace. Glancing over his shoulder, two dark eyes study me. "Nervous?"

"No." Ice travels up my body, coating over the sound of my voice. I grip the necklace tighter and sew my brows together. "Why?"

"'Cause you have a death grip on your necklace."

My hand falls away, taking my posture with it. I'm slouching. "Sorry. It's just..."

"It's okay to be nervous, Bianca." His brow lifts. "I haven't done this before either."

A barb of irritation pokes at me from his assumptions. "I didn't say I've never done this before."

"You don't have to. I can see you haven't."

"Brett—" A warning tone hits my vocal cords.

He chuckles, holding one hand out. "Come on." He winks. "Help me unpack."

I'm across the room, interweaving my unsteady hand through his in a flash. *Damn it.* My teeth grit at how easily I crumble to his requests, especially when he says it so sweetly.

Chewing on the inside of my cheek till I think it will bleed, I sit on the bed, watching him lift the suitcase onto the bed. Silence clouds in the room but it feels like so much more, and my body tingles from the vibrations. Brett orbits around me like he's becoming part of my life, universe. *Crap.* Not good. Each day he sticks around, I discover my soul has sunk another inch deeper into him, and that wasn't in my plans when we started doing this.

*Fuck.* He was supposed to be simple. Easy. A quick fix to kill the hormonal overload he initiated in me, but now with him moving in his items, the primitive part of our arrangement is washing away. I'm worried about the floodgate this will unlock and I don't know why I suggested it in the first place.

We're going to crash and burn, and I never should have said yes. To any of this.

I force a deep breath. *At least he'll be going home soon.* All he needs is his property and then this idea is over.

"...Hello? Earth to Bianca?" Brett's deep voice raises in volume, shattering my wandering thoughts. A smirk spans across his mouth. "Have you heard anything I said?"

"Sorry." I rub at my arm, my cheeks flashing with heat. "I spaced out."

"Obviously." His shoulders lurch with a chuckle. Directing his attention to the black suitcase, he plucks up a pair of jeans and places them down on the bed.

I fixate on them. It's the same pair he was wearing at the lounge when I ran into Lance. My heart thrashes away at my chest walls. Each violent bump coils down my body, making me stiff. I never would have thought a pair of simple black pants could act like a wire stripper to my composure, clamping and tearing away at my nerves till I'm sick and jumbled, yet here I am. Raw. A fine tremor vibrates through my hand as the truth sinks in harder. He's really doing this—moving his things in.

Watching him place a shirt on the bed, I take a hasty gulp of needed air. "Why do you want to bring your things here, Brett?" My shaky question sounds so simple, but there's more weaving through it. Things I can't utter—a question of his truest intentions, a wondering of his motives and how deep they go...the inner workings of his heart. All those topics thread through my words.

From the way he smiles, and the gentle way he answers, I think he knows it. "Because you're different from everyone else, and when you meet someone different, you *do* something different."

I shake my head, expelling a huge breath of air. It depletes my lungs and I'm praying it pushes out all the uncertainty riddling me today. That doesn't happen. Hugging my arms around my middle, I rock in small back-and-forth motions. "Brett, I know you're trying to help me forget that I don't do serious relationships, but I don't think it's going to work."

"And how will we know that unless we try?" His question is pointed, yet comes out so soft that I'm not given the chance to be offended or afraid, just timid.

"But why should I try?" I barely hear the words; however, I do feel my pulse. It springs to life, rapping against the veins in my wrist as Brett rests his weight on the bed and smiles.

"Aren't you tired, Bianca?"

"What do you mean?" Each fiber in my shoulders tightens, drawing them up to my ears.

"I mean, look at our lives." Dark eyes which lack their usual hardness today drop to the bedding. He draws a deep breath and slowly reaches his hand out, taking his time toward his destination. My hand. I'd like to pull it away, but I can't. All I can do is draw a ragged inhale when he connects and gently traces his fingertips over my knuckles. "We've both been driven by revenge, anger, and things that don't last. Don't you want something more?"

The question shoots up through my arm like glass, slicing me wide open before it lands in my heart. "No." I jerk my hand out of his, not able to stop the coldness in my voice. "Honestly, I need those things to fuel me and my writing."

"I disagree." He moves closer to me, never allowing the distance I need. There's a rasp laying deep in his voice. "I've been thinking a lot lately, and I'm wondering if not letting go of our hurts is fucking us up."

My brows pull together and my head jerks back. "You don't mean that."

"Yes. I do." More vigor returns to his voice as he speaks. Arching a brow, he stares into my eyes. "Revenge is a confession of pain."

My eyes widen while a lump forms in my throat. The conviction in his utterance feels so right. Something about it worries me. *No.* I'm not going to give into his words. Whatever I do, I won't feel them. I narrow my gaze. "I think revenge is needed. Necessary. Good." There's calculation in my voice. Something that hasn't come out since I spoke to Dad. "Without anger, where will my inspiration come from?" All I'm used to is thinking about disobeying Dad when I write, or at least try to nowadays. Not having that behind me sounds so odd.

He rubs at his nape. "A healthy source. One that won't have you rubbing gangrene in your heart."

"What?" I wrinkle my nose, head swimming in a sea of confusion. Eyeing him up and down, I curl my shoulders away. It gives me the space I've been looking for. "I don't understand."

*Gangrene.* The word strikes at me with long fangs, digging into my heart till I feel ugly, and for whatever reason it shoots a bolt of guilt down my body. Clutching at my necklace, I'm yanking it hard. It can't funnel out the hot shame, and soon my skin is slicking over with sweat.

"I can't be so sure you're right." A grumble scrapes at the back of my throat. "I need it and so do you. Without revenge, we're screwed."

"Is that so?" His voice is calm, but challenging. "Answer this." Serious lines course his face.

I freeze, gripping the hem of my shirt.

"When did your dad die?"

My eyes widen at the question. "Three and half years ago."

"Mm-hmm." He leans forward. "When did your last bestseller drop?"

"Three and half years ago." My heart drops into my stomach. Why does the time frame seem to justify his ideas? *No.* I pucker my lips out, forcing a bored face. "That's only a coincidence."

"It's not." He's across the bed in seconds, capturing my chin with his thumb and index finger. "And you know it. Let it all go, Bianca. Let it go with me." His head lowers and his eyes dip for my mouth.

"Where is all this forgiveness stuff coming from today?"

"It hasn't been simply today. I've been thinking about this for a while."

"I don't believe it." My gaze studies the perimeter of his face—one that's looking less harsh. Confusion twists across my mouth. "This isn't like you. You're not the type of guy who forgives."

"Not the type? What gives you that impression?"

"Well, just...just—" I gesture at his clothing.

His brows lift so high they hit his hairline, and he huffs out a breath like he's just been punched in the stomach. "You'd seriously shoehorn me into some idea of what you *think* I should be? Based on what? The way I look? The way I cuss?" He frowns when my mouth snaps shut, admitting my guilt. "That's disappointing, Bianca."

*Shit.* I can't think of what to say. Not while shame slices at my core.

"Don't let my tattoos fool you, kitten. Of course I can forgive, and I know you can too." Reaching out, he bundles my hand in his, giving it a firm squeeze.

I can't pull away. Maybe it's his gentle tone, the glow in his eyes, or how right he feels while holding my hand, but there's something here. It lessens the uncertainty that roiled in me moments ago, leaving me parched.

A thick swallow washes down my throat as I lift my gaze to stare at him through my lashes. "How do you know I can forgive?"

"Because I *see* you." He's on his knees, over me, cupping my face. One flick of his tongue to wet his mouth, and my heart roars to life, striking at my ribs so hard I wonder if he hears it.

"Brett..." I pant out that one word.

"*Fuck.*" He scans my face, leaving me emotionally naked. "I see you, Bianca." Peppermint breath trails into my mouth while his lips brush mine. I shudder. "Always have." His fingers grip into my hair. "Always fucking will."

His mouth seals over mine and he groans. The sound hits the back of my throat, piercing right into my chest. I'm climbing to my knees, fisting his hair and tugging on the roots. Brett works me, kissing me, nipping my lips and neck in the ways he knows I like. Much too soon, I'm falling apart, in his arms, and we lie back.

"Fuck, Bianca." He positions his wide frame between my legs, peppering kisses up and down any showing skin. "I love the way you fit against me."

"Mmm." My nerve endings alight on fire when his finger slips under my shirt and I peel my spine off the bed, pressing myself against him, delighting in that perfect fit he's just mentioned as the air swirls around me.

He chuckles, holding me tight, stroking his fingers through my hair. "Are you sure you don't do serious?"

*Fuck.* Panic rolls down my limbs. I'm rigid, not even able to draw a breath.

"Because with you like this—" He sucks at my earlobe and moans. "Jesus, you're so sweet I want to fucking die."

Damn it. I freeze, overloaded by everything circling around me tonight. Him challenging my viewpoints about Dad. Him wondering if I can't do serious after I promised myself years ago that I'd never try again. Brett is flipping my whole way of thinking onto its head, and he's almost winning—sweetly coaxing me to fall into him, trust him. *Crap.* I'm not sure if I can. Panic crashes over me, stealing my oxygen. I can't even get lost in his sizzling kisses. My body stiffens.

"Bianca?" Brett's deep voice calls me back to him. Pulling away from him, our eyes meet. His gaze tightens, brows matching the same pattern, almost meeting in the middle. "What's wrong?"

"I...uh... nothing." Patting him on the chest, I convince him to sit up and smile. "I need to check on dinner." More like I need to get out of here and steal away a few moments to think. Hard.

Sliding off, I'm out the bedroom door faster than he can say anything, making sure my head is high.

It's not till reaching the kitchen that I scratch my head and suck in some needed air. Clutching my necklace, I close my eyes and sense my pulse slow. *Can I do this?* The serious things in life?

Part of me wants to run from Brett, but not only does it feel wrong, I'd also be ditching the most amazing sex on earth and that's dumb.

But maybe I don't need to worry about any of that.

Thinking of his property, my limbs loosen some. I think he's told several people he plans to leave after he gets it.

*It's only until he's gone.* The words loop in my head a few times. *It's only until he's gone.* Soon, he'll have his land and me losing control won't be an issue. For now, I just need to enjoy the hell out of his body, because it can't last too much longer. Nothing fun ever lasts. Nothing. And for the first time in my life, I'm looking forward to something not lasting—that something is Brett.

# Chapter 22

*D*amn. If I ever thought I would die from extreme pain, today would be the day. The curtains to my room are drawn together, blacking out the room. It's still not enough. The horrendous split occurring behind my eyes and encasing my head leaves my vision blurry while blotches of white snow dance outside my field of view.

This headache is the worst one to date and even I'm wondering if I should go to the doctor.

Not that I could go right now, even if I wanted to. A fraction of light is too much, making me think my head will crack in half anytime a beam slips through.

I'm reminded of this very fact when Brett taps on the door and enters, allowing a small sliver of brightness with him. Fresh pain slices through my head.

I moan and toss the comforter over my face.

"Bianca?" His deep voice laces with concern and while I find it sweet, I'm too absorbed with the pain to get lost in the sentiment of it.

"Mmm."

"Baby."

His footsteps drag on the carpet, a slide occurring with each step he takes. The sensitive state I'm in heightens each sound, allowing me to pinpoint the way the wood under the padding creaks from his weight, and how his socks cause static on the thick pile on top. I swear I can even detect the moment he kneels down by my side of the bed. It's like I can hear his joints bending and folding to allow the motion.

The blanket falls from my face, and he extends his hand. I instinctively nuzzle into the palm cupping my cheek. His large thumb strokes over the same area in gentle back and forth, and he sighs. "Bianca, let me take you to the hospital."

"No." I want to say more, but it's the only word I can manage. My voice is hoarse in my throat, tricking me into thinking I haven't talked in a hundred years. This headache is no joke.

"Bianca." He sits on the bed, sinking the mattress down. "This is serious. Something's wrong." Dropping his hand, he latches it onto mine, which lies near my side. "I know you like being tough, but this isn't about that." He drags his fingers across my skin, alighting flecks of comfort across the area he touches. "This is about your wellbeing. I think you should get checked out."

"No." I mumble it out, my brows pulled together.

A grumble slips out of him, and he rakes a hand along the side of his head. "Fuck. Why did I have to meet the most stubborn woman on earth?" He moves, adjusting his weight to slide off the bed.

I don't want that. My heart hammers louder in my ears, picking up in tempo at the thought of being alone again for the rest of the day. He's checked on me a few times, but he's mostly left me in peace, which I'm tired of. I'm also regretting my negative thoughts about not wanting him to move some of his items here from last week. Right now he's the best sight in the world, headache and all. And I need him. Something about his voice and touch makes the headache more bearable.

Flipping my hand up, I grip around the bottom of his forearm, halting his departure. "Brett. Stay." I pulse my fingers around his muscular arm, praying he'll feel the desperation working in me. My heart slows when he listens. It sings when he joins me on the bed.

"Can you lie down on your side?"

I nod, suppressing a groan while a deep throb thrums across my brain.

"Then do that so I can hold you."

Words have never sounded sweeter, and if I could, I'd leap into action. But I can't. Slowly I turn, careful not to jostle my head along the way. Anything faster than the pace of a snail has left me cursing my ancestors for whatever the hell this torment is.

Successfully in a fetal ball, Brett curls up behind me, draping his large hand across my stomach.

"Jesus." His warm breath tickles the hair on my neck. "You're so difficult." The words and tone are all frustration, but I know he's not too upset as he lightly kisses my skin. Trailing his lips up and down on my neck in a few simple passes, he rests a hand to the top of my head and runs his fingers through my hair. "Why aren't you getting tested, Bianca? Don't you want to know what's going on?"

I don't answer. My eyes droop shut and I'm happy talking is near impossible today. It's the perfect avoidance of his question. The real reason why I'm not going is because I'm scared. The panic of how serious this is slithers around inside, snaking around my stomach. And while I'd never admit it to anyone, I'm worried something serious is going on, and who wants to know about that?

Ignorance is bliss. I just need to reassure myself of that.

*It's nothing.* The words repeat, all the way up until I'm lost in sleep with Brett sleeping right beside me, helping me combat the pain— helping me believe that in the morning this will be gone and I can get back to life as usual.

But until then, I'm thankful Brett's here to hold me. The heat of his body, the weight of his hand. *Him.* In the dark, falling asleep to the rhythm of his breaths, he's never felt more right.

Damn, I'm glad he's here.

# Chapter 23

"I still haven't heard from Lizzie." I recline into Brett's sofa, right into his arms, eyes closed. I have no idea what's going on with for Lizzie. She won't return my calls, but I think she remains set on moving. That's the last Cora heard, and while I'd like to dwell on it longer, a moan slips out as Brett gives me a massage. He's so damn good at it, I'm like an addict—a slave to his touch. I elbow him as he tries to drop his arms. "No one said you could stop."

He laughs, and even with my eyes closed, I can imagine the sin-filled smile spanning across his face. "Man, you're bossy." Leaning forward, he flicks his tongue at my ear once.

"You love it."

"I do, even though it drives me fucking nuts." Warm breath rushes against my skin with his chuckle, but the sound is subdued. I already know he's thinking about the phone call he got earlier today—even my shoulders wind up thinking about it.

"So when does Monica's husband want to meet up with you?"

His fingers knead deeper into my muscles at the question. "In a few days. After he gets back from a trip." Brett's voice is calm, but he's nervous.

I'm nervous for him, clutching at my necklace hoping the meeting goes well. Paul, Monica's husband, called saying he had some questions about Monica. Brett tried to get Paul to go into further detail, but he remained tight lipped over the phone. And while Brett and I can guess what the discussion will be about, we obviously don't know the outcome.

"What if he runs you out of town?" While I'm preparing for Brett to leave, I don't want it to be at the doing of Monica.

"I'll try not to let it get to that point." Giving my arms a full squeeze, he places a kiss on my neck. "I'm sure I'll work something out. For now, let's not worry about that."

I relax into him, hungry for another kiss. "Then what are we going to worry about?"

"Turn around, kiss me back, and find out."

"Yes, sir." Giggling, I turn around, cup his face, and close my lips around his.

Moments after, we're both trapped in blaze of our desires. Sometime later, as I chant his name, sweat-drenched and void of my senses, I'm wondering if maybe it would be best for Paul to run Brett out of town.

What we are is only supposed to last until Brett leaves, and it's already been too long. Each moment with him ties me to Brett a bit more, and as I fall asleep in his arms that night, I slip further into him—doomed by discovering I'm starting to want him to stay, but protected by the knowledge of knowing he'll leave.

What should be anxiety-inducing revelations float away with me settling on the idea that he'll leave soon.

Soon, Brett will either get his land or get run out of town. But in either case he'll be gone. And while I'll miss our mind-blowing sex, I'll be safe again.

Alone and in control. Just like I was born to be.

# Chapter 24

Brett walks through the front door of his apartment and I flip my laptop to a close fast, no longer able to focus on writing. Well, it's not like that's been happening anyway. Anxiety has knotted my core and getting out words has been impossible. The door catches shut behind him and I wring my hands so tight my skin burns.

When he doesn't say anything at first and casually strolls for the open kitchen, I jump to my feet. "Well? What did Paul say?"

Brett met with Monica's husband this morning, and the last two hours have been torture while I've waited to see what kind of problems this will cause for Brett. I shift weight from the balls of my feet while Brett takes a swig of water. "Did he talk to you about Monica?"

"Sure did." Damn, he sounds calm while saying it. For whatever reason it makes my stomach swirl.

I clutch my necklace, yanking at the chain. "And?"

"He heard about Monica and I, and wanted to confirm it."

I blink slowly, head tilting hard to the side. "How did he find out? Did Monica say something?"

"Ironically, no." He chuckles. "She complained to a friend about us being together. She told her about our basement session and mentioned you being a poor substitute."

*Ouch.* A sting radiates through my chest. I rub at the ache.

"The funny part is her friend was jealous of Monica since she wanted to be with me. Said friend then went to Paul and ratted her out."

A snort comes through my nose. Damn, life serves up karma in the finest ways at times. Still, the humor is short lived as I look at Brett. My shoulders weigh down and I sigh. "So Paul asked about you and Monica and...? What did you say?"

"The truth." He sets his glass down on the counter, walks around, and smirks. "Thank God Paul had enough sense to ask if I'd been tricked into thinking she was single, and if she threatened me. I guess he's been suspecting things for a while."

Not the outcome I was expecting. My mouth dangles open. "And what did he decide to do?"

"Leave." He shrugs and pockets his hands. "He told me my confirmation was the last straw. Paul's selling everything, taking his kids, and moving out of state."

"And the property? I'm sure he didn't want to offer it up. Not after—"

"Actually, he did. He told me it was mine."

"Really?" A smile beams across my lips. To say I'm elated about Brett snagging something he's been fighting for is an understatement. At least Monica didn't ruin that for him. "Oh, Brett that's—"

"I didn't take it."

"What?" My eyes widen, shock knocking me back a few steps. I could not have heard that right. I blink a few times and try again. "What did you just say?"

"That I turned it down." It rolls off his tongue in a smooth combination, not stuttering or missing a beat. "I don't want the land anymore."

"I-I don't understand." I frown in confusion. "Why don't you want the land?"

"Because it's poison, Bianca." He draws nearer, shoes pounding on the wood of his floor. With each shuffle forward, my pulse ramps up. "Chasing the land, trying to get even..." A frown tugs down the corner of his mouth. "It's not worth it. The sole person I'm fucking over is myself, and I don't want to live like that."

"Well, wow. Uh...good for you." *I guess.* All I've heard is that he's given up on his dreams, but it's Brett's choice. Also, there goes my sex life. With no land to buy, he'll leave quicker than I thought, but I've been preparing for this. Rubbing my palms together, my shoulders bunch up. "I see." I attempt to smile and nod at his baffling choice. "So, I guess when you return home—"

"Home?" Groomed brows snap together. "What the hell?" Running his eyes over my body, I notice he's rigid, and I don't miss the hard shock twisting in his tone. "What do you mean by that?"

My head draws back. "Wasn't that the plan?" A tightness pulls at my sternum, and dread creeps over me with the feeling that everything I'm about to hear is going to be something I don't like."To leave after you got the property?"

"Not anymore." His head tilts after my mouth drops open. "I don't know who you've been talking to, but ever since Saber returned with me, my plan has always been to stay here."

*Shit. No. Shit.* If there was a chair behind me, I'd collapse into it. This isn't part of the plan. I was only supposed to relinquish control of wanting him to last until he left.

"Bianca? Are you kidding me?" A red hue splashes across his face and he rakes through the side of his hair. "Please tell me you're not this far in denial? What's the point of me moving my things into your house if I'm not planning on staying?"

*Fuck.* A fresh wave of panic slaps me across the face. "You can't!" My voice shatters the unusual quiet of the room.

"What?" His brows meld together. It looks like he's eaten something sour. "What do you mean, 'I can't'?"

"Like I said." Something hard coats over my heart, taking my voice with it as I force back the flood of shock that commanded me moments ago. "You're not supposed to stay here, Brett. It's not a part of the—"

He takes a large step forward, and my words die.

Heavy, baited silence looms over us and it lasts for far too long.

"It's not a part of what, Bianca?" His tone is deep, threatening.

I methodically take a slow shuffle backward, ensuring that this time, I get the space I need. "It's not part of the plan."

"*What* plan?" A look of disgust swirls in his eyes.

"It's complicated, Brett." My throat tightens when he moves for me again. I creep back one more step. "*We* are complicated." Understatement of the year. "I think it's best if you leave." I say it, numbing my nerves and injecting the same sound into my voice. A huge part of me wants Brett to stay—wants to believe that we can last and be more...but it's just too dangerous. The amount of control I'll have to give up to be in a real relationship with someone isn't worth the risk.

Taking a huge swallow, I pull my shoulders back and force a glare. "You need to leave."

He mirrors my look and arches a brow. "The fuck if I do."

All the blood drains out my body. When his jaw grits and he takes a deep breath, it depletes all the oxygen in the air during the process. My lungs are heavy, smothering me from the inside out.

"Brett—" I take one more step of retreat. *Shit.* My spine smacks against the wall. I've been so focused on Brett, I've failed to notice my surroundings, and I'm pinned. But that doesn't mean I have to sound weak.

Tossing back the anxiety swirling up my insides, I jut my chin out and steady my voice. "I meant exactly what I said, Brett. You can't stay here. You're not meant t—"

He flies across the room, and he's over me. Two hands on either side of my body—a massive wave of heat wrapping around me.

Smacking his palms to the wall, a loud thud echoes and roars in my ears. "What the fuck is all this bullshit?" His chest bumps mine and a deep growl rumbles from the back of his throat. "Telling me when I can stay and not stay?"

"Yo-you can't," I stammer, my heart thrashing in my chest.

"The fuck if I can't." There's a glower in his eyes. It pierces through me while he lowers his head. "And why do you have this notion that I can't? Are you scared?"

"I'm not." My throat dries up. "I have nothing to be afraid of."

"You have *everything* to be scared of," he counters. "You think I haven't been watching you? Noticing you? You won't say it because you're afraid to be happy. You're always expecting the worst and then when it doesn't happen, you pray it comes true."

*Damn.* Nothing in me moves, minus the hairs on my neck. They ripple upward, standing on end while his truth nails me to the wall. "Please..." My voice is a plea. "Please just leave."

*Please let me be safe.*

"Fuck no." His eyes go dark. "I'm sick of you bossing me around, Bianca." His nostrils flare. "I'm not taking the land and I'm staying. With you," he adds after scanning my face.

*Fuck.* Dread creeps up my body, snaking around each organ inside until it reaches my throat and constricts around my neck. "Brett, no." It wheezes out, like I'm being choked.

"That's a piss poor response." He bears weight into the wall, forcing our bodies to skim across each other. He burns like a forest fire against me, and I want to engulf myself in the flames. Instead, I glue my ass to the wall to keep myself in check. I won't touch him. I won't be consumed. "What is it? Are you afraid of having something deeper?"

"No—no." *Yes.* "It's only because I don't need you."

"Bullshit, you don't need me. You need me as much as I need you. You're simply scared to admit it."

"That's not true."

"It is. I told you I *see* you, because I *am* you. You think I'm not scared to try something real for once? Trust me, I see your fear. Every time you look at me, I see how you try to block me out, but it won't work, Bianca. We're not made to be separated." He brushes his knuckles down my cheek and I shiver. "And I'm here to break you of your irrationality as well as my own. I'm going to show you how twisted your lie is."

"You're wrong." I press more of my body against the wall, hoping to escape the man who's just cut and splayed open my whole existence.

It doesn't work, he feels closer than ever, bound to my soul as he brings our foreheads together—his breath heavy, mine nonexistent.

"Then instead of telling me I can't stay, make it personal and say you don't want me in your life."

My body tenses and my eyes pull wide open.

"Say. It." Hot words trail over my nose, cheeks, and ears. "Better yet," he groans, "say it after you stop me."

Hot greedy lips crash onto mine, abundant weight falls on me, pressing me hard into the drywall—each bump imprints into my back. One taste of peppermint and I open wide, letting him consume me. Own me. *Fuck.* Own me. And I can't stop it. I'm tugging him in, erasing all space between us, wishing he could knit his heart to mine. But it still wouldn't be enough. I'll always be depleted of him no matter how much I receive.

Warm hands secure around my back and he presses me against his marbled frame. He fits my soul. Each jagged piece of him seeps deep inside, marking me as his, and damn if this doesn't feel like this is how my existence should be. *Shit.*

I love it.

I hate it.

Shoving him off me will keep me safe from the storm that is Brett. My hands clench the lapels of his shirt and I flex my biceps, preparing to force him away. "Fuuuck!" Raw electricity coils down my body when his fingers deftly slip under my pants to rub my clit. He circles, and my legs quiver. A whimper trails out my mouth.

He dives in further, brushing my drenched opening, and groans. "So beautifully fucking wet, for me," he says dark and low. "*Me.*"

"Yes." I gasp, unable to stop my confession. "For you."

Black eyes sizzle, branding my skin while his chest expands. "Do you want me out of your life?"

*Shit.* I pinch my lips closed, refusing to spill how weak I am.

After an eternity of examining my features, he smirks. "Very well. You want to clam up? Well, guess what? I won't allow it." My skin vibrates with need at the words. "I'll get the truth today because no matter what bullshit you throw at me, the one thing that can't lie is your body. It always speaks truth to me, kitten."

"Fuck." My throat is arid, each fiber in me trembles. But he's right. One tug at my pants has me spreading my legs, allowing him whatever access he needs.

"Mine," he groans, and I wilt at those words, strength draining out of my limbs.

He draws my panties to the side. The cooling atmosphere forces me to take a sharp inhale of air, and when his finger grazes my opening, the room swims around me.

A finger slips inside. One makes me want to moan. A second one dares me to whimper in ecstasy. A third one has me biting my tongue to refrain from saying his name.

An earth-shattering pump tests the fortitude of my walls, of my knees, of the lies I feed myself that I don't want or need Brett. My nails scrape at the flat planes of the drywall as I search for the grounding I need.

"I feel you, baby." His voice is power, working through the darkness in my head. "I feel how you're drawn to me." He pulls a groan out of me. "There's no way we're so perfect for each other and not meant to be together. Allow us to be happy."

*No. No.* I want to refuse him. I can't. The pace of his fingers quicken—the slickness of my body acting as its own voice, confessing how subjugated my entity is to this man. Another finger crams inside, and he pumps harder. A crack forms across the barriers I've created.

"Brett..." His name flows out of me like honey, and I'm stuck to him.

"Fuck yes. Say my name like that again."

"Brett." I writhe against the wall. "Brett..." More areas of my fortified partitions disintegrating into dust.

"Shit." He's on his knees ramming me, siphoning the fear and denial out of me with each draw and push.

"Holy fuck!" His tongue slides across my clit once. I scream his name, my hoarse cry echoing around the house and through the haze of my climax. His deep voice cuts through it all.

"Look at me."

My eyes snap open on command.

With his pace never decreasing, he licks his lips and furrows his brows. "Do you want me out of your life?"

"Fuck, Brett." My back arches while another climax builds. Close to the edge, I toss my hands over my head.

"Answer me." His pace slows.

I grumble in frustration at how my climax ebbs. "Please." I raise my frame to glide up his fingers.

"No, little one." He shoves my pelvis back, taking no care to be gentle in the way he glues me in place. "Tell me. Tell me if you want me to leave you."

Biting my lower lip, I scowl, anger roiling in my veins. "What do you think?" I bite out.

"I think no." Slow, steady pumps resume, and they pluck at the raw edges of my teetering composure. "Am I right?"

"Yes." I say it breathlessly and wholeheartedly. "Yes." I tilt my hips off the wall. "You're right. You've always been right." Sweat dews on the nape of my neck when he serves a delicious slam. "You've always been right." Fuck. Of course I don't want him gone. Merely thinking about it slashes an ache through my soul. I'm certain he's meant to last. I'm just not sure I can verbalize it.

But thank God he understands. At least that's what it feels like as he moans my name and pleasures me with untamed vigor. Each push inside weakens my knees a little more, and soon I'm slouching halfway down the wall. His name is on the cusp of my tongue when he slows down again.

I squirm in desperation. "Shit. No. Please."

"One last thing."

"What?"

"How do you feel, Bianca?"

My eyes flutter open and he's there. Looking at me, staring into my soul. Beads of sweat climb up my face, kissing my temples, and I'm not sure how to answer.

Smiling some, his voice softens. "With my fingers inside of you, how do you feel?"

"I feel..." My legs partially give out. "I feel..." *Full? Satisfied?* No. My eyes widen as the right words landmine through my being. *Complete.*

"Complete?" He says it so calm and sure, like he knows that's the word my heart found and settled on.

I nod.

"That's how you make me feel, baby. Please, don't take that away."

"I won't..." Air compresses out of my body. "I promise I won't."

"Good girl." The small smile blooms into a full one. "Now cum for me."

A single pump and I shatter. Splintering apart, sliding all the way to the floor, uttering his name. I come hard for the man who owns me. I come hard for the man whom I own, and I do it with my heart so full it wants to bust out of my chest.

He's right. I'm complete.

And that's fucking terrifying.

# Chapter 25

"So how long is Brett gone for?" Cora's voice blares over the speaker of my cell as I pace the bedroom for the millionth time.

"Till Saturday." I sit on what's become Brett's side when he stays here and trail my hand down the bedding. Terror still taps at my heart when I think of him being a permanent fixture in my life, but slowly I'm learning to accept it. I think.

"Cool. And you're holding up alright without your beau?"

I scoff. "Oh, come on. It's not like we're lovesick high school kids. I'm fine without him here."

"Sure," she snips. "And I suppose you being 'fine' is the reason why you've been calling either me every day since he's been gone?"

"Oh, whatever. I have not." My eyes go skyward. "I've been calling you the same amount of times as always."

She barks out a laugh, and for whatever reason, a wash of aggravation hits my chest. "Shit, Bee, let me hang up now so the lightning doesn't hit me through the phone."

I grumble loud enough so she hears it, letting her know she's working under my nerves today. She doesn't care.

"And enough with the grouchy shit." It's an order, but I know she's probably smiling when she says it. "I only see or hear from you these days when Brett is gone, so don't think you're going to pull the wool over my eyes."

"Like you see anything."

"Ha. More than you. Case in point, Monica the hoe."

I grimace. "True that."

A long breath rattles into the phone, and I know she's going to dive into the bombshell that shook our town. After Monica's husband left, hell has kind of broken loose. "Can you believe that one dude that came forward? The one who said she date-raped him?"

My stomach churns and a sour taste creeps into the back of my throat. "Poor guy. I can't imagine the courage it's taking him to step forward."

"No joke. I hope that lying slut pays. I mean, I knew she was bad, but holy fuck."

I rub my finger over my necklace, making small circles. "I hope she hasn't hurt too many other guys."

She sighs. "I guess time will tell. If they do, it only goes to show that women can be predators too."

"Absolutely. I hope Monica never gets away with this again." My stomach growls. I scooch off the bed, ready to dive into the stew I made earlier this morning.

"Are you still in shock about Brett not taking that property?" I hear some background noise but can't make out what she's doing. "I drove by the place the other day and I guess Paul sold it. Looks like it's being worked on."

My head bobs. "Saber bought it." Maybe Brett wasn't keen on the land, but Saber DuBois is. From what Brett said, it sounded like Saber said yes to the land before Paul even finished making the offer. I sigh, thinking about her second part of the question. "And to say I'm in shock is the understatement of the year."

"Why didn't he take it?"

Reaching the kitchen, I go for the cabinets where my bowls are and pull one down. "He had this whole philosophy about not taking it because his motives were wrong and that he thought it was fucking up his life."

"Really? Wow. Sounds like he had a serious matter of the heart check there."

"I guess." I nervously pick at my sweatpants. "Frankly, I don't understand it."I've been trying to sort out his reasoning ever since it happened, and I can't draw up any conclusions.

"What's not to understand?" Cora asks. "He's giving up something that he thinks is toxic. I think it's pretty awesome he's letting something go if he thought it was unhealthy. That shit's hard to do."

"It sounds great. I just..." My frame sags. "Why do it?"

"Seriously?" she quips back. "You're seriously asking why someone should be the better person, or grow in a certain area?"

"Possibly. I mean. Ugh!" I tip my head back in frustration and lack of understanding. "Look, this might sound wrong, but I think sometimes you need resentment to act as fuel." My shoulders rise then fall. "Without Dad making me mad, I never would have had the motivation to write."

"But where is that getting you now? At first, yeah, maybe it gave you a charge, but when it all built up and your dad died, what were you left with?" She pauses, clicking her tongue a few times. "You haven't been able to write at all lately. Have you ever considered trying to move on? Have you thought that possibly Brett is right? That past hurts do screw you over?"

My heart beats quicker. Her words build up anxiety. "But without my past motivations, what will I write? *How* will I write?"

"That's a silly question. You know how to write."

*Do I, though?* I bite down on my tongue, not wanting to voice that logic, and try to focus on anything besides the blood roaring in my ears.

"Gosh, Bee." Cora's voice cracks through my drowning head. "I think I can hear your brain processing over the phone."

I laugh some, but most of it stems from the overload of confusion swirling inside. "I'm just trying to understand." Also trying to figure out where the hell my new motivations will come from if I forget about my dad. I've used the understanding of my writing aggravating his bones as the crutch of incentive for my whole career.

"I'd say that's a good step. It shows you're at least open to change."

Setting down the lid to my Crock-Pot, some annoyance pops up. Cora's talking like she understands, but I don't see how she can. Her life has been pampered. She's never had to go against the stream and struggle. She comes from a solid home, has lots of money at her disposal, and was free to pursue whatever avenues she wanted with full support. Keeping my tone in check, I try to gently remind her that our paths have never been the same. "I think if your family life sucked like mine—"

"That's an excuse. Don't give me that bullshit." She says it kind enough to where it doesn't offend me. "A whole family doesn't mean I've had a perfect one." Her tone softens. "Lots of things have gone down in my life that I've needed to get past. We all get hurt, Bee."

*Crap.* She's right. I know she's right, but there's something more powerful battling my sense of logic. Fear. And fear is an expert at silencing the truth. I wish I knew where this unease and hesitation sprouted from. Maybe it's because I haven't known a different path for so many years. Or maybe it's because anything new in my life has always become disastrous and alarming. I'm not sure. The only thing I do know is that I am terrified. But I don't know how to tell Cora that, so instead I stand there with my heart twisting into the worst knot of my life.

"Last thing I'm gonna say is that the shit that happened with your dad was awful, but you gotta press forward. The built up animosity toward your dead daddy isn't doing you any favors." Her voice drops even lower, and a rawness creeps into her tone. "You've had a string of bad luck lately. I seriously think life will only get better once *you've* moved on."

*Damn.* I don't know why, but I feel small—like the room around me is massive, and I'm a fleck of dust locked inside its overwhelming walls. I hang my head, resting my butt against the ledge of the counters. My vision rests on the floor for far too long while I struggle to conjure a response, or an agreement. There's nothing.

"That's my two cents anyway." Her voice is strong again, shattering the muted aura from moments ago. "Take it or leave it. Either way we all have to make our own path."

Finally, I smirk a wryness springing up inside at her philosophical viewpoint. "Dang. Who's Confucius now?"

"Ha. Whatever. Bye, Bee. Try not to miss Brett too much."

"I'm not missing him." I ignore her laugh. "Bye."

The call ends and I stand there, staring at the deep aqua hues of my kitchen, getting lost in the color. Cora *and* Brett's words repeat in my head. Captions about letting go and moving on float across my mind's eyes, and while forgiveness seems so right, it also sounds intimidating.

I wouldn't be a writer if it wasn't for the grudge against Dad. Each bit of rejection he dealt sunk more fuel into my soul to write better, *be* better at my craft. Work harder at proving him wrong—so why am I standing here now feeling like the emptiest shell in the world?

Maybe Brett's right. But I can't know that for sure, and if I let go, all my writing abilities might die along with it.

Is that worth the risk?

# Chapter 26

"So Lizzie isn't moving after all."

"That's good, right?" Brett's soft laugh fills my ears while he nuzzles my neck while we stand in my kitchen.

"I guess so." That's the best answer I have considering she remains a steel trap, but she's no longer moving. It's the only thing she'd say. A sigh slips out as I push the thought away. Focusing on it will only lead to more frustration. Instead, I press my body into Brett's and smile. I am supposed to be making dinner, but that priority lasted for five minutes after I laid eyes on him.

My hands inch up his torso, breath snagging in sync with every delicious ab ripple. Pressing my tits hard against him, he chuckles again, It switches to a light groan when I plant a reverent kiss on his left pec, my lips leaving an outline on the white, starched article. His large hands clasp around my neck, both thumbs brushing along my jaw bone. "Someone missed me."

"No." I mumble the word out, smiling while I say it—but I totally did, and he has to know that. The idea to flick my tongue over his torso and make him my main course for tonight is sounding better with each heated second. My mind zeros in on having him alone as I start to untuck his shirt.

One of his hands clasps over mine, and he smirks. "You're making me hard."

"Good." I yank at the fabric.

"No. Bad." He stops me, but not before giving me a firm swat to the ass. "I expect to be greeted properly before you break my cock off with your insatiable ways."

"You?" My brow rises along with my voice. "I thought you would have dragged me off to bed right when you got here."

"Ah." He nods slowly. "Well, call me old fashioned." Backing away, he winks. "I need to be sweet talked before you can fuck me."

I snort through my nose. "Is that the word you're using for all the exchanges we had before Thanksgiving?"

"If that's what you want to call it." He smiles wide.

I pat him on the chest, brush a finger along his jaw line, and return to the stove. "If that's the case and we need to talk, then tell me about your trip."

"Pretty uneventful. I'm trying to negotiate a plot of land. I think Starbucks will grab it in the future. It's a prime location." He pauses and rubs at his nape. "Also, I was thinking about moving more items down here from my home in Colorado."

My pulse bumps harder at the words. "So soon?"

"Is it though?" He stretches out his neck, his brows pulling together. "I mean, if I'm staying..."

Every muscle bunches into thick knots. *Shit.* I'm not as ready as I thought, thinking I was past this—the fear and uncertainty, the fast comprehension that Brett's uprooting his life and planting himself in mine.

"Bianca?" As if he can sense it, he steps close, coasting his hands up my arms. "You're too quiet."

"Yeah," I sigh. "I'm just thinking."

"Still nervous?"

"Yes." The confession is a whisper. One that barely hits my ears.

"That's alright." He draws me in, wrapping me in his strong arms. "I've never done this either. We'll get through it together. Fucking terrified and all."

*Damn.* Every ounce of my blood goes warm, heating my skin as he pulls me tight against his chest. We stand there for several passing moments, a gentle calm swirling around the longer we stand. Eventually my pulse slows and the tightness in my lungs vanishes.

He shifts. Our hips and thighs press into one another, like we're glued together and not wanting to escape. Like a match, need flickers on, and I'm consumed for Brett to take me. In a silent request, my head cranes back and I stare at his lips.

"Yes, Bianca." He answers like he's heard me speak. His mouth captures mine, nipping my bottom lip along the way. I'm struggling not to let my head fall back as he finds my breast and grips onto it through the bulk of my sweatshirt. As he palms my tit with an expert touch, I can't keep my hands from traveling down the front of his jeans.

He's hard, ready to go, and I grab onto his length, rubbing at him in crazy desperation, despite the black jeans which block me. My head hums when he hisses at my touch. I smile, his hands coasting down to my legs, drawing us together so we're flush. Reaching up to my tiptoes, I find an open spot on his neck and suck. Smooth skin tasting of soap and cologne brushes my tongue—my pulse spiking from the way he moans.

"Fuck." He's breathless, his heavy pants breaking the silence of the kitchen. "I want you to do that everywhere."

"Mmm," A groan spills out against his heated skin, the lingering of his sweet aftertaste causing my center to grow heavy. I move to a new part of his neck, ready to obey.

"But first..." His voice is tender. Encouraging me to break the kiss, he strokes his thumb along my cheek. "I have something for you, before we get carried away."

Slight irritation licks at me, but I don't let it show. He's trying to be sweet, and while I won't admit it, I'm starting to like this surprising side of him.

"Be right back." He whispers a kiss across my lips and darts off for a moment. When he returns, a long rectangular box wrapped in gold-foiled wrapping paper is tucked under his arm.

"A gift?" I touch the chain around my neck. "For what?"

"Because I wanted to." He places it down on the counter in front of me. What looks like apprehension swirls in his tight eyes as he first glances at the box then me. "I hope you like it."

A smile quirks up my mouth. "I'm sure I'll love it." Tracing my fingers along the paper, I take a moment to admire the oversized red and gold bow on top. I wrap my fingers along one of the velvet tails of fabric and then drag my fingers along the bumps of the gold foil design.

"Open it, Bianca." It's calm, but still spurs me into action.

I pluck off the bow, tucking it away to the side, and finding a folded edge, undo the invisible tape. When that's done, I slide the box out to reveal a white shirt box. Shaking the top off, I hook my fingers under the borders and jiggle till the lid slides off, then I peel back the paper.

"Oh my—" My heart flatlines, blood no longer pumping in my veins. Prickly heat hits the back of my eyes and everything blurs for a millisecond. I'd recognize the floppy bow and cream color anywhere.

It's Mom's blouse. Stain free, looking better than ever. My hands tremble as I reach out to touch it and words choke up in my throat. "It's—it's Mom—"

"It's not." His hand glides down my back. "I had it made." One of his large fingers skims over the fine fabric. "I felt so fucking bad, you have no idea. I went to a designer I know and showed her a picture."

A beautiful hole punches right through my sternum and I bow over as the cavity fills with an abundant warmth that I haven't felt since childhood. Tears drain out my eyes, and I throw my arms around Brett's torso. "Oh my God." I barely hear my own words. "Thank you so much."

He strokes the top of my hair. "It's not hers, but I hope when you wear it, you'll still be able to remember her." The large swallow he takes reverberates in my ears.

Closing my eyes tight, I listen to the sound of his heartbeat, which plunks faster by the second. A smile spans my lips and I toss my head back, looking up at him. "I'll think of both of you when I wear it." I shudder under his touch as he cups my face.

"You sweet, sweet thing." Desperation fractures the fire crackling in his dark eyes, and then his lips find mine.

He works me slow, his kisses echoing off the walls as he pauses between each one to let us breathe. My arms fall limp at my side as he gathers me in his hold, fitting me to his body in a way only he can. He finds the spot where we curve and meld against each other, and when he ducks his head to kiss my neck, I collapse against his build.

My pulse follows his kisses, jumping to the spots where his mouth connects with my flesh. Each area he grazes, he plants one ghosting brush before going back in for a tender suckle between his lips. Fire swirls up my body with each new pleasure point he finds. When he flicks my ear lobe, I groan.

"Oh, Brett." Fever is heavy in my voice, and his response to it spurs my need for more.

"That's it. Say it." He sweeps his thumb along my jaw, his mouth pressing to my heated skin. "Say my name like that again...desperate." His large thumb smooths over the front of my neck. "Say it like I'm the only name that should ever be on your tongue, like I'm the only man you've ever tasted."

I obey—his name spilling off my lips like the sweetest and most intoxicating wine known to this world. It seems to spur him.

He hoists me off my feet and secures my legs around him. "Damn, Bianca." He threads his fingers through the back of my hair while carrying me out of the kitchen. "Look at what you do to me. Two minutes into kissing you, and I'm falling apart."

"Sorry, not sorry," I say, peppering kisses along the one side of his face.

"Didn't ask for an apology." I nip at his ear, feeling his cock thicken, digging into my ass cheek while he continues to walk. I can't stop myself from grinding onto it and gasp. "Fuck. You're going to make me jerk off in my jeans."

"Would that be so bad?" I ask it as he enters my room and lays me on the bed.

"No." He sweeps his fingers between the valley of my breasts, smiling, applying an expert amount of pressure where I strain for my breaths. "But I'd rather go off in you." There's a glint in his eyes followed by one yank at my pants. The elastic waistband of my sweats stretches around my hips. I arch my pelvis up to give him easier access.

Shivers tendril up and down my limbs when he sweeps over my opening. He sighs at my dampness. "So beautifully fucking wet for me, little one."

"Brett." I shimmy my lower half off the bed. "I need you."

He breathes in deep. So much that the buttons of his dress shirt look like they want to fly off and scatter. He drops his pants. Planting one hand on the other side of my head, he leans forward, rubbing his cock against my drenched opening. I whimper in frustration and he chuckles.

Ducking for my ear, there's a darkness to his tone. His teeth nip at my ear, and I yelp, but I am still aware of his words, ones that work down into my soul. "And I need you." It sounds different from the way I say it—makes my heart unsteady in its pace and skin flicker alive with goosebumps. I want to bury the strange sensation.

Brett doesn't let me. "Look here, kitten."

He grabs my face in one hand, fingers and thumb grabbing at my cheeks. With the right amount of demanding pressure, he turns my head, forcing me to lock eyes with him—reminding me that while he's sweet, he's still Brett. Commanding. Powerful. My eyes are already wide, staring deep into his, but I gasp as he slams into me, tip to root in one fell swoop.

"God!" I clutch at the bedding to my left and right, still pinned—a slave to his gaze.

He plants a gruff kiss on my mouth, and I groan when he plants himself deeper—his balls framing the bottom of my ass. I hear my own heart pumping hard for blood as he licks his mouth. "Feel that?"

He completes me so well, I can't fucking move. Nodding isn't even possible as he expands in my walls. I'm too pleased to move, but the way he smiles tells me he sees it in my eyes.

"That's you, Bianca." His grip around my face tightens and I feel his fingertips grind into the frame of my cheekbones. "This is what you do to me." He pauses to moan while keeping still inside me. "You strip me naked." A hard huff expels out his nose. "Usually there's always a barrier, ensuring that the only thing I ever give away is my cock. But you take it all, baby." Bright amber smolders in his eyes while he tilts inside of me. When I mewl and buck my legs, he growls. "Fuck, yes.

You take it all, and you make me like it."

Those words seem to unravel him, and I keep my legs spread wide to watch him fray above me. His sweat droplets, which patter on my naked body, are scraps of his soul, and I absorb everything I can because I love seeing this side to him.

The world sees badass Brett Walker—cursing, drinking, poker-playing, tattooed man that keeps the world at a distance. But me? I get to see him decimated, unhinged with his body glistening and my name hissing off his lips. I witness his rawness as he begs me to squeeze him tighter—just the way he likes. And when he finally falls apart and pumps me full of him, I bite down on my lower lip as he quakes from the aftereffects of experiencing my body.

He gets high off of me. Satisfied from me, and I can't think of anything more gratifying.

Eventually, he falls asleep in my arms as I stroke his hair. A smile rounds the apples of my cheeks as I twist a longer strand around my finger. I kiss his cheek, dreading the thought of tomorrow coming and pulling us out of bed.

*I'd be happy staying here forever.*

With *him* and only him for eternity.

The thought is burrowing deep into my mind while I nestle against his spent body. My eyes droop...*God, I lo—*

My eyes fly open. *Shit.* A tightness captures my chest, pressing out all the oxygen I have. All of a sudden I can't breathe, and my body is too stiff against Brett. *No. No.* The thought I almost had...it couldn't be.

But when I stare up at his peaceful face, a crack of lightning rips across my sternum, and God when we draw a breath at the same time, I think of myself tethered to his soul. All too suddenly I'm aware of a need so intense it makes me tremble. It's like I'll die if he doesn't move the rest of his things here and attach his life to mine. And all too easily,

I identify the new feeling coursing through me.

I'm in love.

These things he infuses in me. The hope and purpose, leaving me to think my heart will shrivel up tomorrow if he doesn't wake with me. It's love.

*Fuck.* That's the most dangerous thing in life. Because while I didn't want him to last before, if life has taught me one thing, it's that the good things *don't* last. Wanting him was one thing, loving him is another, and I know life will find a way to mess this up. It always does.

A tear streams down my face while thinking of all the ways this will go wrong.

*It won't last. He'll leave.* I can see it now. Brett will move his things here, but once I'm dependent, he'll get tired of me, and Brett Walker will vanish. I don't think I can survive the best thing that's ever happened being ripped away from me. The only solution I see is to let him go first.

But can I do it?

My heart beats like mad, the manic pattern hurting my chest with each of its pulses.A battle occurs for the next several hours while I weigh the horrid options. Breaking up with him now will yank tender portions of my heart right off—making me bleed my soul out for who knows how long.

But staying?

When he rips himself from me, the failure of us will spear right through my soul, and I can't survive that. Pulling away from Brett first is the only option I have if I want to survive. And even though it's going to hurt like a son of a bitch, it's exactly what I'm going to do.

I don't have a choice.

Sleep doesn't come tonight. Instead I cry, thankful he's not awake to watch me fall apart as I choose the best option for me, because I'm sick of life deciding for how long things last.

Tonight, I'm going to end something first and beat life to the punch.

Unfortunately, I'm starting with Brett.

# Chapter 27

It's luck that Brett disappeared to Colorado again two days later. He left to go get more items to bring here. Little does he know that I'm throwing his few items into a duffel bag to finish us.

My whole body jerks, nerves raw and shot when my phone vibrates, *again*. It's Brett, of course. I deny the call and send it to voicemail along with his millions of others. When he texts me moments later, I don't read it. I clear it and go back to my job—kicking Brett out of my life.

Slamming his last pair of jeans into the bag, a sob finally bubbles up and betrays the emotions I'm fighting to contain.

A fresh assault of tears sting the back of my eyes as I try to shake them away. The black straps of the duffle bag chafe against my smooth palms thanks to the death-grip hold. Sealing my eyes closed, I force deep breaths. "It won't last." I mutter the words out. *No.* Not *words*. Promises. Bitter truths that are a bitch to swallow, but necessary.

The simple fact is, nothing lasts.

Success? It's not made for longevity, and because of that, it dooms Brett and me.

Safety? When created from others, it's as temporary as the wind. Your safeguard could wake up mad and rip everything from you.

Love? Sure as fuck not lasting. Dad and Mom proved that, and I'll be damned if I end up like Mom—reduced and gray because I depended on one person for too long.

That's not me. Ripping Brett off now like the painful band-aid he is, is better than being gutted later.

But fuck, it's hard. Zipping the bag closed, an ache cuts across my chest, flaying it open. I grip at my ribs, bow over, and shake, refusing to let out the wail that's built up in my lungs from the time I first started packing.

*It won't last.*

I use the words to ground me.

*We won't last.*

Strength surges down my limbs, I hoist the bag over my shoulder.

*He's going to leave me. Hurt me.*

My legs work on their own, transporting me to the front door.

*He never should have come.*

I drop it. It lands to the floor with a thud. A ten-ton weight flying off my chest the longer I stare at the light blue item. Inside is Brett, and when he comes back we're through and I'll be safe once again.

Months after Lance broke up with me, I promised I'd never pass through that heartbreak ever again. I'd never allow my heart to be stripped and battered, or cry endlessly into my pillow. That's what I'm doing now. Protecting myself for whenever Brett decides he's done with me.

Tapping my toe against the bag, I nod and sigh. "Goodbye Brett."

Returning to my room, I turn off my phone and go to bed. Brett will be home in a few days. Hopefully, it's the last time I'll see him. Because falling in love with him is the most unsafe thing I've ever done. Now he just needs to get back so I can tell him we're through. Even though in my heart, I know I'll never be able to fully let go. This is simply so my heart doesn't die when he rips himself from me—because it's not a question of if we'll fail, but when.

# Chapter 28

"**B**ianca! Open the fucking door, *now*."

My front door rattles from the heavy hand of Brett—it still can't match the drumming in my chest, neck, and fingertips. My heart slams harder than his knocks ever will. But it won't stop me from opening the door and getting this over with.

I adjust a curly strand of hair while shuffling toward the entrance and duck to look into my entryway mirror one last time to ensure my makeup is on point. Looking less than perfect for this isn't an option. I've decked myself out in low heels, a sweater, and a tight pair of jeans. Sadness and anxiety pump hard in my blood, and I know I'm going to hate every second of this. Especially as a tear threatens to seep out while I reach for the door handle.

One deep breath of composure, and I fling it open, mid-pound from Brett.

I skitter back while he loses his footing and stumbles forward a step. My back snaps, rigid, when he catches himself and looks at me—heat and fury lashing in his gaze. He holds it, causing my heart rate to quicken, but I don't let it play in my voice.

"Hi." My greeting is dead on the outside, withered and broken on the inside.

"Hi?" Deep red flashes across his face, and his jaw grits. "What the fuck, Bianca? Do you know how worried I've been about you?"

Guilt twists my stomach into a knot. I didn't think about him being concerned for me, and I should have been more considerate. *No. I can't.* I want to apologize, but this will make me crumble. I shove it away and say nothing, forcing my eyes to narrow.

"Now..." He tosses his suitcase inside, hurling it so hard from his grasp it hits the side of the couch before toppling over. I'm sure he doesn't miss the jump that leaves me when he does it, or the way I swallow hard as he takes an authoritative step towards me. "Do you want to tell me what the fuck is going on and why you haven't answered my fucking calls for *three* days?"

The temptation to create distance is strong, yet I glue my feet in place and jut my chin out. "Brett." Maybe I'm not moving, but I have to pause.

"I'm listening." He pockets his hands, his features going dark, matching the cloud of anger I can see around him. It aligns with his voice. It's pressurized, grungy.

Deciding less is best, I let the sight of his departure speak for itself. I cast my eyes to the floor, to the duffel bag and the one dress shirt that's on a hanger, neatly resting on top. I found it in my closest last night and decided not to put it in, so he'd get the message up front.

A beat passes and then with his face screwing up in what looks like confusion, he looks to the spot where I'm fixated on. He gives it a quick head jerk. Halfway to turning his head back to me, he snaps to look again. He freezes.

The silence descending lets me hear how hard my heart jumps against my ribs. I think it wants to bust through my body and land on the floor. I hold my breath to keep from making any noise.

His eyes widen the longer he stares at it, and soon his mouth parts. "No." His voice cracks with the delivery. Shit, it's sad. My heart splinters at the sound.

I bury the sensation away, but it still pulls apart more as his chest shakes for a breath and his shoulders drop.

He directs his eyes onto me, commanding me to him in the way only he can. "You're breaking up with me?" Sickness tugs at his features, and he slouches. The trembles racking his body make it look like he wants to keel over, grab his knees, and hyperventilate, but his voice keeps control and washes over me, making me aware of how angry he is.

I clutch at my necklace and finally take a much-needed step back. "I am." The admittance is weak. My body hating the distance I create. How I'm not sobbing is beyond me. Possibly it's because I know better. Something will go wrong between us. It always does for me. Nothing lasts for me.

"Why? We're past this. We're..."

"I lied!"

"You didn't." His voice pops and he no longer looks shattered. He stands tall, brows furrowing, creasing the skin between his eyes, while a vein bulges out at his temple. "I *see* you, Bianca, and I know you didn't lie."

My face hardens over. "You didn't *see* shit. What you did was finger a confession out of me." *Damn.* The lie is so bitter, and each fiber in me aches, but I can't change it. This is the only way.

"Is that what you're sticking to? Holy shit." He eyes me up and down, disgust swirling in his eyes. "You're a fucking coward."

"I'm not." I ignore the flipping of my stomach and force an icy tone. "You moving here was a mistake. You need to leave. You were right the first time..." My fists clench while I take a huge breath. Pain radiates down my limbs and I want to bow over in agony. "I don't want you in my life." My heart fractures open with the words, but Brett doesn't see that.

His eyes round. "Bianca..." His voice is soft.

*Shit.* My lie is evaporating. He needs to leave. Now. "Brett—"

"I'm in love with you!"

His broken declaration is loud, booming off the walls of my house until it ricochets back and plants into my heart. *Fuck.* That's the worst thing he could have said. Same for the dampness glistening at the corners of his eyes. My knees lock and I stand like I've been electrocuted—in some way I think I have. My limbs are numb and while I hear the loud swallow I take, I can't feel it.

The two sensations I'm aware of are my pulse, radiating hard through my body, buzzing and reverberating out my fingers and through my toes, and my neck. I think I'm being choked. "You..." *Shit.* The word gurgles out, I start over. "You don't mean that."

"The fuck if I don't. What do you think I've been trying to say this past month, Bianca? Me moving here? Me saying how complete we are? What do you think has been going through my mind?"

"Don't," I croak.

"I've been thinking about our future together. How crazy fucking in love I am with you, and how I'd do anything for you." His fists unclench some. "Anything," he repeats in a softer tone.

My stomach won't stop somersaulting. God, I hate hearing this from him, because all it's doing is making ripping him away more painful...heart wrenching. *I'd give anything to kiss him.* To hug the life out of him and confess I feel the same. I wall all of it off by inwardly repeating Dad's words. *It won't last.* Somehow it steadies me. "Seems convenient to tell me now." I send off my accusation like ice pellets, hoping it hits him and drives him away. "If you've been in love with me all this time, why didn't you say something?"

He rakes a hand through his hair. "Because I'm shit at it, that's why. I've never been good at confessing my feelings. I can show them all day, but talking about them is hard."

"Well, I think you're lying." I hiss the words out even though it's forced and try to turn on my heel.

"No!" He grips his hand around my arm and tugs me back. "You don't get to go anywhere."

He feels so good holding me, even when he's mad, but I can't give in. I clench my teeth and try to sound mad. "You don't get to control me." When I try to yank away and he doesn't allow it, I want to turn into his arms and cry.

"Control you?" He laughs a bitter laugh. "Oh, trust me, I know. You're superb at showing me *who's* in control." His lips form a sneer. "It's always about what you like, isn't it? And forget about facing the things you can't let go of."

My head jerks back, his words striking a bitter chord in my heart. "What the hell does that mean? Of course I can let go."

"But you can't," he growls. Darkness seeps through his pupils the longer he stares at me, and I retract my shoulders inward. "Your mom's blouse, the necklace you wear, the grudge you hold against your dad, it all tells me that you can't let go." He ducks his head, bringing our mouths mere inches from each other. "That's gangrene to you, Bianca, and now it's coming between us."

"You're wrong." Straightening my spine, I infuse strength into my voice. "This was a mistake. We're just not meant to last."

"We're not lasting because you're not giving us a chance." He

drops my hand and paces over to the door, his hands shaking. "Fuck!"
He punches the door. The thud his fist causes is hard enough to make my
stomach spiral. He splays out his hands against the entry, then claws his
nails down the white paint. Spinning around, there's something wild in
his eyes. It breaks me from the spot on the floor, allowing me to stumble
back a step.

Kicking him out has never been harder. All I want is to soothe
away his anger and confess all the lies I'm telling, but that's a mistake.
With my shoulders tangled like a cord, more of my resolve cracks. I
know that if he doesn't leave soon, I won't let him leave at all. "You
should leave."

"Why? Because you're a fucking coward who won't talk things
out?"

"Don't call me *that*." I bite my cheek so hard a copper flavor floods
my tastebuds. "And you're lying because I do talk things out."

"Ha!" He grips the door, and it makes him look like he's scrambling
for control. "Tell me one time when you've talked out your problems.
Because you haven't." Flicking his hand, he gestures at my body. "All
you fucking do is put up walls, run away, and shut me out."

"No—no..." The words are bitter on my tongue, and they fight me
on the way up. "That's not true."

"Then you're blind to who you really are, because if you think
clamming up and shutting out your problems is the sign of being a
strong-ass woman, then your way of thinking is more twisted up than
I thought. I mean, look at you..." He scoffs. "All this is, is you running
away."

"I'm not running away." I stand up straighter, the bristling of my
tattered emotions making it happen on its own. "You.." The words cut
off. The hottest lash of blinding pain descends. It's different from all the
rest—ten times worse than normal, but doesn't sink me to my knees like

I'd expect. Somehow I bite back the pain this time. Brett always sees me at my weakest and when I'm most vulnerable, and I won't let that happen tonight. I'm sick of it. This inconvenience won't be my undoing.

"You what?" His voice is a deep grumble. "Finish what you were going to say, Bianca. Have the courage to at least talk to me like a human."

*Fuck.* I'm not sure if I can. I try to shake my head, to jostle the pain away, but my muscles are stiff, tingling from the base of my neck to the tops of my shoulder blades. And the longer I stare at Brett the more it feels like we've done this before, although I know we haven't.

With the tingle creeping up to the left side of my face, I try to speak. "Leaving..." Something tangles up. The room floats. I push on. "Leaving that you have the ability..." *Shit.* What am I saying?

Brett's brows come together. "What?"

It will come out better this time, even though now I've lost my ability to swallow. "My home with not having you to leave."

His breath sucks in, eyes tightening, tone going soft. "What the fuck are you trying to say?"

Nothing comes out. My throat binds up, and every tendon and fiber inside wraps around me, like I'm receiving the hardest, most painful hug in the world, and I might be falling. Everything tilts to one side.

"Bianca?" Brett sounds distant. "Bianca?" He blurs in front of me and his voice echoes. "Bianca."

Everything fades away.

# Chapter 29

I'm in an area I've never seen before. The walls are white. Light bounces off the border of the stark and bare area, making me squint. Looking down, there is no floor, but I don't fall. Taking a few steps, a *click-clack* echoes all around me, but I'm barefoot. My head cocks in confusion. "Where am I?"

"Bianca."

My head jerks up to the voice of my dad. Disbelief strikes at my heart when my eyes see the figure—blonde hair like mine, but shorter, and thin features so slim she could be a doll—it's Mom, even though I heard Dad's voice. She's a few feet away. My hand stretches out and strains for her, to feel her comforting touch once more. "Mom?"

"No." The figure turns away, her white garment glittering in light, and a hallway opens before her.

"Please." My voice cries out. "Don't leave." I chase after her, an odd feeling as I'm weightless yet heavy. Walking is fine, but running is a different issue.

She doesn't wait for me, and it doesn't appear she struggles to move like I do. Reaching the end of the hallway seems easy for her. Gifting me one more view past her shoulder, a sad smile passes across her mouth. She vanishes.

"Mom! No!" An ache cracks my heart in two. Explosive energy barrels me down the hall. However, when I reach the end, there is no teleportation.

Instead, the nonexistent bottom vortexes beneath me, and something crumbles under my bare toes. I jump back and scream just as a chasm opens up, and my heart leaps up into my throat.

Blackness, lightning, and fire cloud my vision and screams assault my ears. I drown out the unholy shrieks, placing my hands over my ears, tears streaming down my face as I wonder if Mom is down there. It doesn't look like a place she deserves to be in. I scream into its depth, but it's not my voice. Instead, other voices break out—ones that sound like me, but are not me.

"Let go," says one voice.

"I love you, Bianca," says another, in a tone closer to my Mom's.

"Revenge is a sign of pain," shouts one more.

"Say you don't want me in your life." This voice sounds like Brett.

I clutch at my necklace, but it's not there. My rigid fingers search for the item for a moment before finally deciding to rest around my neck. A white figure shoots out from the chaos below and hovers across the valley, and a tremble seizes me.

I hate the way it floats closer, even though it appears not to be moving. The more it draws near, the more I move back, until I've tripped and crash landed on my hip. I bump my head on the invisible barrier along the way, and hot searing pain shoots through my skull, letting me know pain is real here.

"Shit." Rubbing at my eyes, I'm hoping to stamp down the ache that rolls behind each socket. It seems to dissipate. Dropping my hands, I open my eyes and scream.

The figure is over me and it's old. Old enough to make me wonder how it exists. With an ancient grace, it floats down, sweeping long gray hair away from its face, and it looks me in the eyes.

Paralysis winds through the fibers of my body.

The figure is me.

Old. Weathered. Grayed out. Permanent tear stains streaking down my leathered face. A bony hand levitates up and reaches out.

I try to withdraw, but can't move fast enough. Her bony finger connects to my shoulder, and a reel spans out before my eyes. There are no words, yet I want to sob as I watch my figure transform from the body I have now to the one I see in front of me.

Helplessly, I watch as my life dwindles away until I am old and colorless. I see myself crying on my bed, alone and cold. In one spot, I push away a tall man standing with open arms who wants to embrace me. He mouths for me to "let go." One reel shows me screaming to an open sky. In one section, all my books lie in a pile, burning to ash as I weep in front of them. Eventually, I see myself on my deathbed, alone, gray, and with no one to care for me.

When the hand pulls away, the movie screeches to a halt. Looking up, I clutch at my neck and although my lip quivers, I manage to form words. "Wh-what was that?"

A weak, broken-hearted smile passes the figure's lips, and she nods. "Your path."

She plunges into the pit below—lightning crashes, shaking the room as she vanishes.

More of the barrier underneath me crumbles away, and I think I'm going to fall into the darkness underneath.

Then the room is black.

Gone.

Like it never even existed.

# Chapter 30

**M**y eyes peel open. I regret it. The room blinds me and I squint, trying to filter the natural sunlight which overtakes the room. *Where the hell am I?* The brightness is a trivial thing as I observe the unusual ceiling above me. I've never seen it before. Large squares hang overhead. They make their shapes by metal dividers running the entire length of the room. It's not like an office. There's a starkness to it all.

My ears perk up at a beeping sound. Then I notice the tubing attached to my arms and the awareness of my surroundings hits me like a freight train. I'm in the hospital. *Shit.* What happened to me?

Twisting my shoulders, I groan.

"Bianca?" I'd know the deep voice in a screaming sea of people. It's Brett. He's at my side, casting a shadow over me before I blink, and maybe my perception is still fuzzy from whatever the hell this is, but I swear dampness forms at the edges of his eyes.

My heart sings at the sight of him, slowing down in its previous rising tempo. Having him here when I'm clueless is like a weighted blanket to my jumbled nerves. He's here, and because of that, everything is going to be alright.

His hand wraps around mine, but the connection is feather light and tender. When he grazes his thumb over my hand, it's so soft I wonder if he thinks me constructed of porcelain. He draws in a breath, but it looks half as deep as it should be, and a deep crease forms between his brows. "Do you know who I am?"

The question and the tight way he says it makes my heart want to fall out, landing at his feet. I force a stronger connection between our hands by squeezing. "Of course I know who you are, Brett."

His eyes widen, his brows hitting his hairline, but the way his brows crumple together makes it look more like overwhelmed shock. Air sucks deep into his lungs, then he expels it all. "Oh thank God." He breathes out the words and places his hand on my cheek. "You can talk." Sniffling, dark clouds dispel from his eyes. They halo with a gentle glow. One I haven't seen before. "The doctors weren't sure you'd be able to when you woke up."

*Not talk.* Anxiety claws at my neck, making each thread of muscle in it tighten. I need to find out what happened. "Brett—" My words vanish as he extends his arm out toward my legs.

The sound of the sheets rumple and he directs every ounce of attention in that direction. "Can you move your legs, can you feel them?"

Wiggling my toes, there's numbness in my calves and shins. *Shit.* Will I be able to walk? The uncertainty has me clenching my fists. My skin pinches thanks to the IV's taped to the tops of my hands. "Brett." His name is hoarse off my lips, the slow panic creeping up toward my neck, causing my voice to rasp.

Looking down, I can now see he's squeezing up and down my

legs, but I can't feel it all that well. Just some pressure. I want to cry. He doesn't notice. "The doctor said you might need therapy, but some feeling is better—"

"Brett." His name crackles out of me and a tear of alarm slides down my face. But at least he's finally looking at me again. With my heart slamming against my ribs, I try to keep my question steady sounding. "What happened to me?"

He returns to my side, bundling my hand in his while his eyes turn downward. "You had a brain bleed." The answer is so soft I barely hear it, but from the gut punch of shock it brings to my senses, it feels like he shouted the words.

For a moment, I can't move. Can't think. When I replay what he said, I stammer over the words. "A-a brain bleed?"

"Yes." Sinking down into the chair, he frowns. "You almost died, Bianca. And you would have if I hadn't been there." His grip around my hand tightens, but only by a touch. "They had to perform emergency surgery to drain all the pressure from your head. When they saw your condition, it shocked everyone that you were still alive, much less talking and walking until the point of your seizures."

I blink as more shock tidal waves through me, causing a raw buzz in my nerve endings. "Seizures?"

"That's what happened, baby. You had it in the middle of..." His shoulder sags and he tears his gaze away.

My head tilts. "In the middle of what, Brett?"

He gives me a sharp sideways glance. "You don't remember?"

*Damn.* He makes it sound important. Closing my eyes, I replay anything that sticks out. When I'm able to see myself throwing his clothes in a bag, I gulp and my limbs tense. "I was..."

Guilt swallows up the words I want to say. I can't finish them when I see how wrong I've been.

Brett Walker. The man I was kicking out of my life—the one I feared not lasting, is here with me and he's talked to the doctors, being privy to all the ins and outs of what I've been through. He's been here the entire time. *Fuck.* I cringe at how foolish I've been.

*Your path.* My choices. All terrible ones that have been pushing me to my own destruction.

My hand covers my eyes, masking the shame that's pulverizing my insides.

"Did it come to you?" He strokes his hand over mine while asking it.

The gentle coaxing makes me feel worse, and my breath goes shaky. "Yes. Brett, I—"

"Bianca." The broken way he says my name forces my hand to fall away, and my heart threatens to crack in two when a tear wells up in his eyes. "Baby, please," he's pleading with me. "Don't make me leave. Don't do this to me. *Us.*"

I frown, my eyes stinging from the river of tears resting behind them. I've been the most selfish, shallow person on the planet with him these past several months—afraid, and unwilling to allow him to prove himself to me, all because I've been too scared to even try. *Crap.* Why he wants to stay with me, I have no idea, but I'm glad he has to show me what a fool I've become and opened my eyes to how I've allowed my past to control me.A past that's dead.

"Brett..." My hand trembles in his. Actually, my entire body does. From head to toe, I vibrate with remorse. "I don't deserve you."

"Bullshit." The first genuine smile tugs at his mouth. "Yes, you do." Standing up to lean over the bed, he captures my chin with his thumb and forefinger. "Do you know how long I've waited to find someone like you? To come across a woman who lines up with all my rough edges?"

I shake my head, swallowing back a sob.

"That's you, Bianca." He ghosts his thumb across my mouth. "From the moment we locked eyes in that basement and you didn't turn away, I knew it was you. Please." The previous smile is stolen away as his lips set in a hard line. "Don't take this away from us. Don't choose fear." His voice cracks. "Not when I'm only now discovering there's more to life than the shallow things I've known."

"Brett." My fingers grip tight into his arm as words pour out of me, ones I never thought I'd utter. "You're right. I'm a coward. I'm scared. I'm afraid, and I'm sorry I hurt you." An anvil of desperation presses down on my chest, and I'd do anything to shove it off. "I'm sorry—"

"You've been through a lot." He tilts his head. "Bianca, maybe I was too harsh—"

"No. You're right. About it all." I shake my head. "I'm not sure if it was a dream or what, but I saw something."

His brows lift as if he's saying it's the understatement of the year. "Judging from how much you tossed in your bed, I think you had a lot of dreams."

My brain spins while I try to determine if what I had was one dream or several. Unable to discern, I finally sigh, and stroke my hand up and down his corded forearm. "Well, whatever happened, I think a message came through that I need to deal with my past."

Each admittance of how weak I've let myself become, of how I've allowed the wrong things to feast off everything I am, makes my throat tighten till I think my windpipe will collapse. Soon, I'm nearly sputtering on my confession, but I don't let myself stop. "I need help, Brett." My grasp goes harder, and tug on him, urging him close, thinking he'll vanish when I say the next word. "I *need* to let go. Please, please stay with me."

I can't track Brett's movements. All I know is that I'm tasting fresh mint and a pair of warm soft lips meld to mine in a flash. He barely applies pressure, but I feel him deeper than ever before—working into the nooks of my soul that I'd forgotten about long ago, and for the first time in years, my pulse jumpstarts to life with a renewed purpose. When he tries to stand, ending our kiss, my fingers wring through his hair, and I lift my head off the pillow. I'm sinking and drowning in the depth of how much I adore this man when he runs his hand over my head. It doesn't run through my hair. The heat of Brett's open palm connects with my head and I realize I'm bald.

I shriek, ending our moment, slapping my hand over my mouth. Brett's vision widens while pulling back. Patting at my head, I can feel that there's nothing and an embarrassed heat hits my cheeks. "I'm bald?" My loud question echoes off the walls.

A soft smile lifts his mouth. "You are." He says it calm and easy, even lifting my hand to his lips to plant a kiss on my knuckles. "They had to shave it for the surgery."

Groaning, I cover my face. "God." My stomach flips. "I'm sure I look awful."

"Oh, I don't know." The lightness in his tone has me daring to look at him again, and I'm not disappointed. The sinful smirk pulling up his mouth is a sight for sore eyes. "I've never gone out with a girl who shaves her head." He winks and my heart flutters. "Pretty fucking hot if you ask me."

A long hard giggle shakes out of me, the lightest, sweetest one I've ever had in my life. It unlocks a warmness in me, one that has my heart floating high and my tongue going loose. Looking deep into Brett's eyes, I get lost in a gaze that's mostly brown today and smile. "God, Brett, I love you." *Shit. I didn't just say that.* But I know I did, and even though I'm a little scared at how easily it rolled off my lips, I don't regret the words. Not one bit.

"Fuck." His eyes glaze over, becoming wet and glossy while holding my hand against his racing heart. "It's good to hear you say that. I love you too."

We stare at each other for a beat until he breaks up the moment by pulling up to his feet.

"Move over if you can," he orders, and I'm already sliding against the bed railing. "I want to hold you. I've missed it so much."

With my shoulders pressing into the gray plastic siding, my brows furrow. "How long have I been out?"

"Only a few days." He hitches one leg over and sits his butt down on the sheets. "But it's been enough to drive me insane. Now, let me hold you and fall asleep with me."

Nestling up to him as he lies next to me, I relish in his natural body heat and scent. Obeying his command has never felt easier as my eyes droop closed. A few moments of being awake and I'm already spent, fatigue pulling at my eyes.

The room swirls around me in a way that makes me feel like I'm in the safest cocoon of comfort while Brett drapes his arm over me, and with everything slipping away to a sweet and peaceful black and my hearing tunneling to the sounds of Brett's inhales and exhales, I'm aware of his lips whispering a gentle kiss to my forehead. The last words I hear paint a smile across my face as I go back to sleep.

"We're going to last, Bianca. We're going to last until we leave this world together, exactly like this."

And I know he's right. I slip into a deep sleep. It's easy to say that it's the best one I've had in years.

*3 Months Later*

"Holy fuck, Bianca, squeeze me hard like that again." Brett's towering over me, my legs dangling off the side of the bed while I lay on my back, enjoying the lovemaking that's been denied us since I've gotten out of the hospital. I giggle. He's just ordered me to do his favorite thing, and you'd think from his tone that we're having the hardest session of our lives, but we've hardly broken a sweat.

He's been so gentle with me that a few times I've frowned. I'm more than ready for slow, long nights where we make love to our heart's content, but this is a little *too* soft. I bust out a friendly reminder for the second time since we started.

"Brett, you can pump a little faster."

His eyes flood open and I see the frustration swirling in them. "Hell no, I can't. We're lucky to be doing this at all." He sweeps his hand down the valley of my breasts. "You're not fully recovered yet, Bianca. We can't push it."

Biting down on my bottom lip, I grin. "Oh, but you can. Your pushes feel real good."

His head tilts back, and he laughs. "Glad I have a fan." Winking, he pulls out of me, ignoring my grumbling protest. "Shut it, we have to go to physical therapy."

"But you didn't even get off."

"Tonight I will." He pokes his tongue out, resting it in the corner of his mouth while a coyness flicks in his gaze. "You can watch me. Seeing you squirm would be nice."

I chunk a pillow at him. "You're awful."

"You like it." He pulls up his briefs, collecting himself in a snap. "Ready?"

Extending his hand to me, I don't take it. Rather, I sink my frame into the bed. "I don't want to go."

"Too bad, kitten." He captures my wrists in his sure hand, gluing our connection as he grips me finger by finger. "You fell yesterday, remember? You need the therapy."

"It's frustrating." My spine obeys his tug off the bed.

"Simply because you're having to relearn something. Don't worry." He runs his fingers through my reappearing hair. My locks are short, but at least I have something. "Pretty soon you'll be walking like normal. The therapist said a full recovery was certain."

A sigh slips out of me and I want to protest more, but as he helps me off the bed, I'm realizing once again, he's right. Only a couple steps in, and if Brett wasn't here, I think I'd fall. The sensation is weird, like my legs want to go on autopilot but have forgotten the sequence that allows me to move forward. *Crap.* I bear more weight on Brett, using him as the anchor I need when my feet threaten to trip up once more.

Reaching the sink, he makes sure I'm standing before going to his side of my bathroom and arranging his hair while I work on fixing my makeup. The necklace I no longer wear catches my eye. It's hanging on a nail next to my mirror. I stopped wearing it shortly after I was discharged. I'll always miss Mom, and I'll always despise the way her story ended, but I've learned I don't need to brew in sadness any more or use it as a token. There are bigger things to live for now. Light glints off the shiny K and I smile. I'm fixing smudged eyeliner when Brett captures my attention.

"How's the new book coming along?"

A warm smile creeps across my face and my head is bouncing up and down with an enthused nod. "Good. Fantastic." Which is an understatement, really. So far, this book is flowing better than any of my others.

He smirks. "And your agent likes the sound of a bad boy who meets a jaded and spurned romance author?"

"So far." My voice is bright.

"Good," He flicks back a piece of hair trying to curl forward. "Excellent choice by the way, giving your guy some tattoos."

A flush tingles in my cheeks and I smile so big the apples of my cheeks round. "Inspiration helps."

"Hmm." He lifts his head once, a sparkle in his eyes, and slides his gaze along the counter in the mirror. "Can you pass me my jeans?"

He's left them on my side of the counter and they rub against my elbow. Wrapping my fingers around them, I lift them up, but as I swing them around, something falls out, clattering to the floor.

My line-of-sight jerks to the tile. I gasp.

A navy-blue, velvet ring box rests at my feet, and of course I already know what it is, but my body can't move.

"Wow." Brett says it in the most peaceful way I've ever heard. "Looks like you need to pick that up."

My body obeys the words, and I'm bending down, my descent slowing as Brett reaches out and steadies me with one strong hand.

Brushing my fingertips against the box is a jolt of reality, and it unlocks a tremor in my hands that trails up my arm, working to my lips. My chest lurches, desperate for oxygen, yet hardly any reaches my lungs. "Oh, Brett." A fresh onslaught of tears blur the article as I lift it up and pull it open. One sob of uncontrollable happiness spills out when a gorgeous oval solitaire glows in my vision. "I...I..." Gurgling over my own words becomes my only option.

Next thing I know, I'm sobbing while being scooped into Brett's arms—my heart so full it presses against my ribs.

Brett's hand cups the back of my cheek, his deep voice rumbling against my ear, making my pulse skip a few beats. "Do you like it?"

"Like it?" I can't even believe he'd ask something so ridiculous. Tossing my head back, I pepper a few kisses along his jaw, which makes him sigh. "Darling, I love it." Glancing down at it again, some of the joy ebbs away while thinking about all the progress I still need to make in life.

There are still bad days. Days where I'm angry at Dad, losing Mom, and I struggle. Struggle to be fueled as a writer by understanding my purpose and realizing I create stories because the love for writing resides in my heart. Simply put, I'm making progress, but the road ahead of me to fully healing is going to be a long one. Damn, I feel unworthy of the second chance I have.

Nestling harder into Brett, I frown. "Brett, this is so beautiful, but I—"

"Don't even tell me you don't think you deserve it." He plants a gentle kiss to my temple and tightens his arms around me. "You're the only woman who does."

Lightly tracing over the diamond, more wetness sprouts from my eyes while I attempt to accept how he feels for me. "But I have so many shortcomings. Why do you want me?"

He chuckles softly. "We all have them, baby. We all have scars. We're all mangled in some way, shape, or form. The hard part in life is finding someone who we don't mind showing those issues to, and that's us. We're meant to be and heal together."

*Damn.* I'm weightless. My stomach flutters high, taking my arms with it as I fling them around his neck. "Oh darling, thank you. How can I ever show you how thankful I am for believing in me?" Dampness from my cheeks absorbs into his shirt. "Tell me."

Capturing my chin, he tilts my head up and smiles deep into my eyes. "You can marry me and never think about kicking me out of your life again."

Cupping his face in my hands, I give him one long kiss, then pull back and return his smile. "I can't think of anything that sounds better."

# Chapter 31

*One and a half years later*

"Bestselling novel." Brett raises his glass to me from across the table and beams wide. "*Annnd.* And..."

A laugh slips out of me as he draws the word out. Rubbing my finger along the stem of my drinkware, I bite down on my lip, waiting for him to continue.

"In the talks to be bought out for a movie."

Another one of my girly squeals comes out. My latest novel has blown up and swept almost every bestseller spot available. The cherry on top? I received the news this afternoon that Fox Studios is interested in buying my manuscript. Of course I'm going to say yes. They could make my main character a green octopus with laser eyes, and I'd still say yes.

"I'm proud of you." Pushing his seat back from the table, he pats his knee, asking for me to sit on his lap. "Get over here, baby."

I'm on my feet, settling down on his leg in not even a second.

"Are you happy?" He nuzzles his nose in the valley of my neck, causing goosebumps to prick at my skin.

"Thrilled," I moan, reaching my hand down. Finding the plain gold wedding band around his fingers, a smile splits open my mouth as I run my fingers over it.

We got married five months ago, when I could finally walk by myself again and could trust my legs. Recovery was a long hard road, but Brett stuck with me day in and day out, and without his strength or his light, I don't think I would have been walking at all. I would have given up.

He breaks me from my thoughts, and my head falls back as he slips a hand under my shirt, skimming his thumb across my bare stomach. Nipping at my skin, I'm near a tipping point, but somehow I stall him long enough to talk about a trip we thought of this afternoon.

"Shouldn't we be calling Lizzie and Cora to tell them we want to go to Vegas in a few months to celebrate all of this?"

"We will. Eventually." He sucks gently on my neck for a moment. "For tonight, however, I want to focus on us. I want to celebrate *you*, Bianca."

"Mmm." My hands clasp around the back of his neck as his other hand secures me around my back. "Any ideas?"

He stops kissing me and looks up into my eyes. "Several." Nodding toward the room, he smirks. "To the bedroom, kitten."

Hopping off his lap, I grab his hand, threading our fingers together to make sure we depart as one. Somehow, even with one hand tangled up, he finds a way to spank my ass, which makes me jump, then squeal, then laugh.

Moments later, he's stripping me down to nothing, removing my bra straps with his teeth and making me call his name more times than I can count. As our night goes on, and we make love in the slowest way possible, and I relish knowing most of my demons have been banished away.

There is no more anger taking up all the room in my heart, crowding out the one person who was supposed to live in it all along.

And the words Dad used to say were nothing but lies. Horrid projections of his own evil ways that twisted my mindset and poisoned my heart.

I've learned over this time with Brett that Dad was wrong.

Things do last...and I found what that is in my life.

It's love.
It's Brett.

## The End.

# Saber

*13 years old*

Eliza Morgan.

The most beautiful girl in our school. One I can single out in a crowd. Some call her Lizzie. Her friend Jake, calls her Liz. Both are awful and don't match how gorgeous she is. Pouty pink lips, pale skin, cornflower eyes… she's perfect.

Been so since kindergarten.

A warmness floods my chest while stealing a glance at her across the cafeteria.

She sits in her everyday spot. Last table in the far right corner, pizza and chocolate milk since it's Thursday. It's what she eats everyday unless it's Friday. Then it's eggrolls, salad, and a burger. So much food for such a small thing. Maybe she needs all the calories, because whatever spell she has me under has to be draining.

I try not to make it obvious how much she demands my attention. It would make me look weak, but whenever she's in the same room, I feel her pulse… almost like it's locked under my skin.

I sense her.

I see her.

But I never look at her.

Whenever I punish someone or beat up a *stronzo* for getting in the way, she's there. Staring at my target with horror in her gorgeous eyes.

It kills me everytime, and I wish I could explain.

I don't like being like this.

Control here is all I have. Everyone at this school thinks I'm hot shit. That I own it all.

Truth is?

I'm nothing. Home is hell, Dad is a monster, and there's no escaping him.

Catching one more glance at Eliza, I frown. *Does she know?* But I know the answer to that. She can't know. No one does.

No one knows that in those moments of pain while I'm at home, Eliza's there.

It's her I see.

When I'm under dad's belt, covered in welts and bruises, being cussed at and kicked— it's her eyes I think about. Sometimes I see her gaze sad, like they are sharing the whipping of the leather with me. Other times they come to me happy, showing off that twinkle that happens when she's talking to Jake Goode and laughing.

Either way, it's her. Always her. Getting me through the pain. Making it possible to hold back the whimpers and tears. Her light is my guidance when I'm shoved in the dark, allowing me to believe that everything will end soon. And on those nights I can't sleep on my back and can only lay on my stomach, I stare at the moon lit skies out my window and drift to sleep imaging her.

Always her.

Always there.
Eliza. My beautiful, Eliza.

Lizzie and Saber's story will be coming to you in the fall of 2021.

Preorder *Stay* today.

# Acknowledgements

Holy moly, where do I even start with something like this? There are so many people who've
helped me get to this point that I'm not sure where to start, but I'm going to try.

**First off, to my love, R.**

Baby, I can't thank you enough for everything you've done for me. For all those times you've taken care of house stuff and life while telling me to "go write." To letting me miss out on big events so I could rework that chapter, or bringing me big glasses of water and asking me if I ate so I wouldn't die like a neglected house plant, thank you!

Thank you for believing in me even when I had nothing to show for my work, and for letting me write till all hours of the night even when there were no plans to publish. Thank you for listening to all my book ideas even though you don't always know what's going on, and for encouraging me when I complaining about the tough times in this author life. I love you with my whole heart, and I couldn't do this without you.

*To my dearest friend, Lee Jacquot.*

Lee, what an amazing experience this whole publishing journey has been with you. This book wouldn't exist without you. From your guidance to all my scenes, to rereading all the parts I reworked, all the brainstorming ideas you listened to, and those ten minute long voice memos where I rambled about nothing…thank you! Your support has meant everything to me. Thank you for putting up with all my impostor syndrome slumps, and for telling me to "write the damn book" and for believing in me when I didn't believe in myself. You're the best, and I'm thankful you're in my life.

**To the best person ever, Shayna Astor:**

Girl, we've only known each other for such a short time, but it feels like so much longer in the best way possible. Thank you for reading everything. For your amazing feedback that made my story even better, for being my cheerleader, and for all the late night talks. Most of all, for not letting me back down even when I'm scared. Your support has meant everything to me, and I can't imagine my author journey without you. I'm so happy to call you my friend.

**M.L. Philpitt**

Thank you for your sharp eyes and for challenging me to make the second part of the book better than I ever thought it could be.

**A.V. Asher**

Thank you for being the last piece of the puzzle. You gave me the right feedback in the right places, at the last second. Because of you, I felt like I was able to put the bow on the top and make this story nice and pretty.

To my PA, **Amber.** Girl thank you so much for giving me guidance in this whole post writing phase. Writing is the easy part, but the rest is tricky. Thank you for helping me out and for helping me navigate through the marketing side of things.

To all my amazing Beta readers thank you for your time, for loving this book and having faith in me.

To my graphic designer, **Cat.** Girl! There are no words to describe how incredibly thankful I am for you and your work. Thank you for taking me on! Thank you for creating a cover that made people even want to pick this book up in the first place. Thank you for each wonderful graphic and teaser you made, and for making this book so incredibly beautiful with your formatting. Thank you, thank you, thank you. I just adore you.

To my editors, **AI and Rochelle,** thank you for your amazing guidance, for sharpening my words, and for loving this story as much as I did.

To my Arcs, bloggers, and bookstagrammers, thank you, thank you, thank you for your enthusiasm and support. I felt each and everyone of you during the post writing phase. I can't thank you enough for your energy and amazing love.

And last, but so importantly, to you the reader. Without you, writing is pointless. Thank you for picking up this book, for trying out a brand new author with her book baby. Words can never express how much it means to me that you read my book. Time is precious these days and it seems like life has a way of making the hours way too short. Thank you from the bottom of my heart for taking your precious time and for using it reading my story. It means the world to me. I hope you enjoyed it.

# About the Author

Garnet Christie is a romance author who loves serving up hot Alpha males who are searching for a true connection and looking to fall in love. When she's not writing, she's spending too much money on K-pop merchandise, drinking tea, eating chocolate, and avoiding falling asleep at a normal human hour.

Website: www.garnetchristie.com
Instagram @authorgarnetchristie
TikTok @ authorgarnetchristie
Join my Facebook group: Garnet's Societea and catch all the tea to stay up to date.

Made in the USA
Las Vegas, NV
08 June 2021